"You didn't have to take her dress off!"

"I didn't," he insisted. "She took it off herself."

"Well, you didn't have to take her to a private room at an inn."

"Darling, what could I do? Where else could I take her in the middle of the night, in the winter?" Suddenly his voice became low and seductive as his fingers crept up her arms and began pulling her closer by small degrees. "You knew when you agreed to marry me, dearest, that I sometimes have to do unusual things in my work," he said in a voice as sweet and smooth as honey, enfolding her in his arms.

ROYAL REVELS

JOAN SMITH

FAWCETT CREST • NEW YORK

A Fawcett Crest Book
Published by Ballantine Books

Library of Congress Catalog Card Number: 85-90626

ISBN 0-449-20637-8

Manufactured in the United States of America

First Edition: July 1985

Chapter One

The Dowager Duchess of Charney's drawing room was noticeably cool on that morning in early January. Wind drifted in around the ill-fitting window frames and rustled the draperies. A sluggish fire smoldered in the grate, emitting more smoke than heat, till she felt some fear of being kippered alive. Though the duchess was bundled into a stout shawl, she was chilled to the marrow and was impatient, waiting for her guest to arrive.

"It seems to me that Belami might make some effort to be on time when he comes to visit his bride-to-be," she told her niece with a scowl from her close-set eyes. "I should never have allowed the match. I can't imagine what possessed me to do it after his behavior at Beaulac," she added, tugging at the ends of her shawl to block out an errant breeze.

"Now, Auntie, we've all been through that," her niece replied calmly. It was easy to be calm now that she was, indeed, betrothed to the only man she had ever loved. Nothing could dampen Miss Deirdre Gower's spirits. Not her mean-spirited chaperone, not the faded Mustard Saloon in which they sat, not the dreary view of snow turning to slush beyond the window, not even Dick's tardy arrival. "He could hardly tell the Prince Regent to hurry, as he has an appointment with his fiancée," she said to remind her aunt that Dick was late for such a royal reason.

It was quite an honor for Belami that the prince wished to

consult with him on a personal matter, and the magical words *Prince Regent* always managed to bring a smile to the raddled countenance of the duchess. When she spoke again, however, her tone was irritable. "If it weren't that he is with the prince, I should bolt the door and not let him in." Really, it was only impatience and curiosity that jangled her nerves so. She was on thorns to learn what scrape Prinney had fallen into that he required the services of Lord Belami, sometime investigator into criminal matters for his friends. Prinney had been settled down with Lady Hertford as his flirt anytime this past decade. As the lady's husband was entirely agreeable to the arrangement, it was unlikely that Lady Hertford was the cause of it. Blackmail, Belami had mentioned. After women and drink, spending inordinate sums of money was Prinney's little weakness. Had he borrowed privately and found himself unable to pay up? The cent-percenters might be nipping at his heels, threatening some dire revenge or revelation.

But Belami would fish him out of hot water. He had just rescued his own reputation and the duchess's diamond when the latter—and much more important in the lady's view—had been in jeopardy. A clever rascal, Belami, but she did not care for that proclivity for dabbling in criminal matters. After he rescued Prinney, whom she could not abandon in his hour of need, she must either persuade Belami from his avocation or persuade Deirdre from marrying Belami. Neither course would be easy. Her thin lips assumed the unnatural position of a smile to contemplate the challenge.

While the duchess schemed and Deirdre sat in a happy daze, dreaming of her honeymoon in Italy, Lord Belami was led through the sumptuous rooms and passages of Carlton House, the prince's London residence. The private chambers were situated at the back of the south side, to afford a view of St. James's Park and perhaps to necessitate passing through the rest of the house to admire such treats as the Blue Velvet Closet, the Crimson Drawing Room, the Chinese Parlour, and the Library. Belami bit his lip to control the wayward smile that wanted to peep out. Such vulgar opulence, with gold upon gold everywhere, quite overwhelmed him. His own preferred mode was understated elegance.

Colonel McMahon, the prince's private secretary, was Belami's guide. "You've met the prince, of course," McMahon said as they walked briskly along.

"Only at public gatherings," Belami replied. Though he would sooner have lost his hair than admit it, he was nervous.

"He's easily pleased. Pretend you're amazed with his banalities and he'll love you forever."

"Can you give me any idea what's troubling him?" Belami asked.

McMahon wore a worried frown. "Truth to tell, Belami, what's troubling him isn't what's troubling the rest of us. When he finishes discussing the blackmail with you, try if you can to urge him on to the subject of a certain Mr. Smythe. It won't be difficult," he added grimly.

"Who is Mr. Smythe?" Belami asked, already thinking it sounded like an alias.

"God only knows. Some American who turned up at Brighton and has been more or less added to the royal retinue, but in no official capacity as yet. It would be appreciated if you'd do a little looking into the fellow's background—see if you can learn who he is and what he's up to."

McMahon stopped at a pair of high, broad doors embellished with gilt and panels. A page in dark blue livery, trimmed in gold lace, opened the door, revealing the Prince Regent. His Royal Highness sat alone with a glass in his hand, smiling sadly into it. He had not yet dressed for the day. He wore a mauve silk dressing gown with an embroidered pocket and looked like an overaged, overweight satyr. He looked up and made a beckoning gesture with one graceful hand. Belami followed the colonel into the very hot chamber, wishing he had worn a summer jacket. It must be above ninety degrees, he thought.

"Kind of you to come, my dear Belami," the prince said in weary but cultivated accents. He made a sort of nominal motion of rising, but his corpulent body didn't actually leave the chair.

Though the prince was only in his early fifties, a life of indulgence had not been kind to his appearance. Despite, or perhaps because of, the various ointments and unguents he lavished on his face, it had assumed a waxy quality. His gray eyes were bleary and his chins sagged, to be caught up and concealed in the immaculate folds of a high neckcloth. He wore this device even with his dressing gown. His brown hair was artfully brushed forward to conceal time's ravages on the hairline.

"You may leave us now, McMahon," the prince said, motioning Belami to the chair beside him. A flick of the royal wrist sent the page boys hopping from the room, hastened forward by the colonel.

"How can I be of help, sir?" Belami asked.

The prince looked at the lean, young face before him and felt an awful pang of envy. Once he himself had been known as an Adonis. Really, Belami was not so much an Adonis as a Corsair, out of a poem by Lord Byron. There was a whiff of danger in those coffee-black eyes and of romance in the exaggeratedly long lashes that a girl might covet. It was a marvel how the skin sat so tightly against the classical bones of the lad's face. And he wore a fine jacket—Weston, of course—upon a fine set of shoulders. Damme, but time was a traitor.

"A mere trifle," the prince replied indolently. "McMahon feels it would be best handled by an objective third party whose discretion could be counted on, and he suggested you. Can I offer you a glass of wine?"

"Thank you," Belami said, accepting the glass. The warm, sweet Madeira being poured into it would do nothing to assuage the glaring heat of the room.

"It will involve a jaunt to Brighton," the prince continued.

Belami did not betray by so much as a blink that this was
dismal news for him. He was newly engaged and wanted to
be with his fiancée, wanted to get on with the marriage and
to plan the honeymoon in Italy.

"You're welcome to stay at the Pavilion, if you wish,"
the prince added.

This was a rare favor, and one to be avoided at all costs.
Belami dodged the invitation by saying, "What is to be handled at Brighton? McMahon mentioned blackmail. . . ."

"That is a harsh word. *Pressure*, perhaps, is closer to the
mark. There is a young lady who wishes to sell me certain
objects of a personal nature. She has set an inflated price on
them, as she appears to think she can exact a high sum from
the newspapers," he said, his florid complexion deepening
with anger or embarrassment.

"Letters, I take it?" Belami asked, showing no censure.

"A few notes written in a sentimental mood after a lonely
spell in which I sought solace from a glass of wine," the
prince explained. "I met the woman—Lady Gilham she
calls herself—one afternoon at St. Ann's Well last autumn.
My—better friends"—Belami quickly translated this into
Lady Hertford—"were in London at the time, and the
woman invited me to call upon her if I happened to be passing nearby. A man gets so desperately lonely," he said with
a quick peep to see if he was eliciting sympathy. He saw
none on the impassive face before him. The young were all
brutal. Lady Gilham was brutal. Who would have thought
that that sweet-faced chit would betray him?

"I quite understand, sir. All I shall require is the lady's
address and your instructions. Do you wish to purchase the
letters or have you something else in mind?" *Pay, you fool!*
he said to himself and feared for a moment that he had said it
aloud. The prince was looking at him oddly, with a dissatis-
fied expression. Belami felt he was doing well by wiping all

emotion from his features, not knowing he was expected to simulate sympathy as well.

"She must be silenced. Five thousand pounds she's asking for the letters. Out of the question. See her and tell her one thousand is what she'll get, not a penny more. There's nothing salacious in them, Belami. Nothing of the sort. I believed at the time she was a lady and was very proper," he said earnestly.

"Five thousand *does* seem very high," Belami agreed, frowning. "There must be *something* incriminating if the newspapers have offered her five thousand."

"Bah, the newspapers! They make bricks without straw. They'll twist and cut and paste my phrases till they have me offering to marry the wench. You're old enough to remember how the Hunt brothers vilified me in the *Examiner*, and to try to suppress those fellows is worse than letting them have their say. There'll be another raft of caricatures in shop windows. I tell you, my lad, it's no easy thing being a ruler. The royal crown cures not the headache, as the admirable Ben Franklin so succinctly put it. I'd gladly trade all the royal trappings in for a simple cottage away from the cares of the world," he said, allowing his eyes to roll sadly toward the window.

Belami looked around the ornate chamber and took tacit leave to doubt this pious nonsense. "She may be happy enough to settle for one thousand and have done with it," Belami suggested. "She's bound to ask for more than she expects to get."

"That is the sum McMahon suggested. *You* would be well informed on such matters, I make no doubt. The colonel will give you her address and the money. It's kind of you to take care of this little matter for me. Naturally you must get all the letters back from her—six in all. You might make a bid for a certain locket as well. Gold with a small heart picked out in diamonds on the front. A mere trifle, but the miniature of myself inside is something I promised to one of my sisters. It was only a sentimental gesture. She has a few other gewgaws—get them all back if you can.''

If the other trinkets were also laden with diamonds, Belami began to think, the price he had suggested was too low. "Perhaps another hundred *douceur* for the trinkets . . ." he suggested.

"Yes, yes, whatever it takes. You're the expert, my good fellow. I have no experience in these matters. I certainly don't want any more scandal at this time," he said irritably.

Belami lifted one mobile brow, wondering why "this time" should be of particular importance. The words of McMahon were in his mind and the name of Mr. Smythe. "Is there a reason why the present is particularly inauspicious?" he asked carefully. One never knew how far he might intrude on the prince's patience and privacy. In the proper mood, he'd bare his soul to a perfect stranger and, a moment later, he'd insult his bosom beaus.

A beatific smile lit up the waxen countenance, and the bleary eyes sparkled. For a fleeting instant, Belami caught a glimmering of what people a few decades ago had found to admire in the man's looks. There was a certain something—a charm.

"As a matter of fact, there is," the prince replied. Belami sensed an expansive mood had come upon him and encouraged him on to revelation with a smiling nod of interest.

"It is incredible, something out of a fairy tale." The prince sighed. "One hardly knows where to begin. It all started so long ago. I met her over thirty years ago," he said dreamily. This tipped Belami the clue that they had reverted to the days of Maria Fitzherbert, and his heart plunged. In a long line of troublesome mistresses, Mrs. Fitzherbert had taken the lead. Her affair with the prince had nearly toppled the government. What she could possibly have to do with a Mr. Smythe was unclear, but there was surely some connection between them.

"Maria Fitzherbert is the only woman I ever loved," the prince continued, still gazing fixedly into the air, seeing a vision of his love. With a maidenly blush he pulled a locket up from his neck and turned his eyes to it. "You didn't know her when she was young. A vision of loveliness, with her golden hair and the sweetest blue eyes ever bestowed on woman." A tear swelled in his eye and trembled over the waxen cheek.

Belami's memory of the lady was more recent. She was a tall, portly dame with a hooked nose and an overly elaborate manner of dressing. Gossip had it the prince had actually married her, but he later denied it. A twice-widowed Roman Catholic of undistinguished birth, she was quickly sloughed off when his official wedding was performed.

"I've heard her cried up as a great beauty," Belami said vaguely.

"And a good woman, Belami. A *good* woman. She is my wife, you know," he added with a sudden change of intonation. He looked sharp now, alert, ready to defend this outrageous statement with all the royal prerogative at his command.

Belami was too astonished to reply. The whole world knew his wife was Princess Caroline of Brunswick. "Oh" was the only sound to come from his lips.

"You are surprised," the prince said, in perhaps one of the understatements of the year. "Definitely, Maria is my true wife. Oh, they foisted that German princess on me when I was too young to stand up for my rights. There was coercion brought to bear, Belami. I was in debt at the time, due to the miserly bit of an allowance I was allowed. Yes, Maria Fitzherbert and I were married by the Reverend R. Burt, an Anglican curate, on December 15, 1785. The happiest day of my life," he said simply.

"Where did this take place?" was the only question that occurred to Belami.

"It was in Maria's drawing room. Certainly the marriage is valid," he answered confidently.

"But she's a Roman Catholic," Belami reminded him. "According to the Act of Settlement, you and your heirs would forfeit the right to succession if you married a Roman Catholic.''

''Some things in life mean more than a crown,'' the prince said calmly, though his next speech showed he had no intention of giving up his much-maligned crown. ''Actually, there exists some doubt in *my* mind that Maria remains a Catholic after being married in front of an Anglican minister. It is possible she became a *de facto* non-Catholic when she married me, in which case the Act of Settlement would be irrelevant.''

''There's still the Royal Marriage Act,'' Belami reminded him. ''You were under twenty-five at the time and hadn't the consent of the king. Without that consent, no legal marriage was possible.''

''My dear father is, unfortunately, so confused in his mind that he no doubt has only the vaguest memory of those days, if he has any memory at all,'' the prince answered with a very sly smile. Was he planning to claim a *spoken* agreement by the king?

''Surely the consent must be formal and written,'' Belami said, but he had, in fact, no idea if this was the case.

''We are wallowing in details,'' the prince said impatiently. ''The fact is, Maria and I married in good faith before God and the wedding is *morally* valid and binding. Are we to put man's laws before God's? These 'acts' can be managed as King Henry VIII was obliged to do. Not that I mean to say I want a divorce. Nothing could be further from my mind. I want only the right to call my true wife my wife,'' he said with a noble attitude.

''What about Princess Caroline?'' Belami inquired, carefully avoiding the words ''your *real* wife.''

The prince lifted his hands and hunched his shoulders. ''That is another detail to be worked out. Some honorary title and a settlement must be made.''

''What has brought you to this decision?'' Belami asked, guessing he had only seen the tip of the iceberg.

"It is not for myself," the prince assured him. "No, it is for England and for my son."

"But you don't have a son; you have a daughter," Belami said, almost beyond rational thought. He felt as if he had fallen into a nightmare.

"I *do* have a son, Belami!" the prince declared, wearing the reckless smile of a gambler. "I have, and I have found him. Maria had him shipped off to America, never telling me of his existence, the naughty girl. You must know there were periods of regrettable disagreement in our marriage. For long periods I didn't see Maria, and it was during one of these that our son was born and shipped off to America."

Belami held his face under tight control. One did not laugh or scream at a prince. "What is your son's name?" he asked, but he already had a good notion of the reply.

"He goes by the name of Mr. Smythe—George Smythe. You understand the significance of this?" he asked, staring hard at Belami.

"Is it that George is your own name?" Belami asked in confusion.

"Just so, and Maria's maiden name was Smythe. Fitzherbert was her second husband's name. It proves, in my mind, that George Smythe is my son. But you must see him and judge for yourself. He has Maria's eyes, I think, with something of his father's hair and physique."

Belami heard a strange ringing in his ears. Had poor old Prinney finally gone completely mad like his father? What could be in his head to be rooting about in the past, unearthing such mischief? What did he plan to do with his real wife, the king's cousin, and with his daughter, Princess Charlotte, the most popular woman in the kingdom? Did he actually think his subjects would sit still to see her consigned to illegitimacy?

"I speak of my youthful physique, of course," the prince was saying when the ringing in Belami's ears stopped.

"Is he here now?" Belami asked.

"Ah, no, McMahon and some of my advisers thought it

wiser to leave him in Brighton till I get these few details ironed out." Ridding himself of a wife and daughter and repealing two acts of Parliament were sunk to "details." Certainly the man was mad.

"Might I see Mr. Smythe when I go to Brighton to take care of the other business?" Belami asked. He was eager to get away now and talk to Colonel McMahon.

"I hope you will look him up. He isn't well connected with the right sort of chaps because of being raised in America. I would take it as a personal favor if you would befriend George, show him his way around society. You will be a very proper model for him, Belami. We admire your style," the prince said with a smile and a bow of his head.

"I'm eager to meet him."

"It will be best if you not tell him you act on my request. He will be more at ease if he thinks you just a friend and not an emissary."

"Yes, that might be best," Belami agreed. "I'll go and find Colonel McMahon now," he said, then began bowing himself out.

"You're a fine fellow," the prince proclaimed, chatting amiably from his chair as Belami inched away. "A dashed well-cut jacket you have got on. We must take George to meet Weston, what?" A glass of wine teetered in his fat pink fingers.

Belami got out the door and closed it behind him. It was not only the infernal heat of the chamber that caused him to wipe a film of perspiration from his brow as he went in search of McMahon.

The colonel was awaiting him around the first corner. "I judge by the blank look on your face that His Highness has let you in on it," McMahon said in a sardonic way. He was a tall man with a military bearing and a down-to-earth manner.

Belami shook his head, dazed. "Where can we go to talk in private?" he asked.

McMahon led him to his office and poured him a glass of

wine. McMahon leaned his shoulders back against his chair and propped his feet up on the desk. "The cat sits poised to swoop amongst the pigeons," he said in an ominous voice. "You're an intelligent man, Belami. I'm sure the consequences of such rashness as we anticipate is clear to you. The prince is barely able to hang on to his position by the skin of his teeth as it is. If he takes it into his head to inflict Mrs. Fitzherbert's bastard on the populace as their ruler, there will certainly be a revolution."

"Is it true then? Is Smythe her son?"

McMahon sat silently for a moment. When he spoke, he said, "I don't honestly know. There's a superficial resemblance. Fitzherbert *could* have had a son and had him shipped off to America."

"Hasn't anyone *asked* her?" Belami inquired in astonishment.

"This is entirely a new turn. Smythe only fell into favor during the New Year's festivities at Brighton. The prince has written to Mrs. Fitzherbert, but she hasn't answered his letters in years. She sends them back unopened. Actually, she wouldn't have received the latest yet. It was sent to London from Brighton, and when we arrived here we learned that she had gone out of town for the holiday. She had her house closed up. We haven't been able to find out where she has gone. She lives quite out of society nowadays. But it makes little difference whether Smythe is her son or not. He's illegitimate in any case."

"True, but if he's not even her son, it will be easier to turn the prince away from this folly," Belami pointed out. "It sounds like a ruse to me."

"If you're fingering Smythe as a rogue, I'm afraid you're mistaken. He was more surprised than any of us. He makes no claim to being of royal blood. It's all Prinney's idea."

"Does he not have a set of parents?"

"No such luck. He's an orphan. A nice, simple lad, good-natured. It's the coincidence of his name being George

Augustus Smythe that did the damage—along with a certain physical resemblance."

"Half the male population of England bears the name of the royal princes. That's pretty flimsy," Belami said doubtfully.

"Their last name isn't Smythe," McMahon pointed out. "I feel partly responsible myself. I am the one who brought them together, quite by chance."

"How did you happen to meet Smythe?" Belami asked with quick interest.

"He came to England last autumn, hung around London for a while, then went to Brighton, probably because living was cheap off season. He met an old army acquaintance of mine at the Old Ship Hotel, where Smythe is staying. They played cards there at night. I dropped in and invited the army man—Captain Stack is his name—to the Pavilion to join us for faro there. Just as an afterthought I asked young Smythe to join us. Company was thin at the time and Prinney likes to see a new face. I could see right away that Smythe was a success. It seemed harmless, another friend of the Beau Brummell sort, I thought. Smythe was invited back again and again, each time the party shrinking in size, till, the last night before we left, it was only Prinney and Smythe. It was after that meeting that we were hit with this misbegotten theory. I dragged the prince back to London at once, hoping the thing would die a natural death, but it's taken such a hold on his imagination that it's become an obsession."

"It's a pity," Belami said, shaking his head.

"Yes, but a perfectly understandable one. The people hate the prince. He's hissed and jeered at when he goes about in public. His wife has left him to traipse through Europe with a ragtag and bobtail caravan of foreign ruffians, and his daughter seems unable to produce an heir. She's miscarried twice since her marriage. The prince is ill and worries about the succession. Securing that would bolster his popularity. He longs for a stout-bodied son to carry on and has convinced himself he's found one," he explained.

"How did he convince himself the son is legitimate?"

"Power and folly are old friends. We're all quoting Benjamin Franklin these days. He's Mr. Smythe's favorite author, you know. The prince *did* undergo some sort of wedding ceremony with Mrs. Fitzherbert. He knows in his mind the marriage is invalid."

"He's beginning to worm his way around the various acts of Parliament that forbid it. He'll never convince Parliament, but if he convinces himself, he'll be hard to hold back," Belami said, frowning into his glass.

"He's convinced himself, all right. He forgets the divine right of kings is history. He believes that if he brings Smythe forward and the lad becomes incredibly popular, Parliament will go along with him to avoid an uprising. If Fitzherbert doesn't deny it and claims herself a non-Catholic, he might just pull it off. And furthermore, she just might abet him. She's ambitious," McMahon said, shaking his head.

"We don't even know if he *is* Fitzherbert's son. If she's as ambitious as you think, she wouldn't have sent him off into anonymity all those years ago," Belami pointed out.

"They had tiffs, then would get together again. She might have feared a son would prevent a reconciliation," McMahon said thoughtfully.

"The likeliest spoke to stick in the wheel is to find out who Smythe is, and I mean to tackle it," Belami said with an air of resolution.

"You're welcome to it, but it won't be easy to trace down a twenty-five-year-old orphan from America. This is really why I urged the prince to call you in, Belami. Lady Gilham was only a pretext to get you off to Brighton without alerting the prince that you were involving yourself in his affairs, the Smythe affair, I mean."

"I confess it's the Smythe affair that interests me more," Belami replied with a smile.

"It's extremely urgent. Prinney is champing at the bit to

bring his son forward. I'd say you have about a week before all hell breaks loose.''

"Then I'd better get to Brighton," Belami said and arose. "Ah . . . Lady Gilham's address and the money to buy her silence. What's the real story on her?" he asked with mild interest.

"Nothing very interesting there. She's just a clever, pretty hussy who set her cap at Prinney and managed to attract his interest for a few weeks.''

"Does she, ah, *pass* for a woman of virtue or is she the other sort?''

"She passes for respectable in Brighton. Pure as the driven snow to hear her tell it, but I believe the snow has a few paw marks in it. She was cunning enough to get him to write her billets-doux and knew enough to hang on to them. It shouldn't be necessary to pay her sort anything, but the mood the papers are in, it might be best to keep her quiet if we can," McMahon replied.

He drew open a drawer and handed Belami a bag of gold coins. "There's something in there to cover your expenses as well. His Highness won't be ungenerous in his nonmonetary rewards," he added vaguely. He was hinting at some court sinecure, Belami supposed, but didn't press the matter.

"As to the more important affair, Belami, I don't know if you are an ambitious man, but the government would be extremely grateful if you could circumvent a new scandal. You could name your own price if you bring off this one. Lord chamberlain, an earldom, relatives on the Civil List—anything within reason."

"Deciding will be a pleasant diversion from business," Belami said lightly.

"Where will you be staying if I need to be in touch with you?''

"At my own place on Marine Parade," Belami said.

"I expect to see you soon. I won't be able to keep Prinney

away from Brighton for long, when his *soi-disant* son is there. Godspeed.''

McMahon accompanied Belami to the door and along the passage to the courtyard, discussing further aspects of the case. ''We must at all costs keep Smythe from moving into the Royal Pavilion. That would be too close for comfort. He has carte blanche to do so if he wishes. It's strange he didn't jump at the chance, is it not, when his pockets are to let?'' McMahon asked. He directed a long, curious look at Belami.

''Very odd,'' he answered with a considering frown.

This was the detail that occupied his mind as he hastened to Belvedere Square and Deirdre. Why did Smythe refuse to stay at the Pavilion where he could mix with the well-to-do, who might land him a good position? McMahon had intimated he was not well off. But then Smythe probably found the prince's company suffocating, and the old cronies roosting there would hardly be to a young man's taste. That must account for it. Or perhaps he'd found himself some female company that was not fit to introduce to polite society. His mind veered to Lady Gilham for a moment. He little thought what pranks that female had in store for him. He allotted half an hour to handling her case.

Chapter Two

"So we are off to Brighton! An odd season for it, I must say," the duchess exclaimed when Belami informed them that he had to go there.

His black eyes opened wide in horror at the mental vision of this dragon's company. His work would involve him with rakes, rattles, and roués—every one of whom the duchess would hate on sight.

"What fun!" Deirdre exclaimed, her large gray eyes shining with delight. Belami gazed at her and found his heart softening to the idea. It wouldn't take him twenty-four hours a day to handle Lady Gilham and Smythe, and it would be good to have Deirdre near him.

"It might be best if I go alone," he said, but in no very firm way. Within a minute Deirdre had pouted her way to success.

"You realize what I have told you is in the strictest confidence," he told them.

"We are not gossips!" her grace informed him with a gimlet shot from her sharp eyes. "Naturally I would *never* breathe a word to bring discredit on the dear prince. But just between ourselves, Belami, what do you make of this Smythe fellow? Is it possible he is indeed of royal blood? Fitzherbert was always fat as a flawn. It would be hard to know till the last few months whether she was *enceinte*. She hid herself away every time she and the prince had a tiff, so

17

it might easily enough be true. I almost wish the prince could carry it off. The tales coming home from Italy about his wife are enough to turn us all into Republicans. I hear she runs about in outlandish states of undress, naked from the waist up with a pumpkin on her head, and dances with her servants. It would be a blessing if we could get rid of her once for all.''

"But what of Princess Charlotte?'' Deirdre asked. "She is the only member of the royal family who is in the least degree tolerable. The Whigs will work to dump the prince and put his daughter to rule the country.''

"Even she is more than half hoyden,'' the duchess said severely. "We must avoid it at all costs. When do we leave for Brighton, Belami?''

"I plan to leave as soon as I can get a few jackets thrown into a case. Why don't I run along today and have the servants make the house ready for your arrival tomorrow?'' he suggested.

"Tomorrow? Rubbish, we can be ready in a trice,'' the duchess countered. Actually a week was her preferred packing time.

"I'll go and tell the servants,'' Deirdre said, hopping up in her eagerness.

"I'll take my own carriage and follow you. Is an hour too long a delay before parting?'' the duchess inquired.

"That will be fine,'' Belami said, blinking at her eagerness.

She was so hot to be on the trail of Prinney's son that she elbowed her niece aside at the doorway and darted down the hall, leaving Deirdre alone with her fiancé, a situation usually avoided.

Deirdre turned and smiled at Belami. "It seems we must postpone our trip to the travel agent to arrange our honeymoon,'' she said.

"This won't delay our wedding,'' he promised rashly. "I'll apply to the bishop for a special license as soon as we get back from Brighton and we'll get married right away.''

"Actually, Auntie has been speaking of having the wedding at Fernvale. Our friends and relatives aren't in London at this time," she said, looking for his reaction.

"I don't want to wait a minute longer than necessary. The spell I had cast over her might wear off before then," he said lightly. "She'll rescind her permission, and we'll end up darting to the border for a wedding over the anvil."

"Then you'll just have to get Herr Bessler out of Newgate and have her mesmerized again," Deirdre said, as this was the spell originally used to bring the duchess into line. A light laugh escaped her lips at what she had just said. She would never have thought it possible to be involved in such havey-cavey goings-on as she had since her betrothal to Belami.

Now the quickening of her blood told her another spree was about to begin. She was every bit as eager as the duchess to fly off to Brighton and meet up with the new set of characters Belami's strange avocation threw in his path.

His dark eyes softened as they regarded her. Deirdre was rapidly emerging from the chrysalis that had enshrouded her to spread her radiant new wings and enchant him. Her upbringing by the duchess had been severe, but beneath the antique gowns and hairdo there lurked an unsuspected flair for fun and fashion. He was never quite sure which he preferred, the innocent girl with the lingering trace of shyness or the new woman of fashion that peeped out at times. No matter, both had the raven-black hair, the stormy gray eyes, the short, straight nose and the full lips.

"Her grace is not the only one who is mesmerized," he said softly and pulled her into his arms. He sensed the reluctant girl holding herself back, felt the quiver that ran through her as he pressed his advances, and began tightening his grip for the final transformation.

"Deirdre!" The shrill notes of the duchess sent them flying apart.

"One of these days . . ." he said through gritted teeth, then left.

His friend, Pronto Pilgrim, was waiting in Belami's drawing room when he arrived home. It was a case of opposites attracting between Pronto and Belami. Pronto was an ungainly man whose major talent was for bungling things. His undistinguished appearance—short, small-shouldered, bow-legged, with a face whose most noticeable feature was a broken nose—was strangely at odds with Belami's elegant physique and striking good looks.

"When are you and Deirdre getting leg-shackled?" was Pronto's first speech. There was a hangdog look about him today. He had just recently decided that he, too, loved Deirdre Gower.

"As soon as can be. Right after I get back from Brighton, I hope," Belami answered. "I'm in a bit of a rush today, Pronto. Do you want anything in particular?"

"Brighton? What the deuce are you going to Brighton for when you've just gotten engaged?" Pronto asked suspiciously. "Damme, Dick, this is no time to be oiling around some bit of fluff!"

"Bite your tongue, you ridiculous object!" Belami answered with a laugh. "It's not *my* bit of fluff I'm chasing this time."

"All the worse, poaching on some other man's. 'Pon my word, Dick, you ain't changing your ways a bit. You promised you'd swear off the muslin company."

"This is business, Pronto. Confidential business or I'd let you in on it. I'll be back in two shakes of a lamb's tail. I suggest you have your monkey suit pressed up and be ready to stand as my best man next week." Belami looked impatiently at the clock on the mantelpiece.

Pronto sniffed and began nibbling on the corner of his thumb, a great aid to concentration. "Charney don't like your dabbling in crime if that's what it is," he felt obliged to remind his friend. "Just might be enough to turn her against you again."

"She likes it well enough this time," Belami said nonchalantly.

"You don't mean she's gone and lost that dashed diamond again after we just found it for her!" Pronto exclaimed indignantly.

"No, no, it's an entirely different matter, but mum's the word." A shapely finger was raised in admonishment.

"I'll be off then and let you get packed," Pronto said with a suspicious alacrity. He normally reacted at the pace of an aged tortoise. "I'll drop in and entertain Deirdre for you from time to time," he offered with a cagey light in his blue eyes.

"She's coming with me, but thanks anyway for the offer. I'll look you up as soon as we return. I really have to go now, Pronto."

"I won't detain you," Pronto said and ambled out, muttering into his collar.

Dashed Belami thought he was so clever just because he had solved a couple of crimes. Anyone could do his deductions when he got the knack of it. Motive, method, opportunity—Pronto had heard him say so a dozen times. That's all there was to solving these cases. Who did it, when, and why, in other words. And *how*—that was the trick. It was as plain as a pikestaff, after some basic deducing over a couple of ales at the Daffy Club, that Belami was nipping off to Brighton to pay off some lightskirt he had under his protection. And simple-minded enough to let Deirdre go with him, which naturally meant Charney went too.

Whether he knew it or not, Belami would require the help of his best friend, Pronto Pilgrim. Who had arranged for the time and the privacy for Herr Bessler to mesmerize Charney in the first place and make her give Belami permission to marry Deirdre? Pronto Pilgrim! Who had done half the work in finding the diamond stolen from the duchess? Pronto Pilgrim! Who *always* helped Belami out of his scrapes? The same Pronto Pilgrim! And if by any chance Charney *did* learn of the matter, who would throw himself forward to rescue Deirdre from heartbreak? Pronto Pilgrim! But he wouldn't do a thing to expose Belami. He was a gentleman, by Jove.

He nipped smartly around to his apartment in Albany and had his bag packed for a short visit to Brighton. He'd put up at a spot convenient to Belami's house on Marine Parade. The Old Ship was a decent hotel. Even had a spot of dancing in the evenings and a card game on Wednesdays as he recalled. He'd drive like the wind and be there before nightfall, if only the night would behave itself and not go getting dark in the middle of the afternoon, as it had the habit of doing in the winter. Prinney had made the trip in four and a half hours, or let on that he had at any rate. Pronto didn't see any reason why he couldn't better that record.

There were three carriages with disgruntled passengers on the trip to Brighton. Belami regretted the slow pace he had to set to allow the duchess's ancient carriage and team to follow him and resented that she wouldn't allow Deirdre to go with him. Deirdre was also unhappy with her aunt, while the aunt saw no reason for Belami to trot his team along at such a wickedly fast pace. She preferred eight miles an hour, and, with a bit of ice on the roads as there was today, six seemed a more ladylike speed.

Pronto Pilgrim was miffed that Dick hadn't invited him along. After all the sprees they had been on together, why was he left out now? But that's how it would be once he was hitched. By the living jingo, it would serve him well if Deirdre caught him with the lightskirt.

The unhappiest person of all on the trip was Pierre Réal, Belami's groom. A dashing trip along icy highways was balm to his soul, but to inch along, holding in the grays all the way, gave a bitter foretaste of how marriage would change things.

Matters did not improve much when the first two carriages reached Marine Parade. Unalerted to their master's arrival, the servants had no fires laid upstairs and insufficient food in the larder to please that excellent trencherman, the duchess. Her bedroom was inhumanly cold, but she had the bed heated and remained in it, rolled in blankets, till food was brought in and cooked, and the drawing room made habitable by a roaring fire.

Pronto, on the other hand, found the Old Ship so warm and convivial that he decided he would delay his own private investigations till the next morning.

Deirdre amused herself by looking over one of her future homes and planning renovations. She was much too happy and excited to mind the cold.

After Belami had spoken to his servants, he changed his shirt and cravat and went to call on Lady Gilham, to get the minor detail of her blackmail out of the way. The address was the corner of the Dyke Road and North Street. It was not a fashionable part of town, but the house was a decent brick building of modest proportions. He knew he should have written first asking for permission to call, but when one is the prince's emissary, permission seemed unnecessary. A dark-suited male servant answered the door. This was in keeping with the establishment, not a liveried butler but not a female servant either.

The door to the saloon was closed, but he heard voices from within, a woman and a man speaking in low tones. A curled beaver hat and a pair of York tan gloves sat on the hall table. He smiled to see that the lady already had another suitor on the line and regretted that he was apparently not well to grass. The nap of the hat was worn around the edges and one finger of the gloves was out. He handed the butler his card and said that he was not expected, but that he had a message from the Royal Pavilion. The butler carefully showed him into another waiting room and closed the door, depriving him of a view of the other gentleman, who was heard taking his leave immediately. All the view he had from the keyhole was of a pair of dark breeches.

Belami darted to the window to try for a look as the man left, but the butler came at once to the door and called him.

He was very curious to see what sort of female had attracted
Prinney.

His usual flirts were plump, aging, managing women
with a superficial softness concealing a spine of iron. They
invariably led him by the nose, procuring favors for themselves and their families. Belami had a mental picture of another such specimen. She wouldn't actually be an intelligent
woman, but she'd be clever, cunning. He'd have to tread
lightly to outwit her.

The servant opened the door into the saloon, and Belami
beheld a woman much like the one he had been imagining.
She might be any middle-aged, respectable matron. Prinney
liked them respectable-looking. She wore a dark evening
gown, displaying a plump collarbone and round, dimpled
arms. As his eyes moved up to her face, he found himself
being closely examined by a pair of very sharp blue eyes.

"Lady Gilham," he said, and bowed.

"You are mistaken, sir. I am Lady Gilham's companion,
Mrs. Morton. Lady Gilham is indisposed this evening. I
shall be happy to relay any message from the prince, however. Is he back at his Pavilion?" There was a hungry gleam
in those eyes.

"No, ma'am, he is still in London. And my message, I
am afraid, must be delivered to Lady Gilham personally.
When might I see her?"

"I don't believe I caught the name, sir?" the woman said,
making a pointed, inquisitive perusal of her caller. In fact,
she held his card in her hand, but the news that he was here
from the prince had upset her to such a degree she forgot
what was on the card. She had observed the quality of the
jacket, however, the expensive emerald ring glimmering on
his finger, and the haughty manner that bespoke the aristocracy. She could also see quite clearly that he was extremely
handsome, such a young gentleman as might amuse Lady
Gilham.

"Belami," he answered simply.

"Pray be seated, milord," she said, peering at the card.

Her manner softened to welcome. "I'll send up and see if Lady Gilham is feeling better. It was only a touch of megrim. Company will cheer her up. This business with the prince has been hard on her," she explained with an air of offense, but somehow she managed to imply that the offense had not touched the caller.

Then she called into the hall to summon the servant instead of using the bellpull. Mrs. Morton poured him a glass of wine, and they chatted about inconsequential matters till Lady Gilham had been sent for and finally appeared at the doorway a quarter of an hour later.

Belami arose and stared in amazement at the vision before him. She was only a girl, not much older than twenty, and she was quite startlingly beautiful. Something about her reminded him immediately of Deirdre and engaged his sympathy for that reason. Her hair was dark as night and styled simply. She had a soft, doe-eyed look about her and her pale cheeks were flushed with nervousness. Her toilette was simple—a dark gown with a strand of pearls at the neck and no other jewelry except her wedding band. She had a girlish figure, small-waisted but full-bosomed. She hesitated a moment at the doorway before tripping in, looking fitfully from her companion to her caller.

"Good evening," she said softly, and smiled. There was a sad, poignant quality in the smile, as though it were wrung from her at high cost. Almost as though she had forgotten how to smile.

Mrs. Morton performed the introduction. "Lord Belami has a message for you from the Prince Regent," she added with a meaningful look at the young woman.

"A *private* message," he added, emphasizing his words with a pointed look at the companion.

"Oh, don't leave me!" Lady Gilham exclaimed, her white hands fluttering helplessly.

"I shall be right in the next room, my dear. You must not judge all gentlemen by your most recent and unhappy encounter." With this little jibe, the dame sailed from the room, and Lady Gilham turned a frightened gaze on her caller.

"Won't you—that is—pray be seated, milord," she said nervously.

She perched on the edge of an upholstered chair and began pleating the material of her skirt with twitching fingers. Her eyes were downcast, with long lashes fanning her cheeks.

Belami smiled and attempted to put her at her ease. "I'm not going to bite you, you know," he said playfully.

"What is the message?" she asked without any alleviation of her nervous state, but at least she lifted her eyes to his face.

"It concerns the letters you received. I am directed to buy them from you."

She drew a sigh of relief. "Thank God!" she exclaimed. "Do you have the money?"

"I have one thousand pounds," he said quietly.

"But that's not enough! We need five thousand. Five thousand was the price!" she exclaimed, a worried frown forming on her pale brow.

"I'm afraid that is the price, ma'am. You must know five thousand is exorbitant," he added, carefully watching her reaction.

She sat silently a moment, thinking. Then she lifted her head and looked at him, her dark, doe eyes filled with worry. "No, it is not enough," she said simply. "I must sound like a dreadful shrew. I wouldn't insist if . . . I can get more elsewhere, you know," she said with that frightened look still in her eyes as though fearful of his reaction. But he just sat, looking. "That is my message, my final decision," she said and arose, glancing at the door.

"Wait!" Belami called, jumping up and taking a step toward her. "Lady Gilham, do you really want the disgrace and degradation of having those intimate letters published for the world to snicker over? You won't remain untarnished yourself."

"I am already thoroughly tarnished, milord. Your royal friend has seen to that," she said, quick anger flashing across her lovely face. "As he has seen fit to boast of his conquest of me, I might as well have some recompense for it. I am ruined for any chance of a respectable marriage. I must have something to live on."

"I assure you the conquest is not spoken of abroad," he told her.

"If he can sprinkle titles and sinecures on his other mistresses, he can give me a paltry five thousand pounds. It is reasonable, considering his alternative," she said with a toss of her head. Anger had washed away that air of the shy, young girl. What Belami was looking at now was a very determined woman.

"You refer to the publication of the letters," he said, his interest piqued at her sudden change of mode.

"That will do—for a start," she said.

While he stood looking, the anger faded and tears welled up in her eyes to splash down her cheeks. She was back to being a frightened little girl, and he felt an urge to gather her up in his arms and comfort her.

"Perhaps if you could let me see the letters . . ." he said, as something had to be said. Negotiations must not be severed entirely.

"We can't talk now. Not with her listening at the keyhole," she said in a low voice, tossing her head toward the door through which Mrs. Morton had recently departed. Belami felt that he had at least ingratiated himself with Lady Gilham. Earlier, she had wanted the chaperone to remain in the room. It was an easy leap to suspect the chaperone was behind the exorbitant sum asked.

"When then?"

"She goes to visit a friend at Devil's Dyke tomorrow. Can you return then? I shall be quite alone."

"At what hour?" he asked eagerly.

"She leaves at ten. I shall be home all day alone. Do come early. I *must* get this settled. It's driving me to distraction.'' She shook her head and dabbed at her tears with a handkerchief.

''I'll come at ten-thirty,'' he promised.

She nodded her agreement with a little sniff to stop her tears. ''What—what did he say when he sent you on this mission?'' she asked hesitantly.

After a brief, thoughtful pause, Belami saw no reason to encourage her hopes. ''He said he hoped to avoid scandal and was willing to pay the sum I mentioned for the letters. That's all.''

The forlorn expression hardened into bitterness. ''That's all I was to him, just a possibility of future scandal. He is a *wicked* man, your friend. Wicked, treacherous, deceitful—like all men,'' she finished with a disillusioned look. Such beautiful youth as he beheld ought not to be disillusioned, he thought sadly.

''I don't suppose it's easy being a prince,'' Belami said, hoping to assuage her anger.

''He should try being a pauper!''

''He's surrounded by sycophants. It's enough to make a saint a cynic. We'll discuss it tomorrow.''

''Very well, but unless you are prepared to raise the price, there is nothing to discuss. Good evening, milord.''

She turned her back on him and walked away, not out the door, but farther into the room, leaving him to show himself out. There was a scurrying sound in the hallway, leading him to believe their discussion had indeed been listened to. Tomorrow they would have a chance for a better, longer chat. He had some hope of talking her price down and some fear she might talk his up.

As he drove home, he pondered what tack to take with Lady Gilham. She was hurt, offended, and she was angry. She was also, apparently, poor. ''We need five thousand,'' she had said. Who was that ''we''? Mrs. Morton and herself? Five thousand was out of the question, but he might have to bump it up to two thousand or twenty-five hundred. It was true the prince lavished more on flirts who didn't need it as badly. Belami felt out of sorts with the world and disillusioned himself, till he remembered Deirdre was at home waiting for him. How fortunate, how positively blessed he was to have found and won her. And when he at last got her away from the duchess, things would be perfect.

Chapter Three

The duchess had not yet made her toilette, which allowed Belami a few moments alone with Deirdre. Without quite being conscious of it, he was mentally comparing her situation with that of Lady Gilham. Here was Deirdre, heiress to her aunt's large fortune and betrothed to himself, who also had a fortune. Life seemed unfair. Poor Lady Gilham had to haggle and bargain and risk her reputation for a meager competence. He admired her spirit in tackling Prinney, even if circumstances had placed him on the opposite side of the matter.

"What was she like?" Deirdre asked eagerly when they pulled their chairs close to the grate.

"Rather like you, in appearance," he said, smiling at the memory. "Much younger and prettier than I expected. More a victim than a predator, I think."

"Oh, really?" Deirdre asked in a voice a shade less friendly than before. In fact, a definite shadow of apprehension flitted across her face. Dick was far too broad-minded and French where young women were concerned. "Apparently she is much livelier in disposition. *I* would never be so dashing as to have an affair with Prinney. Neither would I threaten to publish his letters when he jilted me."

"You might be a little more charitable in your assessment," he suggested. "She hasn't your advantages, Deirdre. I must say I admire her courage. She seems to be in desperate need of money," he added, gazing into the flames.

"Does she have children?"

"No. That is, she didn't mention it. Perhaps that's it," he added, frowning. "She did mention that 'we' need the money."

His fiancée knew by Belami's frown that his mind was still back at Lady Gilham's house, and she resented it.

"How is her establishment? Is she living in a hovel?" she asked.

"No, no, it's decent, but by no means grand."

"I should think Gilham left her something," she said, hoping to wear away Dick's sympathy for the attractive young widow.

"I suppose so."

"You didn't tell me whether or not she agreed to the prince's offer."

"No, she's adamant about her price. I have to return tomorrow. There was a companion there this evening. She wants more privacy," he explained with a shocking naiveté for one of his experience.

"You're returning tomorrow to see her *alone*?" Deirdre asked, disliking the affair more by the moment.

"Yes."

After a brief, strained silence, she said, "Why don't you invite her here instead, Dick? It will be easier for you, and the surroundings so much more pleasant."

He cut through this charade with ease. "Don't you trust me?" he asked. She tossed her head, but didn't answer. "I don't know whether I'm flattered or angry. Both, I think," he decided.

"Of course I trust you," she said then, but with patent insincerity.

"Then it's Lady Gilham you mistrust? She's not what you think at all, Deirdre. She's young, vulnerable. I felt sorry for the girl," he was foolish enough to admit.

"Indeed! You must not go transforming her into a saint,

Dick. She's a widow who had an affair with a man old enough to be her father, and now she's holding him to ransom. I don't call *that* very vulnerable!''

"You're a hard judge."

"*You* are no judge at all. How much are you going to give her?'' she asked with a definite stiffening in her posture.

Before the discussion disintegrated into a lovers' quarrel, the heavy tread of the duchess was heard on the stairs, and soon she had herself bundled up before the grate, placing herself carefully between the lovers.

"Let us hear all about the trollop who is out to fleece Prinney,'' was her opening remark, uttered with great relish.

Deirdre saw Belami stiffen up and felt, for the first time since her betrothal, a doubt as to how firmly she had caught him. He had been a famous womanizer before the engagement. And the engagement was not even a week old. A tiger didn't change his spots overnight. She must keep a sharp eye on the negotiations with Lady Gilham or it would be Dick who was supporting the hussy next.

When he had repeated his tale to the duchess, she said, "She sounds a proper conniver to *me*. She conned the prince, and she has conned you, my lad. Take care she don't set her cap for you. She oughtn't to be given a penny. The cart's tail is the place for her sort. Is dinner ready yet?''

During dinner, there was more of the same sort of talk, with the duchess deriding Lady Gilham, Deirdre adding a few comments, and Dick mounting a defense of the woman, which was soon talked down. Dick began to stiffen. He regretted having brought the ladies to Brighton with him. He'd have done better to come alone and finish his business quickly. Right now he should be at the Old Ship, trying to scrape an acquaintance with George Smythe, instead of arguing black was white with the duchess.

"You have remarkable confidence in your judgment, ma'am,'' he said as dinner drew to a stormy close. ''You're ready to stand judge on a perfect stranger.''

"I know a trollop when I see one," the duchess answered, eyeing the table for any remaining treats.

"But you haven't seen this particular one," he pointed out. Then he added hastily, "And, in *my* opinion, she is not a trollop but an unwise girl."

"All gels are unwise," she said comprehensively, but definitely including her niece in her condemnation. "Their greatest error is to think they can trust a man. I shall give you one short hand of cards before I retire, Belami."

As the duchess liked to eat early, he had time for this before going to the Old Ship. After half an hour the duchess yawned and shoveled her ill-gotten gains into her reticule (for she always cheated at cards) and announced that she and Deirdre would go to bed now. It was eight-thirty.

"I suppose you will go chasing after Mr. Smythe?" she asked before leaving. He nodded.

"I've been thinking about your visit to that Gilham female tomorrow, Belami. Deirdre shall accompany you," she told him.

"I'm afraid not, ma'am. It's not the sort of place you would want your niece to visit," he explained, trying to hold his temper in check for Deirdre's benefit.

"Very true, but it is the sort of establishment she will be drawn into, now that she is betrothed to you," she answered tartly, staring at him as though he were a toad. "You might as well get accustomed to it," she added in an aside to her niece before returning her fire to Belami. "Furthermore, it's clear the hussy has wound you around her finger. We need an objective third person present to hold her wiles in check. I don't suppose she will be brass-faced enough to cast herself on your shoulder in front of another woman."

Belami counted to ten, then cast a commanding scowl on Deirdre, tacitly ordering her to refuse.

"I shall be very happy to go with you, Dick," she said with the greatest alacrity.

"Excellent. Then it is settled," the duchess said. "We take breakfast at eight, Belami. Gammon and eggs, coddled eggs. Try, if you can, to convince your cook not to overcook them, as he did the fowl tonight. I feel a wretched bout of heartburn coming on. After you return from visiting the Gilham woman tomorrow, you might take Deirdre and myself around to Donaldson's Library. I notice there is nothing fit for a lady to read in your book room here. Good night to you.'' With this amiable speech she hauled herself from her chair.

"Good night, ladies." Dick performed a stiff bow, holding in all his anger against the interfering dame. Nothing to read, indeed! There was a room full of the best literature available. Foolish old bint! What she meant was that she wanted the latest maudlin Gothic. And coddled eggs! He hated coddled eggs. A steak and a glass of ale was what he would order. Or here, by the sea, some smoked herring would be a pleasant change.

On top of it all, he hadn't had more than a minute alone with Deirdre, and that he had destroyed by praising Lady Gilham. He felt some anger, too, that the duchess might be right about his susceptibility to that woman. Ladies in distress were his outstanding weakness. He'd be on his guard tomorrow. Part of his anger he saved for his fiancée. Now that she was betrothed, she should be allowed more freedom; she ought to *demand* it. But what did she do? She trotted meekly up to her bedroom at eight-thirty without even sneaking back down to kiss him good night.

He put his curled beaver hat on his head at a cocky angle, threw his many-caped great coat over his shoulders, and struck out of the door. The Old Ship was close to home, not worth having the horses put to. It was just around the corner, at the meeting of Grand Junction Road and East Street.

He was still wearing a scowl when he entered the hotel and stamped the snow from his feet, but the friendly chatter from the card room, the warmth and the aroma of wine, ale, and tobacco soon raised his spirits. If Smythe weren't here, he could at least have a game of cards with somebody who didn't cheat. He stopped at the doorway into the card room and looked around at the tables, hoping to see an acquaintance. He wasn't slow to recognize the broad face and bent nose of Pronto Pilgrim.

Pronto saw Belami even sooner. He lifted his cards to hide his face, but of course he had to peek above them to see if Dick had entered, and when he looked, Belami was smiling at him. Looked downright happy to see him, which was a shock. He was sure Dick would give him a rare Bear Garden jaw for coming down uninvited.

But, no, Dick was pacing forward with his hand out. "Pronto, you old son of a bachelor, what are you doing here? You might have stepped around to Marine Parade to say hello—or better, have come down with me as I was alone in the carriage."

"Eh?" Pronto asked suspiciously. "Thought you was coming with Miss Gower."

"Not with her, three steps in front of her, at a mad gallop of eight miles an hour."

"Is Réal sick?" Pronto asked in alarm. Pierre Réal, Dick's groom, was a famous fiddler.

"He is now after that funereal pace. What are you playing? Is there room for one more?" he asked, looking around at the other gentlemen. He didn't recognize any of them and concluded that Pronto had taken up with some other travelers. There was no one at the table who fitted the description of Mr. Smythe.

"We've just finished the game," Pronto said quickly. Very quickly. His blue eyes darted sideways to the gentleman on his left. "Let's go into the common room and have a wet," he suggested. "It's thirsty work, cards." There was a glass of ale at his elbow, but Belami knew this was only a ruse to get away.

He glanced to the left and saw a perfectly ordinary gentleman of advanced years. He wasn't much younger than sixty, with silver hair and a weathered face. His clothing was not the work of Weston nor of any of the first-rate tailors, though it had aspirations beyond the provinces. There was a sharp, crafty look on the man's face and a good pile of money on the table in front of him. He deduced that Pronto had been fleeced and knew he must rescue him. He gave a civil, blanket sort of smile to the assembled group at the table and departed with Pronto.

"Demmed Captain Sharp fleeced me of a pony," Pronto complained. "I watched him as close as could be and couldn't figure out how he did it. The cards wasn't shaved, but he never lost a hand."

They walked along to the common room and took up a table near the fire. "Who is he?" Belami asked, hardly interested.

"Name's Stack, Captain Stack," Pronto said angrily. "Irish, as you might expect."

"Captain Stack!" Belami exclaimed sharply. "Lord, no wonder he cleaned you. He's a gambling friend of Prinney's set. Too sharp for you, my friend."

"How do *you* know him?" Pronto asked, but as the waiter came along at that moment and he had some involved explanations to deliver regarding the preparation of his rumbo, he missed hearing Belami's explanation.

"'Eh?" he asked when the waiter departed.

"He plays with Prinney. You're out of your league, but if he only took you for twenty-five pounds, it's not worth getting yourself shot over. Was there a Mr. Smythe in the room at all? Did you hear anyone mention him?"

"No, there was a Mr. Staynor and a Sir Giles somebody or other."

"You're sure Smythe wasn't there?"

"Damme, no. What has Mr. Smythe to do with anything? I still have a good mind to call Stack out."

"Don't count on me as your second if you do," Belami cautioned.

"Say, where's Deirdre?" Pronto asked suddenly. "Has the duchess carted her back to London on you? I knew it was foolishness, bringing them along. Did you see the ladybird?"

"I did, and she's some bird of paradise," Belami said, then gave an approving nod. "How did you know about Lady Gilham?" he asked suddenly.

"Is that her name? I didn't know who she was. You told me you was coming down to chase some ladybird. Told me yourself this very morning."

"So I did. It seems weeks ago. Since you're here, you may be useful to me, Pronto. The fact is, I'm involved in a case," he said. "Perhaps we should take our drinks to your room to discuss it, if you're interested."

"Dash it, you know I'm interested. Why else do you think I jogged all the way down here? Knew you'd be needing me. Demmed risky to have brought the ladies with you."

They met the waiter at the door and carried the bowl of rumbo upstairs themselves. When it was stirred and poured and the fire lit, they settled down to a recital of the case. Pronto listened with the keenest of interest, only slightly disappointed to learn that there was no falling out between his friend and Miss Gower.

"So that's it," he said, shaking his head. "Old Prinney is at it again. Don't see why McMahon couldn't have handled Gilham."

After a little soul-searching, Belami decided Pronto's staying at the same hotel as Smythe was too good an opportunity to waste, and he divulged the more important matter of the Smythe case as well. "You understand, of course, this is strictly *entre nous*, not to go an inch past this room."

"You never have to worry about that, Dick. Mum's the word. And is it George Smythe you're talking about all the while?"

"That's the name. He's supposed to be staying here, they tell me."

"Of course he is. Old George and I are bosom beaus. We had dinner together. We're the only men here under fifty years old, it seems to me."

"What can you tell me about him?" Belami asked eagerly.

"We ate in the common room. There wasn't a private parlor to be had, Dick. Shocking the shifts a gentleman is put to when he leaves his home. He's a bang-up fellow. American, you know," Pronto told him.

"So I hear."

"Well, here's something you might not have heard," Pronto said with an important face. "He reads Ben Franklin. Forever spouting his sayings."

"What?" Belami asked, expecting some more impertinent information.

"Ben Franklin. Odd he didn't mention being a royal duke. Or would he be a prince?" Pronto asked.

"Neither one, I assure you. He isn't boasting of it then?" Belami inquired, visibly relieved.

"Never mentioned the word. Can't be true. The fellow's not at all well to grass. Was leery of ordering the second pigeon as he's short of blunt. I treated him to it. Seems a shame a gentleman must go hungry. Funny thing, pockets to let never stopped Prinney from spending like a nabob."

"He didn't mention what he was doing this evening?" Belami asked.

"No. I asked him to sit down with me, but he had an appointment. With a lady, likely. He's a looker."

"You've got to introduce me to him as soon as possible."

"That'll be around lunchtime tomorrow. Meeting him in the common room. You're welcome to tag along. I'll nip over to Gilham's place with you after, if you like," Pronto offered.

"I already have Deirdre tagging along," Belami said wearily.

"No! Dick, if you ain't a jingle brain. You can't take a lady along on such an errand."

"Charney has decreed. What *would* be a real help to me is if you'd entertain the ladies for me while you're here in Brighton and leave me free to do what I must do for the

prince. They mentioned Donaldson's Library in the afternoon.''

"Ain't much for libraries,'' he said doubtfully.

"You could pick me up a copy of Ben Franklin while
you're there. It helps measure a man's mind to know what
he reads,'' Belami added.

"Ain't a reader myself, but I'll be happy to oblige you,''
Pronto decided, smiling fondly at the opportunity this would
give him to cast himself in Miss Gower's path. If Belami
didn't recognize red-hot competition when he saw it, it
wasn't his fault.

Then it occurred to him that perhaps Deirdre, too, mea-
sured a man's mind by his books. "Maybe I'll pick up
something for myself while I'm there,'' he said with a sly
look at his friend. That would certainly impress Deirdre.
She gobbled up books as if they were bonbons. Yes, by
Jove, he'd take out a *big* book to impress her. Get a few
lines off by rote—lines with words like *viz* and *ergo* and
other foreign obscurities that Belami garnished his conversation with.

Belami remained at the hotel till midnight. As the rumbo
sank lower in the bowl, Pronto began to notice many unhappy references to the duchess were creeping into the conversation. It was clear as a bell that Belami was already
becoming disenchanted with his romance. What he actually
said was that Charney was always on Deirdre's skirt tails,
preventing their having a minute alone, but a close friend
could deduce (if he had the knack) that Deirdre was not as-
serting herself in the desired manner. A docile girl wouldn't
suit Belami in the least, but she was exactly the article for
Pronto, who was easy-going himself. He didn't say a word
against the match, but he let a doubtful frown pleat his brow
and admitted that the future would certainly be "different"
once the wedding took place.

"It certainly will,'' Belami said firmly. "We'll get away
from that old harpy and be able to enjoy ourselves.''

Chapter Four

When the duchess came tripping into her niece's bed-chamber the next morning, Deirdre was sure she had changed her mind about allowing her to go with Belami to Lady Gilham's. She was surprised that her aunt had suggested such a thing, but the real reason for it soon came out.

"I want a close description of her to relay to Lady Hertford," she said, spite running amok on her thin face. "No one in London has heard a word of her. Take a good look at her and also at her establishment. Of course I shan't breathe a word till everything is settled, but once it is the story is bound to come seeping out, and there can be no harm in having a few tidbits. I have half a mind to go myself, but I don't think Belami would like it. He was none too pleased with *your* company," she added spitefully.

"I'll give you all the details," Deirdre assured her.

She made a very careful toilette to ensure looking every bit as good as Lady Gilham. She meant to behave in a perfectly ladylike manner and to show Dick by her behavior the difference between a trollop and a lady. When she entered Belami's carriage, she wore a fashionable new bonnet and a warm, sable-lined cape against the raw weather. She also wore an expression of ardent curiosity. It soon turned into a different expression.

As soon as the carriage pulled away from the house, Dick said, "I've figured out how we can handle this visit, Deirdre. I'll have Réal drive you around town while I speak to Lady Gilham and come back to pick me up in, say, half an hour.''

"No," she declared swiftly. "I want to go with you."

"Why? To ogle and stare at the poor, unfortunate woman? This is no place for a lady," he said stiffly.

"I'm not a child. As I already know the whole story, it won't debauch me to have a look at her. If it were not proper, my aunt wouldn't have permitted me to go," she said very firmly.

"I suspect 'having a look at her' to run tattling back to her crones had something to do with it. This is not a freak show. I will deal better with Lady Gilham alone," he insisted.

"If you don't plan to let me go in, turn the carriage around now, this instant, and take me home," she said, with that square-jawed determination that occasionally came over her.

He weighed his options. Back to Marine Parade would soon become back to Fernvale, Charney's country estate. Charney was looking for an excuse to rescind her permission.

"Very well, but you'll carry no tales. Is that understood?" he asked grimly.

Deirdre observed the rigid set of his shoulders and the angry glitter in his eyes and answered carefully. "Have you ever known me to gossip? I just want to be a part of your life, Dick, to share your adventures. You're always busy; when can I be with you if I don't occasionally accompany you on business? Who knows, perhaps I'll even be able to help in some manner."

Her answer softened his mood. "Keep your eyes and ears open then. Oh, by the by, Pronto's in town. I met him last night."

"Did you get to meet Smythe?" she asked.

"No, he was out all night. I just hung around with Pronto," he answered casually.

"Why didn't you come on home if Smythe wasn't there?" she asked.

"At nine o'clock at night?" he asked, and laughed to cover his annoyance. "Your aunt may have you on a string; I hope she doesn't plan to tell me what I may do."

"Auntie didn't say anything. I am asking for my own information. I would have been happy for your company," she added, to have an excuse.

"You're not much company tucked up in bed," he pointed out quickly.

"What time did you come home?" she asked.

He felt a hot jolt of anger at the question. It had been more than a decade since he had been required to account for his comings and goings. Pronto had told him how it would be once he was married, but the actual experience was worse than he had anticipated. "I didn't think to look at my watch," he said with studied indifference.

This was the mood between them when the carriage pulled up in front of Lady Gilham's house. Belami helped Deirdre from the carriage without a single word. She did not feel inclined to take his arm as they approached the door. The manservant admitted them, his face showing some surprise to see Belami accompanied by a young lady.

"Lady Gilham is awaiting you in the saloon," he said and led them forward.

Deirdre felt exactly as though she had a front-row seat at a melodrama when she looked into the saloon. Lady Gilham had seated herself on the sofa in a shaft of sunlight that came like a stage light through the partially opened drapes. It caressed her bent head and drooping shoulders while the rest of the room faded away into shadows. At the sound of the servant's voice, her head lifted on her white, swanlike neck, and she turned her face slowly toward them. One lone tear wet her left eye. The right was perfectly dry. Upon seeing Deirdre, her sad expression changed to shock. She looked in confusion past Deirdre to Belami, then arose with great dignity and straightened her shoulders. Auntie would be interested to learn that Lady Gilham wore an unexceptionable morning gown of deep plum color, with a white lace fichu and a pearl brooch at the collar. Her appearance was demure, and her face was lovely.

"I thought you would come *alone*," she said to Belami in accents of gentle reproof.

"This is Miss Gower, my fiancée," he explained. "Naturally she is privy to . . ."

"To my disgrace," Lady Gilham finished for him with a sad smile and came forward to shake Deirdre's hand, while Belami completed the introduction.

"You must forgive me if I was startled, Miss Gower. Naturally I hoped to keep this entire affair as private as possible, but I'm sure your discretion may be counted on."

Deirdre murmured her agreement and wished she had not intruded after all. She felt gauche, *de trop*, at this unsavory meeting.

"Shall we proceed at once to business?" Lady Gilham said, walking back to the sofa. She had a packet of letters, tied up in white ribbons, on the table. Deirdre noticed that there was also a bottle of wine and two glasses on the table. "You wished to peruse these, I believe, Lord Belami?" she asked, nodding to the letters with a simple dignity that showed her distaste for the business.

"Yes," he answered, and took the packet up. While he opened them and quickly read the contents, Deirdre attempted to chat with Lady Gilham. The wine on the table was ignored by them both.

"I hope you don't mind my coming," Deirdre said.

"Not at all. I hadn't heard Lord Belami was engaged. Is the betrothal recent?"

"Yes, it just happened over New Year's," Deirdre replied, ill at ease.

"How nice for you. It is a great relief for a lady to have a husband and protector." She emitted a wistful sigh. "My late husband, Sir John Gilham, would be heartbroken to know what has become of me. He took such care of me—too protective, really. I never realized how horrid the world is. We lived quite isolatedly in the country, you must know. I lost the estate when he died. It was mortgaged, and I had not the knowledge to hold on to it. I retired here with Sir John's cousin, Mrs. Morton. She is visiting friends today.''

"Do you like Brighton?'' Deirdre asked, hoping to shy away from such personal and sorrowful reminiscences.

"I *did*,'' the lady answered wanly, letting the past tense speak for itself. "Now I must leave, of course. I'm thinking of Ireland. It shouldn't be too expensive—a little thatched cottage on the coast. I do love the sea. So much water it might even wash my stain away,'' she added humbly.

"And is that why you want—*require* the money?'' Deirdre asked.

"Precisely. All I want is enough to run and hide myself away from the world. He owes me that much,'' she said. Her searching gaze demanded agreement. "He robbed me of my position. I had received an invitation to live with Sir John's sister in London, on Upper Grosvenor Square, for she knew my situation was desperate. When she heard of my disgrace, she wrote and let me know that I was no longer welcome. He actually *told* her about us! The prince did, I mean,'' she explained. Belami's head lifted from what he was reading, and he slid one quick glance at the speaker.

"Life is so contrary,'' Lady Gilham continued after some murmured condolences from Deirdre. "He only met Mrs. Lehman—Sir John's sister—at a formal party. They chatted for all of five minutes, but somehow it came out that I was living here in Brighton. She assured the prince that he wouldn't know me, and he informed her that on the contrary he knew me well, very well. *Intimately*,'' she added with a satirical edge to her voice.

Deirdre bit her lip and examined her hands in her lap. She couldn't think of a word to say. It was ill luck indeed for Lady Gilham, but, on the other hand, if it were not true, it would not have been said.

"And Mrs. Lehman refused to receive you after that?" Deirdre finally asked.

"She wrote first and asked me if it was true. I would not add lying to my other sins—I told her it was true. We have not been in touch since. I told her if she wished to forget me, I would understand. It was the least I could do," she said sadly.

Belami was rustling the letters on the end of the sofa, and Deirdre continued the difficult conversation, unaided by him. "How did you meet the prince?" she asked.

"I had hired a mount and groom and was riding at St. Ann's Well. I dismounted to walk and twisted my ankle. The prince was there and offered his assistance. He escorted me home—I was most impressed when I learned who he was. He hinted he would like to call. How does one refuse a prince?" she asked simply.

"It would be difficult to say no," Deirdre said.

"He came a few times and behaved with perfect discretion. Then as he became better acquainted, he learned on what days Mrs. Morton would not be here. I considered him almost a god. The first gentleman of Europe—who would have suspected he would not be a gentleman at all? But it is partly my own fault. I was so naive, so trusting, so very much in love," she said, her voice sinking low.

"Did you go out with him in public?" Deirdre asked.

"A few drives, mostly in the countryside. He was ashamed to be seen with me, if the truth were said. I wasn't high enough in society for him. He never invited me to the Royal Pavilion. But he was kind, generous."

"Perhaps you could sell . . ."

"Oh, not jewelry! I did not consider myself his mistress. I never took money or valuable jewels. No, he used to bring the game he had shot himself and have his chef prepare it for us. Carème is considered the world's finest chef," she added proudly. "He also brought some of his own silver and fine china for us to dine in style. I still have it. Perhaps you'd care to see it?" she invited.

Deirdre glanced at Belami. He set down the letters and joined the conversation. "May I tag along?" he asked.

"By all means," Lady Gilham said, and led them to her dining room. "I leave it on the table for display," she explained. They looked at the table, set with beautiful Wedgwood and silverplate, with the royal crest. "If he doesn't pay me what I deserve, I shall set a sign on my front door and invite Brighton in to dine from the prince's plate—for a fee." She gave a teasing smile to Belami. "There are other little gifts as well," she continued calmly. "In the boudoir. I could practically open a museum. Put the letters under glass and add the locket he gave me. It bears his likeness in miniature. It's the only jewelry I ever accepted from him. Of course if only he will give me the five thousand pounds I require to leave the country, I shall whisk all of this off to Ireland with me and lock it up for my grandchildren."

"Do you have any children, Lady Gilham?" Deirdre asked in a conversational way.

"Sir John's sister is keeping my daughter in London. She's five years old. Till I can set up a decent establishment for her, I won't demand her back. I'm afraid she would go to the law to keep Stephanie from me, but I *will* have her back, if I must go there myself and kidnap her," she said in a firm voice.

"You must have married young," Belami said. He thought she was not much above twenty herself.

"I did. Sir John married me right out of the schoolroom."

"Where did you and Sir John live?" Deirdre inquired.

"In Cornwall."

"Brighton is very far from there," Deirdre said.

"When I lost the estate, I wanted to get away from the memories. I had read of Brighton by the sea. I like the sea."

"Couldn't you return home? You must have friends . . ."

"I fear the scandal would follow me. I wouldn't desecrate Sir John's memory for any consideration," she said, surprised at such a question.

They all returned to the saloon and sat down again, still ignoring the wine and the two glasses. "So about my money, Lord Belami," Lady Gilham said, glancing at the letters.

"As I told you, I am only commissioned to pay a thousand pounds for the letters and another hundred for the locket. It's strange the prince didn't mention the china and silverplate and—other items. The letters are not terribly incriminating," he pointed out.

"There are passages," she told him, her manner very confident. "In this one, you see," she said, riffling through them to pick up one particular letter. She read: " 'I will come to you Wednesday when you are *alone*.' That speaks pretty clearly as to his reason for coming. And in another"—she flipped to the last and picked it up—"here it is. 'I have known true happiness only in your arms.' That is not very ambiguous. And this one: 'We shall dine tête-à-tête in the country.' " She raised one brow and smiled. "*Dine* was not his full meaning," she assured them.

"But the letter *does* say 'dine,' " Belami pointed out.

"Folks can read between the lines. Actually that is where he first seduced me. I know I sound perfectly vile and vindictive. Perhaps I am. If only he had treated me with the least vestige of respect after . . . But, no, he met me on the street and looked the other way. Lady Hertford was with him on that occasion. He never contacted me again once she came down to Brighton. He was supposed to come that Wednesday. I sat at the window waiting for four hours till it grew dark," she said, her voice breaking on the last word to reinforce the pathetic image her words conjured up.

Deirdre bit her lip to control a sniffle that wanted to come out. Belami handed Lady Gilham his handkerchief, and she dabbed daintily at her tears.

"What else can I do?" she asked, looking from one to the other. "A person must go on living even if her heart is broken. I must raise my daughter. He deprived us of a home with Mrs. Lehman, and he must restore us to decency. He *promised* me I would not lose my reputation. He told me his mistresses were all perfectly respectable, and they are! So why is everyone so horrid to *me*? It's Lady Hertford's doing. She won't let anyone speak to me. I haven't had a single caller since losing the prince,'' she said. ''I'm all alone with that awful Mrs. Morton lecturing me day and night.'' Her voice broke, and she buried her face in Belami's handkerchief.

''Why don't you get rid of her?'' Deirdre suggested, her sympathy easily stirred by such a strict chaperone.

''She is Sir John's pensioner—been with us forever. She has nowhere else to go. I am *desperate*. And if I don't get my five thousand pounds, Lord Belami, I shall sell my letters to the newspapers. I know it will ruin me forever in England, but I shall take Stephanie and go abroad, where no one knows me. We'll change our name. I won't be cast aside like a piece of soiled laundry, and you must tell the prince so. Tell him I refuse his thousand pounds. When he is ready to talk business, I shall be here. But my money is running short. One week from today, the correspondence will be in the papers and my whole story to go with it.''

''I think you should reconsider,'' Belami said calmly. Deirdre was a little surprised at his lack of sympathy for the woman. ''Eleven hundred pounds will get you to Ireland with some shred of privacy and decency. You'll meet some gentleman—a beautiful woman like you.''

Her lip curled in distaste. ''I've given my trust to a *gentleman* for the last time. I want my money. He *promised* to take care of me. If he refuses to keep his promise, then I must take care of myself. You give that message to the prince,'' she said with a long look at Belami.

Then she arose with an imperious toss of her head. ''Nice to have met you, Miss Gower. I shan't ask you to return. A lady's reputation is too precious to trifle with, as I have learned to my sorrow, but I look forward to seeing Lord Belami again. On business,'' she added, playfully lifting her brow behind Deirdre's back.

Belami gazed at her for a long moment, trying to interpret that glance. There was something of the coquette in it. There was also a challenge. His sporting blood warmed to it, but when he replied, his voice was cool.

"It will take a day or two to work out a counteroffer," was all he said. Had Deirdre not been present, he might have said more, but she was waiting for him, and they left.

Réal had been walking the horses. He arrived as they came into the street. "I've walked our bloods around the block," he told Belami.

"Fine, we'll be going straight home," his master told him, helping Deirdre into the carriage before him.

"They're not getting enough exercise," Réal cautioned severely.

"That's your job. See that they do get their exercise," Belami told him, and closed the door.

"What did you make of that?" he asked Deirdre, when they were settled in with the blanket around them.

"Oh, Dick, I feel such a fool, and so cynical! You were right about her. She's just a pathetic girl in trouble. I went there prepared to despise Lady Gilham thoroughly and ended up feeling sorry for her," she said. She placed her ungloved hand on top of the blanket, silently inviting Dick to hold it.

He ignored it. "You don't mean you were taken in by that Cheltenham tragedy!" he exclaimed, and laughed.

"Do you think her story is untrue?" she asked, astonished at his behavior.

"Five percent of it may be true, but the whole is highly embroidered. She obviously *did* have something to do with Prinney, or she wouldn't have those letters, and he wouldn't be willing to fork over a thousand pounds. He's well past the red-hot sort of affair she's painting. It's suspected the extent of his dalliance with Hertford is laying his head on her bosom, and from the tone of those letters, it sounded the same lukewarm sort of thing with Gilham—if that's even her name. You don't import your chef and footmen and dally for hours over dinner either. I think he just wanted a pretty woman to sympathize with him.''

"She *is* remarkably pretty,'' Deirdre admitted.

"Didn't I say she reminded me of you in appearance?'' he asked with one of his smiles that always sent her heart capering. "But only in appearance. As for the rest of it—the overprotected and naive little wife, the daughter in London—I take leave to doubt every word of it.''

"But you said yesterday . . .''

His finger went to her lips and tapped them into silence. "I thought over what you and your aunt said and viewed her in a clearer light today.''

"She sounded very honorable, outside of having had that affair with Prinney, I mean. She won't turn Mrs. Morton off, and you *know* what a trial an ill-natured chaperone can be. There I feel akin to her. She dealt very properly with Sir John's sister, too. Imagine Prinney telling Mrs. Lehman he had an affair with Lady Gilham. I knew he was ramshackle, but I never thought he would be so mean,'' she said in vexation.

"He's not mean, and he's not a fool either. That's exactly what confirmed my feeling we were being led down the primrose path. Lady Gilham has no notion of how gentlemen of the higher social class conduct their affairs. A gentleman would never boast of such a conquest. They save their boasting for acknowledged courtesans, not vulnerable widows of unsullied reputation. Such an admission would be more damaging to himself than to her,'' he pointed out.

"Maybe he was drunk,'' Deirdre suggested.

"Very likely he was, but even so, he'd never blurt out such a thing, and certainly not at a public party. Prinney knows he's unpopular and walks on eggs when he's out in society.''

"What are you going to do about it?'' she asked.

"I'll pack Réal off to London to sniff around. He'll enjoy a nice brisk voyage in the cold and snow. Upper Grosvenor Square she mentioned as Mrs. Lehman's residence. He'll speak to Mrs. Lehman and see if there is any five-year-old girl there as well.''

"I had no idea you were so cynical, Dick," Deirdre said, unconvinced.

"A newborn babe would smell a lie there. It has all the earmarks of fiction. The façade of respectability, her being a widow with a chaperone but one who conveniently disappears when required. Haste is another feature; you notice she kept insisting on speed. She's afraid something will blow up in her face, someone will recognize her, or some such thing. Then the claim of naiveté—that's another pretty good sign. But she was experienced enough to get something in writing and to hold on to it. And, to cap it all, she comes from Cornwall, the farthest corner of the kingdom, so that checking her story is impossible in the short time she's allowed us. What does confuse me is all that stuff Prinney gave her. Why the devil did he fill up his carriage with china and silver?" he asked, frowning at his fist.

"It might have been more private to visit her house than to be seen in public. I wonder what little goodies she has hidden away in the boudoir," Deirdre said, becoming convinced by Belami's arguments. She was relieved that the woman's beauty hadn't blinded him to her character. If he were falling in love with Lady Gilham, surely he'd be at least a little blind. "I expect if I hadn't been along you'd have seen the boudoir by now," she added, with a cunning smile at him from under her lashes.

"That's a distinct possibility. I'd have a glass of wine in me, too."

"And is that why you were so reluctant for my company, so you could go to her boudoir?" Deirdre asked archly.

"There will be more opportunities. You notice *you* were politely invited to refrain from returning, whereas *I* was asked."

"It was all very theatrical, as I consider it. Her pose there in the shaft of sunlight was very melodramatic, too. I wonder how she got a tear to form in only one eye."

"Maybe she's only half a witch," Belami joked. "Witches can't cry, according to legend."

"I expect you'll have to be in touch with McMahon," she mentioned, her fears all assuaged now that she knew Belami had not fallen under Lady Gilham's spell.

"I'll drop him a note. Investigating Mr. Smythe is my real chore. Lady Gilham was only a pretext to let me come down and snoop around. But I will check Gilham out. The real estate offices might be a good start. I'll find out how long she's been here and possibly where she comes from. I doubt it was Cornwall."

"Poor Lady Gilham doesn't know she has an expert on her trail," Deirdre said, not without sympathy. Whatever her true story might be, she was not in a pleasant situation.

"My duties will keep me pretty busy, darling. I hope you don't mind that I asked Pronto to take you and your aunt to the library this afternoon. I want to get busy and solve these cases, so we can arrange our wedding."

"In that case, how can I object?" she asked, perfectly satisfied. "Besides, I always enjoy Pronto's company. Did you know he's half in love with me?" she asked with a pert smile from the corner of her eyes.

"Only half! I thought he had better taste. I made sure he was totally infatuated," he joked, and finally took up her fingers in his, to make a little love during the remainder of the trip home. Peace was restored between them, for the present moment at least.

Chapter Five

It was a vast relief to Deirdre, and an even vaster one to Pronto Pilgrim, when the duchess decided the weather was too inclement for her to walk from the front door to the carriage, and from the carriage to the lending library.

"Bring me home the latest novel by Madame d'Arbley, and if they haven't got that, I'll take anything by Mrs. Radcliffe," she said. "You know what I like, Deirdre," she added, waving them from the drawing room. What she really liked was a Gothic tale, the scarier the better.

As Donaldson's was just around the corner, they had stopped and chosen their books within a few minutes. Pronto was unable to find anything by Ben Franklin for Belami, but decided the very thing to impress Miss Gower was Plutarch's *Lives of the Noble Romans,* which he took out for himself. He set it ostentatiously on the seat beside him, drawing her attention to it by tapping it with his knuckles.

"What's that you've borrowed, Pronto?" she asked.

"It's all about the Romans," he said, feeling this was a safe guess.

"Oh, dear, how very dull," was her disappointing comment. "I had no idea you read such heavy books."

He assumed she was weighing his brain, as Belami mentioned he used books for. "It'd weigh four or five pounds," he decided, hefting it, before letting it plop to the seat, its job done in impressing her.

She nibbled a smile and said, "I don't have to return home immediately. Since we're so close to the Royal Pavilion, shall we drive by and have a look at it?"

He couldn't believe his simple plan was so effective. Just one glance at Plutarch and here was she, throwing herself at him. Pronto lowered his window and hollered to his groom to "go on up Pavilion Parade past the Chinese place." They both gazed out at the conglomeration of domes and minarets, pinnacles, the arcade of arches and columns—all bathed in a golden winter sun. The garden looked derelict in its dusting of snow.

"Now that's what I call a house," Pronto said, smiling in pleasure.

"It's certainly a building at least," she agreed, trying to think of a word to describe such a macedoine of styles, all rolled into one incongruous whole. "It looks as if it might have been drawn by Fuseli."

"I've heard the name Nash mentioned and a somebody Holland," he said, eager to set her straight.

"Yes, they're the architects. Are you in a hurry to get away, Pronto?"

"Not at all. What else can I show you? There's a dandy little cemetery not too far away, just by St. Nicholas's Church."

"That's a little too lugubrious for me."

"Hate 'em myself," he said with relief. "Seems to me we have a deal in common. Just say the word and I'll steer John Groom."

"It was a real estate office I had in mind," she answered.

"Eh? Don't tell me you're planning to put Dick's house up for sale? He won't like it a bit, my girl. Nothing likelier to put him off than you cutting up such rigs without asking him," he said sternly.

"Don't be so ridiculous. Of course I'm not selling his house. I want to inquire about another house, a much cheaper one. How would you like to marry me, Pronto?" she asked as calmly as though asking the time of day.

"Well, upon my word! I haven't even *read* the book, Miss Gower. Truth to tell, it ain't likely I ever will. I only took it out to impress you. Have you and Dick had another tiff?" he asked suspiciously.

"Another tiff? What do you mean?" she asked, startled.

"He told me all about it last night. About you hopping around to Charney's tune and not paying any attention to him. I could see trouble brewing, but I never thought it would get here so soon."

"What did he say exactly?" she asked swiftly.

"Why, nothing. Nothing at all. I'm sure you could reel him back in all right and tight with a little clever angling," he advised her.

"I wouldn't call it a tiff exactly," she said pensively, concluding Belami had voiced his dislike of her aunt.

"Fight might be closer to it. Don't want to get him riled up all the same. Wouldn't be quite the thing for me to marry you today. Thank you all the same. I'll bear it in mind for the future."

"All I meant," she told him, slowly shaking her head, "was that I want an excuse to go to a real estate office, and if we pretend to be a married couple, we could let on that we're looking for a house. Somewhere around the corner of North Street and the Dyke Road."

"North Street! No, no, it's the Marine Parade or Promenade Grove we want. North Street is a highway, bustling with traffic from dawn to dark. Steep as may be, too, and loaded with coaching offices."

"I'm trying to help Dick," she finally said in plain English. "He wants to learn when Lady Gilham hired her house. And if we should learn she means to leave it soon as well, that would be interesting. So we'll say we want a house in that exact neighborhood," she outlined patiently.

"I'll let you do the talking," he decided wisely. It occurred to him, as they drove along looking for real estate signs, that they might just as easily pose as brother and sister. Funny that hadn't occurred to her. No, what popped into her mind was that she was his wife. Deirdre was hard put to understand the fatuous smile Pronto wore.

They stopped at two offices without any luck. A glance at their toilettes and the agent was trying to peddle a house on Marine Parade. It was at the third office, a seedy one on North Street itself, that they finally struck some luck.

"I don't have anything right on North Street at the moment, but I just might . . . When do you need the place?" the agent asked, nibbling the end of his pen.

"As soon as possible," Deirdre answered eagerly. "Preferably by February, but we could wait till March."

"I just might have a place opening up in February. I have one customer, a Lady Gilham, who's hired the McLean place by the month. She said when she took it she might have to leave on short notice."

"What's that you say, Lady Gilham?" Pronto asked, starting up from his reverie.

"Why, yes, do you know her?"

"No. no. We never heard of her," Pronto said, blushing pink. "How much does her place cost to hire?" he asked, feeling a husband ought to ask or he'd be taken for henpecked.

"By the month or the year?" the agent inquired.

"The year," Deirdre said.

"I'll just look it up for you," the man said and went to his file cupboard. Deirdre's heart beat faster as she sat, willing him to bring the file to the counter, but he only opened it where he was and began riffling through it. She was forced to another shift and advanced to the cupboard.

"Would it be possible to get a glass of water? I feel rather faint," she said, fanning herself with a handkerchief.

"Why didn't you tell me, Miss Gower?" Pronto exclaimed, trotting after her. She glared at him for using her own name, but the agent hadn't appeared to notice.

"Have a seat. I'll get some water at once," he said and left.

She quickly picked up the file of the McLean house and

took it to her chair. The very top item in it was a letter from Lady Gilham, addressed from the Redstone Hotel in London and dated in late August. Beneath the letter was a copy of her rental agreement. She had taken possession on the first of September. Deirdre felt as though she had won the Derby.

The agent returned with the water. Deirdre gulped hastily and said, "We'll think about the house and be back later."

"But I haven't told you the price by the year," he pointed out.

"That's all right," Pronto said helpfully. "We'll take it."

"I'm not at all sure Lady Gilham will be vacating it. I have a much better place . . ."

"No, no, we want Gilham's place. Thankee very kindly," Pronto said, pressing a half crown into the astonished agent's hand as he and Deirdre fled to the waiting carriage.

"What did you find out?" he asked eagerly.

"She's only been there since September. Pretty fast work! She must have scraped an acquaintance with the prince the first week she landed. Her first letter from him was dated the first week of September, Dick said."

"That business of her possibly having to run off on short notice was havey cavey as well," he pointed out.

"She's certainly up to something," Deirdre agreed. "Furthermore, she didn't come from Cornwall at all. The address was a London hotel."

"She could have stopped at London along the way," he said thoughtfully.

"London isn't *on* the way from Cornwall to Brighton."

"Oh. Never been to Cornwall myself," he explained, so she wouldn't take him for an idiot. He was so busy noticing the little dimple in her cheek when she smiled that he didn't wonder why she was smiling.

"You are a noodle, Pronto," she said, patting his arm.

"We make a pretty good team, if you ask me," he answered fondly. "Of course, so do you and Dick," he added scrupulously. "Would you like to go back to the library? I might just pick up another book," he added suavely.

"I'd better go home. Auntie will be wondering what has kept us."

"No, she won't. She'll be playing cards, fleecing the servants. I'll tell you what we'll do. We'll stop off at a tea shop and have a cup of hot cocoa. You can tell your aunt you was thirsty. She won't know you just had a glass of water at the real estate place."

"You mustn't tell her we were there! She would dislike it very much. It's our little secret from her, Pronto," she said, thinking his simple mind would enjoy having a secret. She was rewarded with a doting smile.

"I'll tell her *I* was thirsty. *I* insisted on stopping for cocoa, and if she cuts up stiff, you just sic her on me," he said gallantly and signaled the driver to stop at the first tea shop they came to.

Jaunting around a seaside resort in the off season with an extremely unattractive gentleman might not have been high entertainment to an ordinary young lady, but, for Deirdre, it was excitement of a high order. Everything about her dull life had been enlivened since meeting Dick. She thought of him most of the time. And if Dick thought she was hopping to Auntie's tune, this day's work would prove him wrong. He'd see she could be very helpful to him in his work.

She was smiling and talking some nonsense to Pronto as they went toward the little tea shop. Her cheeks were rosy from the cold wind and her gray eyes sparkled with pleasure. She formed a very attractive picture for Mr. Smythe, who sat at a window table, regarding her from inside the tea shop. It was great luck for him that she was accompanied by that funny fellow he'd met at the Old Ship. He could get himself presented.

"It's Mr. Pilgrim, isn't it?" he said, rising as they came near his table.

"By Jove, if it ain't Mr. Smythe," Pronto said, peering around to see if Dick was still with him. "It's Mr. Smythe," he said to Deirdre with a significant lift of his eyebrows and a wink. "Speak of the devil."

"I hope your friend hasn't been speaking ill of me behind my back." Mr. Smythe laughed. He cast an admiring look at Miss Gower.

"We haven't been talking about you at all," Pronto told him, offended.

"My mistake. I was sure I was the devil you referred to. I don't believe I have the honor of the lady's acquaintance," he added, returning his gaze to Deirdre.

"This is Belami's fiancée," Pronto told him severely.

"Miss Gower," Deirdre added, a good deal less severely.

"What a coincidence! I had lunch with Lord Belami not two hours ago. Brighton is a small town after all. Won't you join me?" he added, looking from one to the other.

"How very nice of you. We'd be delighted," Deirdre said at once. She couldn't take her eyes from Mr. Smythe's face. It wasn't his beauty that held her gaze, though he was handsome. Tall and well-formed, with a reddish-brown lock of hair falling boyishly over a wide forehead, he had bright blue eyes, full of mischief, a Roman nose, and a strong jaw. But what held her eyes was a search for any resemblance to the Prince Regent. She could find none. If there had ever been any, it was long since buried under the sagging flesh and fading eyes of the older man.

"Now that's what I call a coincidence," Pronto said two or three times. He knew from Belami's lessons that a coincidence was always suspect, but, try as he might, he could discover no evil in this one.

"What brings all you fashionable folks to Brighton out of season?" Smythe asked. "I had thought I'd have it to myself."

Deirdre sought about wildly for some coherent reason. "We came to look over Belami's summer home. My aunt was particularly interested," she said, knowing it for a paltry excuse.

"I always taggle along with Belami," Pronto said.

"I expect you'll be darting back to London now that you've seen the house," Smythe said. There was no suspicion on his face, but the eyes were sharp and alert.

"Perhaps we'll stay a while," Deirdre said. "My aunt will want to rest a little before returning. And Brighton is nice, even in winter. Mr. Pilgrim has just taken me to the library. Have you been there yet, Mr. Smythe, or are you a newcomer to town?" She listened sharply for any word that might betray him or his origins.

"I've been here a few months, but I haven't been to the library. I was in London when I first came from America."

"Mr. Smythe comes from America," Pronto inserted, since pretending to an ignorance about him was apparently the route being taken by Deirdre.

This unusual fact was discussed till the cocoa was ordered and arrived. It was interesting to hear from his own lips that he had gone to America a quarter of a century ago as an orphan, but the information was hardly new. They knew this was his story.

"What part of America are you from?" Deirdre asked.

"My father had a small tobacco plantation in Virginia," he said briefly.

"Had? Your father is dead, is he?" Pronto asked.

"Yes, he passed away a year ago. I returned to England with some notion of setting up a hop farm, but I found my money didn't go far. The trip was expensive, of course, and being an innocent, I managed to lose a fair bit in London with card sharks."

"You want to stay away from Captain Stack," Pronto cautioned.

"I know it well. I've had a few hands with him. He's too sharp for me. What I must do before I'm completely in the basket is find myself a position. Farming is so expensive when all one's help has to be paid," he added. "My father had slaves in America to do the hard labor. It's unconscionable, of course."

"You won't find a position in Brighton," Pronto told him. "London is where the positions are. All the MPs hire secretaries. Lords as well."

"I don't feel at home in a large city. I hope to find a place as a bailiff or steward on some gentleman's farm. The trouble is, my experience is all in tobacco and of course it isn't grown hereabouts. But I shall find something," he said cheerfully.

This innocent talk certainly didn't make it sound as if he planned to palm himself off as the Prince Regent's legal son and heir.

"Have you met many people in Brighton?" Deirdre asked artfully to lure him into more revealing conversation.

"You'll find it hard to believe, Miss Gower," he told her frankly, "but I have been to the Royal Pavilion and met the Prince Regent. Pretty good for a young colonial! They won't believe it when I write the story home to my friends in Virginia. He's a famous fellow, the prince, but a bit of a queer nabs."

"It's the drink," Pronto said knowingly.

"He does drink a good deal. I was invited one evening for a game of cards, and His Highness took a liking to me. I expect it was the novelty of my being from America."

Mr. Smythe was a good talker. The conversation never flagged for a minute, but when they parted half an hour later, nothing of any significance had been learned.

"Auntie will be wondering what happened to us," Deirdre said. She felt a twinge of guilt at how long she had been away.

"I'll just drop you at the door," Pronto told her, his gallantry forgotten in the face of the formidable duchess. "Run along to the inn and read my book. Looking forward to it," he mumbled as she descended from the carriage.

"Don't forget our little secret," she reminded him. "Don't tell Auntie we've been house hunting," she said with a bantering smile. "And thank you for a perfectly wonderful afternoon, Pronto."

He blushed up to his ears and stammered himself back to the carriage.

Chapter Six

"Dick, you're back already!" Deirdre exclaimed in surprise when she entered the saloon.

He had been enduring the duchess's indifferent company for over an hour and had become edgy. "Already? I've been waiting an age for you. You were so impatient for my company that I made a special effort to be home in time to drive out with you this afternoon."

"Ring a good peal over her, Belami. It will save me the bother of doing it," the duchess said, also in a huff. "Did you get my book?" she demanded, turning to Deirdre.

"Of course I did," Deirdre said, handing it over and tossing an apologetic smile at both her accusers. Between the smile and disliking to be in league with the duchess on anything, Dick was persuaded to forgive her.

"*The Necromancer of the Black Forest* again! I have read this stupid thing a dozen times," the duchess said with an annoyed *tsk* and put it on her lap, where she was soon browsing through it again.

Belami led his fiancée to the farthest sofa, pretending to point out to her the mist rising from the ocean, but of course wanting privacy to learn what she had been up to. He mistrusted that sparkle in her eyes and the unusually bright flush on her cheeks.

"Let's hear it. You didn't keep Pronto happy in a library for over two hours. Where were you?" he asked.

With a peek across the room to confirm that her aunt was engrossed in her book, she answered in a low voice, "I have information for you. Pronto and I followed Lady Gilham's trail." She went on to open her budget of all its secrets in that regard.

"I'm delighted with your findings, but in future I would prefer that you let me know first what you're up to. And what would folks think if they heard you were house hunting with Pronto?"

"We're not flats! We didn't give our own names," she said, piqued. "I think it looks very suspicious that Lady Gilham was living in London, don't you?"

"You mentioned a hotel was the address. It looks as though she went there for a holiday en route from Cornwall. It's not far out of the way and would be a major attraction. Of more interest is that the shy and wilting violet cast herself in Prinney's path—and to such good avail!—within a week of landing here."

"If she claims poverty, why wouldn't she stay with Sir John's sister on Upper Grosvenor Square when she was visiting London?" she asked with an odious air of having outthought her mentor.

"Because ten to one there is no Mrs. Lehman. That monthly lease looks as though she'd poised for flight—it would have been cheaper by the year. You haven't asked what *I* accomplished," he said. His manner indicated that he, too, had had some success.

"I see you are about to tell me all the same."

"If you insist," he said with a dashing smile that made her heart rush. "I had lunch with George Smythe. He claims to come from Virginia, but was reluctant to pinpoint his home more closely."

"Tobacco-growing country, I believe," she said with a nonchalant nod. "That's what he told me, in any case."

"*You!* You mean you met up with that rattle!"

"We met him at Lipson's Tea Shop when we stopped for a cup of cocoa. It was unplanned," she said, smiling complacently. "Luck is important in this sort of work, is it not?"

A quick gasp of shock came from the sofa, causing conversation to halt, but the duchess only turned a page and continued reading.

"An amateur must count on luck. I make my own luck," he said, burned to the quick that his accomplices had prospered without him.

"What did you learn from him?" she asked.

"A few items of interest. He offered me a sample of snuff, purportedly from his papa's plantation. It was Spanish Bran, the most common sort. It comes from Spain, as the name suggests. To compound the offense, he had drenched it with scent to freshen it. A man who knew anything about snuff or tobacco wouldn't have done so. In short, I don't believe Mr. Smythe has ever been in Virginia."

"He spoke of it a good deal," she said, harking back to the conversation.

"Oh, yes, perhaps even knowledgeably. He's taken a couple of books about Virginia out of the library."

"He said he'd never even been there!" Deirdre exclaimed.

"Well, he lies. I wanted to do a little research, hoping to trip him up, and he has the two books on the subject checked out of Donaldson's this minute. They're overdue," he added irritably.

"That does look a little suspicious," she admitted.

"There were other things as well. I notice he called himself a 'colonial' a few times. I should think *real* Americans consider that a term of contempt since their break with England. He spoke, too, as though his father still had a good spread of land when he died, yet Smythe is penniless. If he'd lost a fortune in gambling, people would have heard of it," Belami said.

"Perhaps the plantation was mortgaged," she mentioned. "If you don't think he's from America, who do you think he is then?"

"It's too early to say. He wears provincial tailoring. *Provincial*, not American, and his clothes aren't new, not purchased within the past few months. The nap's off the cuffs and the edges here and there. And if that's an American accent he has, I'll turn in my ears. Some slight drawl in it suggests Devonshire. He's educated, but not terribly well educated. He holds his American upbringing to account for knowing no Latin or Greek. I'd say he was tutored by some country parson and has done a bit of reading on his own. I don't know what to make of him," he said, tossing up his hands.

"He didn't mention being connected to the Prince Regent, though he *did* say he'd met him. He called him a queer nabs, which is not at all a filial thing to say."

"He said the same thing to me. Since he's not pushing forward a claim of kinship with the prince, there seems no point in falsifying his background. Unless he's wanted for some crime in Devonshire or wherever he comes from," Dick said, frowning in perplexity.

"Couldn't he have had his jackets made in England and sent to America?" Deirdre asked.

"The odd dandy might go to such extremes, but that sort of gentleman would send to Weston or Stultz, not to an unknown provincial tailor. And it wasn't only the jacket. His curled beaver, his shirt, his boots—every stitch he had on was English. I've met a few Americans over the years. There are little oddities, differences in their tailoring. The buttons are different and the stitching—just little things, but they add up to a look. Smythe didn't have the American look."

"You'd think he would have taken care to get the look if he meant to hazard such a project as passing himself off as the heir to the throne," Deirdre said with a puzzled frown.

"For such an ambitious project as that, it would have been worth his while to *go* to America for a year or so, to learn the accent and customs and to outfit himself with all the required bits and pieces. His only bit of Americana is an occasional quote from Ben Franklin.''

"He probably got that from Donaldson's too. Pronto couldn't find it on the shelves,'' she said, disgusted with Smythe.

"You know, I begin to think he doesn't even want this title of royal prince shoved on him. He didn't mention it to you, and he didn't breathe a word of it to me. He didn't move into the Royal Pavilion either, when the Prince invited him to.''

The duchess looked up at the mention of her favorite word, "prince.'' The couple knew their time was limited, and Belami said rather urgently, "There's one more thing, Deirdre. I think Smythe is a bit suspicious of me since I asked Pronto to arrange a meeting. He quizzed me rather closely as to why I'm in Brighton out of season. I told him I'm doing some research into the history of Brighthelmstone for a literary quarterly.''

"Oh, dear! He asked me the same thing and I said Auntie wanted to see your summer residence. He must suspect us already!''

"I'll smooth it over next time I meet him, say the reason I brought you and your aunt with me is to allow you to refurbish this house. Mind I don't want you transmogrifying it into another Royal Pavilion on me,'' he added lightly.

The duchess overheard "Royal Pavilion,'' and decided she was missing some good conversation. "What's that you say, Belami? Are you speaking of the prince?'' she asked. Her commanding eye beckoned them toward her sofa and soon her lips repeated the command. "Come here to the fire. You'll both take your death of cold standing in that wretched draught.''

"Dick was just saying the prince invited Mr. Smythe to stay at the Royal Pavilion,'' Deirdre invented swiftly, "but he refused.''

"The ninny! Why would he do such a thing?''

"It was a bit reckless of the prince to invite him," Belami said.

"The prince? I mean why did Mr. Smythe refuse?" she clarified, offended at being misunderstood.

"I expect he didn't care for Prinney's friends," Deirdre said.

"Hmph, doing it pretty brown for a mere foreigner," the duchess decreed. "What else had he to say, Belami? Give me your opinion of the young man."

Belami repeated those things he had already said to Deirdre. As her aunt appeared to hold no particular grudge against Smythe, Deirdre decided to admit she, too, had met him. She felt one secret kept from her aunt at a time was enough.

"But he seemed gentlemanly?" the duchess asked.

"I only had lunch with him," Belami pointed out. "He manages his knife and fork like a gentleman and is well spoken enough."

"The trouble is," Deirdre explained, "we don't really know what the prince looked like when he was young. If Mr. Smythe resembles him, it's difficult for us to see it."

"My thoughts exactly," the duchess said in a rare expression of good humor. This gave her the excuse she craved to have Smythe presented to her without revealing vulgar curiosity. "I am a little leery about the wisdom of it, but I see no other way but to have you bring him here, Belami," she announced.

"But in the eventuality that he is an impostor . . ." Belami began and was summarily cut off.

"I believe my reputation can bear the strain," she said, donning a haughty stare. "I remember dear Prinney very well when he was a quarter of a century old. Such charm, such grace, and the eyes! We were all madly in love with him. It seems like yesterday. I also knew Maria Fitzherbert well. I am the logical one to assess Smythe," she decided. "Tomorrow morning at eleven you may bring him to me, Belami."

In fact, Mr. Smythe came to call that same evening after dinner. Pronto had met him in the common room at the Old Ship and happened to mention that he was going to visit Belami after dinner. It seemed unsociable not to ask him along, and from there it was an easy step to discover an excuse to do so. It would be an excellent way to keep an eye on Smythe and to study him further. When he learned Smythe had a letter from the prince in his pocket, the matter was settled. Old Charney wouldn't close the door on a fellow who had a letter from the prince inviting him to a private dinner the next night. Even the fact that Prinney was hastening toward Brighton would cheer the old girl up no end. Been sweet on him forever.

It was a strange evening altogether. Just as Charney had been bedazzled by the prince three decades before, she now became infatuated with Mr. Smythe. The feeling was perhaps more maternal than loverlike, but it was noticeably warm. Smythe had no sooner entered the door and made his bow than she arose and performed an extremely awkward curtsy. Prime ministers she greeted from her chair, but there was something in Mr. Smythe that got her to her feet. She was as startled as the others when she realized what she had done and tried to ignore the deed, but for one strange moment she thought she beheld the reembodiment of the young prince.

It was only Mr. Smythe who did not realize the honor he had received. He was quite at his ease. "I am delighted to make your acquaintance, Lady Charney," he said. Even his reducing her from "your grace" to a mere "Lady Charney" didn't rattle her. Pronto stood with bated breath waiting to be castigated for bringing him, but no such thing happened.

The wine was brought out immediately, and, as it was Belami's wine, it wasn't watered. For the first fifteen minutes, the conversation skirted uneasily around Mr. Smythe's coming from America and conditions there. Belami assumed Smythe had been looking into his books from the library when he now located his father's plantation on the

banks of the James River. Belami had found a book on tobacco growing in his own library and tested Smythe's
knowledge.

"How do you manage the weakening of the soil after
growing tobacco? I understand it leaches all the good out in
a few years."

"We had to do a deal of fertilizing," was the vague answer.

Before Belami could inquire what fertilizer was used, the
duchess barged in. She was firmly convinced that she had a
gentleman of royal birth in her saloon and didn't seem to
care much that he was from the wrong side of the blanket. It
was time to wade forward from polite platitudes and get
down to the hard core of the case.

"So you have a letter from the prince!" she said glee-
fully, reverting to an earlier conversation. "He seems
mighty fond of you, Mr. Smythe. Is there a special reason
for it?" Anyone but a moonling would realize she knew
something of the matter. She was fairly drooling with antici-
pation.

Smythe blushed and said, "I can't imagine what he sees
in the likes of me. But then I've heard he takes these inexpli-
cable likings for people of no particular consequence. Beau
Brummell, for instance, a few years ago, and at present his
physician, Sir Henry Halford."

"Come now!" the duchess teased. "A little bird told me
there is more to it than that!"

"Where did you hear such a thing?" he asked, sincerely
shocked, and not happily either. All three of his young ex-
aminers later agreed he wasn't pleased at the rumor's being
let loose. "Surely they're not talking about it in London!"

"A whisper here and there, nothing to signify yet," the
duchess assured him. "I take it you disagree with the prince
on this matter?"

"It's too farfetched to be possible," Smythe said simply.
His broad, handsome face never looked more noble. "It's

true I don't know who I am, but I know I'm not a royal prince."

"How do you know it?" the duchess asked, pretty sharply. "Were you adopted out of an orphanage?" All shilly-shallying was left behind as she got down to business. "Mrs. Fitzherbert would never have put a royal bastard into an orphanage."

"No, I wasn't actually. My father—the man I called Father till he passed away last year—was always very vague about my origins. He told me my mother died when I was born. There was such a reluctance to discuss it that I suspected I was born out of wedlock. My natural father, he said, was a gentleman of high birth, but he never so much as hinted he was of royal blood. I thought he might have been my mother's landlord—the local squire or some such thing. My adoptive father was some kin to my natural mother—or perhaps only a connection. He had just been widowed, losing both wife and son in childbirth. He decided to emigrate to America and start a new life, and took me along, to take the place of the son he had lost. It was a fortunate day for me when he made that kind decision," Mr. Smythe said. He wore a look of gentle wonder.

"Your natural mother died, you say?" the duchess asked.

"I was told so, but have no way of knowing whether it is true and no idea what her name was. It seems strange now, when it has become so important, that I can't be more informative. The fact is, we hardly ever discussed it. I just thought of myself as Alexander Smythe's son. I never knew any other father."

"The resemblance to the prince is very striking," the duchess told him with a fond smile. "A Hanoverian face. Still, it is odd he is so certain you are his son. I mean to say, there are half a dozen princes, and between them the nation is littered with by-blows. I can't say I see much of your mother—Maria Fitzherbert I mean—in you. What caused him to insist you are *her* son?"

"It is this little ring that got him started on it," Mr.

Smythe said, holding up his left hand. On the little finger he wore a very plain gold ring with a domed top. He slid it off and took it to the duchess. He turned it over to reveal a clasp beneath, which he opened. Contained in the cavity was a lock of brown hair. "He says he gave this to my mother, meaning Mrs. Fitzherbert. I suppose there are dozens of similar rings," he said doubtfully.

"Where did you get this one?" Belami asked, coming forward, as they all did, to view it.

"This is the only thing I have from my natural mother. I always thought it belonged to Ada, Alexander's late wife, when I saw it in his room. He kept it in a box on the dresser. When I was twenty-one, he gave it to me and said my mother wanted me to have it when I was of age. It's not much of a legacy, but as it's the only thing I have of hers, I always wear it. The prince spotted it when we were playing cards and later asked me if he could see it. He opened it and that's when he told me. 'That hair is from my own head,' he said. I thought he was making a joke and laughed. But when I looked up, there were tears in his eyes. He threw himself on my bosom and begged me to forgive him, to pardon him. It was terribly embarrassing," he said, looking around at his spellbound audience. "I mean, what *does* one say, in such a circumstance?"

The duchess dabbed at a tear and said in a gruff voice, "You say he is forgiven, if you are a gentleman."

"Then I am not even a gentleman, for I told him he was mistaken," Mr. Smythe said. "I hardly understood what he was getting at. I felt as if I'd been thrust onto a stage without knowing what the play was or what my lines were supposed to be."

Belami took the ring and walked to a lamp with it. "It's inscribed," he said over his shoulder. "I'll get a magnifying glass and see what it says."

"It says *love me true*," Mr. Smythe told him. "The prince assures me that was the message on the ring he gave

Mrs. Fitzherbert, but he could be mistaken after so many years.''

Belami went for his magnifying glass, and both ring and glass were passed around the circle for all to verify the inscription. ''Did he assure you that was his inscription before or after he had read this?'' Belami asked.

''After,'' Smythe told him with a knowing look.

''How could he be expected to remember the wording thirty years later?'' the duchess demanded angrily. ''I don't suppose you claim to remember things you wrote three decades ago?'' she asked Belami.

As he was thirty years of age, he could hardly claim such an incredible feat as writing at all then, much less remembering it verbatim.

The duchess went on fondling the ring. ''I've seen this before,'' she assured them all. ''This is the ring Maria wore before their marriage. For the actual wedding, it was Georgiana, the dear Duchess of Devonshire, who had to supply a ring, as the prince didn't have one with him. I wish Georgiana were alive today. She could tell us so much.''

She didn't blink on the word Devonshire, but it clicked into place in Belami's head. ''Where was your adoptive father, Alexander Smythe, from?'' he asked Smythe.

''Devonshire,'' Smythe told him blandly.

''You inherited his accent from him,'' Belami said.

''Yes, I don't have much of a Yankee accent. Our plantation was isolated, and our neighbors were also from Devonshire, so that something of our homeland accent remains with us till this day.''

''That explains it,'' Belami said, but it didn't explain how a plantation on one of the major rivers was ''isolated.'' ''Your father must have been fairly well off, to have been able to migrate to America and set up a plantation,'' he said leadingly.

''It's a rum thing, that,'' Smythe said, not reluctant to follow up anything he was asked. ''The tales he told me of life in England were hard, but he came into a little money around the time of his wife's death, and that was what got him to America and set up in the new line of work. We didn't have one of the finer plantations, of course,'' he finished.

The duchess nodded her head in satisfaction. "It's clear as daylight what happened. Maria wanted to hustle you out of the country and made a settlement on Alexander Smythe to be your guardian. They were beginning to put pressure on Prinney to marry a German princess by that time. A son out of wedlock would have caused him no end of embarrassment, and that is why your mama took the precaution of sending you away. She didn't dare to tell anyone who you were. I'll tell you frankly, there were plenty who would have been happy to see you buried. Her great friend, Mrs. Mallory, was from Devonshire and likely arranged the details of it, which accounts for its being a Devonshire man who did the job,'' she said, looking around for praise of this deep reasoning.

"The prince places great importance on my father's name being Smythe,'' George told her. "It was Mrs. Fitzherbert's maiden name, I believe?'' he said, making it a question.

"Who else would Maria trust but family on a mission of such importance?'' the duchess asked in a rhetorical spirit. "No doubt she chose a trustworthy relative, but I'll warrant Mrs. Mallory handled the details. They were the greatest of friends, and Mrs. Mallory was often home in Devonshire. It's a pity you hadn't come home while your papa was alive, so we would be able to confirm it. Mrs. Mallory has passed away as well, just last year.''

"Do you have relatives still living in Devonshire?'' Belami asked.

"I stopped at Ottery but couldn't trace the family at all. My father's family was from a farm a few miles north of there. He had a spinster sister who died over a decade ago. No one could help me at all.''

"There must be someone still around who would know,'' the duchess said, becoming cross.

"Mrs. Fitzherbert is the obvious one," Belami mentioned. "As soon as we discover where she's holidaying, we can check these matters." He slid a surreptitious glance at George as he spoke, but if that gentleman was wary of meeting his alleged mother, he didn't betray it by so much as a blink. Neither did he claim any eagerness to meet her, as he might have done if the pair of them were working together. Belami's own impression was that Maria Fitzherbert knew nothing of this hoax going forward.

Eventually she would be contacted and quizzed, but meanwhile he would be busy on his own. The prince's return to Brighton spoke of his eagerness to bring Smythe forward and to throw the nation into a paroxysm. He needed help in managing this case. Someone had to get after Mrs. Fitzherbert—he could count on McMahon for that. Someone had to go to Devonshire and trace Alexander Smythe's history, and someone had to stay here and keep a sharp eye on Mr. Smythe, who, despite his facile claims of *not* being the prince's son, had every detail arranged to support the belief that he was. And, on top of it all, someone had to haggle or romance Lady Gilham into a reasonable settlement. Barring that, the letters and other memorabilia must be stolen from her.

He saw a busy week looming up before him. It hardly left a moment free for his fiancée. If she weren't entertained, she'd be throwing herself into his investigation, probably with disastrous results. Already Smythe suspected he was under investigation. Why else had he asked Deirdre why she was here after he himself had given him a reasonable explanation? Why else had he come to Marine Parade this very night, but to nose around and see what he could discover? His vexation was complete when the duchess invited Mr. Smythe back the next day for "a good, long cose."

When Smythe left, the duchess turned a radiant face to Pronto Pilgrim. "What a splendid notion it was for you to bring Mr. Smythe for me to view him, Mr. Pilgrim. Swift thinking for you to know I was the only one of the proper age to verify his origins. There is no doubt in my mind that he is Prinney's natural son. He has an aristocratic manner, has he not? So easy-going and natural. None of that stiffness you find in the respectable middle class. That man was born spurred and booted to ride, not saddled and bridled to be ridden. Breeding will tell in the end.''

"We haven't one single piece of proof that any of his story is true,'' Belami said dampeningly.

"He has Maria's ring,'' she reminded him happily.

"He has *a* ring, of a not uncommon sort,'' Belami countered.

"What of the inscription and the lock of hair?''

"The hair was remarkably similar to his own, and anyone can have a ring inscribed,'' he countered.

"Aye, his hair is exactly like his papa's,'' was the duchess's fond remark.

"He knows the details of the prince's affair with Mrs. Fitzherbert, and, as he's young himself, that suggests he's working with an older person,'' Belami said pensively.

'' 'Twas old Captain Stack that introduced him to McMahon,'' Pronto reminded him. "He's the right age.''

"Hardly the proper social background, yet you never know,'' Belami said consideringly. "Till we can get hold of Fitzherbert herself, I must discover who her friends were in the old days—surviving friends, I mean,'' Belami said, looking to the duchess for help.

The duchess sat rigid as a gargoyle for a long moment. When she spoke, it was only to throw a spanner into the works. "No, we'd best leave Fitzherbert out of it,'' she decided. "It *could* be all a trick on her part to win back Prinney and the throne into the bargain. She was always ambitious. Nothing would suit her better than to get her broad *derrière* onto a throne. Even if she knows nothing of the matter, she might back up Smythe's story to discomfit the prince. Let her go on holidaying well away from society. She still has connections who would egg her on to mischief. I wouldn't put it an inch past Brougham and the Whigs.''

"How else can we learn the truth?" Belami asked impatiently. "Give me a name—some old friend who still lives here."

"That's your job," she told him simply. "I only saw Maria in London. Her friends here were not at all the thing, you must know. You claim to be clever at these little problems. You'd best get busy and solve this one quickly, Belami. Much as I like the prince's son, I cannot feel I want to end my days in the midst of a revolution. It was the unconscionable behavior of the rabble that killed off our class in France. All that will happen if the prince convinces the world his wedding to Fitzherbert is valid is that he'll be dumped, and we'll have York on the throne. I prefer Prinney."

She settled her shawl around her, gave a commanding nod to Deirdre and said she would retire now. Deirdre gave Belami a meaningful look and trailed after her aunt obediently.

"I fancy she'll be back," Pronto told him. "Slipped her the clue this afternoon."

Chapter Seven

Deirdre darted out her door and downstairs the minute she heard her aunt's door close. Belami gave an approving smile and held one shapely hand out to her.

"Well done! We'll have you reformed into a hoyden in jig time," he complimented. He led her to a sofa, and the three sat down to discuss the case. These were some of her favorite moments, when she was taken into Dick's confidence.

"What's the verdict on Smythe?" she asked.

"Didn't look spurned, booted, and riddled to me," Pronto said with a sniff.

"What?" Deirdre asked in confusion, thinking she had missed this bit of their talk while upstairs.

"What your aunt was saying about his aristocratic bearing. Looked more like a demmed caper merchant to me. Imagine him not knowing a duchess ain't a lady. Ain't *called* one, I mean. Call her your grace, no matter if it don't suit her."

"They don't use titles in America," Deirdre told him.

"What's to do then, Dick? Tell us what you want. We're raring to go," Pronto said.

That casual "we" alarmed Belami to no small degree. Pronto's intrusion into the case alarmed him. Introducing Smythe to the duchess and Deirdre alarmed him. That was bound to be laid in his own dish when the recriminations were eventually ladled out and the man proved a scoundrel. It seemed wise to get Pronto out of Brighton, and he'had just the job for him.

"If you really want to help, go to Devonshire for me and find out everything you can about this Alexander Smythe. Who he is, where his sudden inheritance came from that saw him off to Virginia. Find out, if you can, where George suddenly materialized from—if there even is such a person as George Smythe. It's my belief he's the illegitimate son of Alexander's spinster sister and the father put up the money to spirit them out of the country."

"You said he wasn't even from America!" Deirdre exclaimed.

"I don't think he is, but what Pronto will investigate is his *claimed* origins. We've got to start somewhere."

"Devonshire! Damme, that's miles and miles away!" Pronto objected.

"That's why I can't spare the time to go myself," Belami told him. "I need a really reliable man to do it for me. It's actually the most important feature of the case, Pronto. You won't be out of it by any means. You'll be at the very vital core of it all. Probably bring us back proof that solves the whole thing."

These carefully chosen words appealed strongly to Pronto's imagination. The "vital core" was obviously the place to be, and solving the whole case also charmed him. "How would I set about it then?" he asked.

"You'd better get out your pad. We'll make a list. One, look at the church records, the local registries in Ottery itself, and see if you can pinpoint exactly where Alexander lived. Two, go there and check their parish books. Ask around for the family. Who do we know from that part of the country?" he asked, rubbing his forehead to aid his concentration. "I wish Bertie were here. Mama knows everybody."

"Willie Wyckerton," Pronto said at once. "Lives *in* Ottery. Knows everyone, by Jove. A regular old lady for gossip and family connections. He even knows what a once-removed relative is. And his mama is worse. They're in London now, I believe. That'll save me a long haul in bad weather. I'm off to London,'' he said, squeezing the list into a ball and tossing it toward the grate.

As long as he was off to somewhere, Belami didn't mind. The trip to Ottery and back would take four or five days, and the time involved in tracing Smythe would take another two or three—too long to be of much real use. The prince would have gone public before that if they didn't stop him. The Wyckertons just might prove helpful too. They were as Pronto had described them, busybodies with a good knowledge of their neighbors and neighborhood.

When Pronto had left, Deirdre turned to her fiancé. ''What do you really think of all this, Dick?'' she asked.

''I think Mr. Smythe is a more cunning adversary than McMahon told me. He's convinced everyone he's nothing more than an innocent tool of the prince, but in fact he's done his homework well. I wonder where he got that ring and if it's actually the one Prinney gave Fitzherbert. If I could be sure, I'd have somewhere to start. It must have been lost or stolen—she'd never give such a gift away.''

''He smiled and said the prince only remembered the inscription after he had read it. He always seems to be cutting the ground from under his own feet.''

''Its purpose was to convince the prince, not us. Once that was achieved, he wasn't eager to convince me. He doesn't want to be revealed as a crook when the thing blows up in his face. All he has to do is raise his hands and say, 'I told you so!' ''

''But what does he hope to get out of it?'' she asked.

''Money, probably. A quiet settlement from Papa—the prince—and a gentlemanly offer on his own part to remove himself from the public eye. A perfect gentleman, you see. That must be why he keeps the whole thing so low key.''

''But where did he get the ring? Where did he even get the idea?'' she asked.

"I smell an older person behind it, and Captain Stack is the only one who's turned up thus far. Keep hounding your aunt for old friends of Fitzherbert. She must know someone I could talk to."

"I will. There's Mrs. Morton, Dick. She is fiftyish, the right age."

"Morton?" he asked, surprised. "You've got your cases mixed up. She's part of the Lady Gilham affair," Belami reminded her. "That's what we get for coursing two hares with one hound."

"So she is. I forgot for a moment. Yet there are a few similarities between the two cases. An older woman and a young lady on one side; an older man—Stack, I mean, and a younger man on the other. Both trying to relieve Prinney of money. You have mentioned the importance of method in the past. Their methods are vaguely similar."

"The timing, too, coincides," he said, always ready to consider all angles. "Gilham came in September and Smythe not much later. Both were in London before that and both from an inconvenient distance. It's an interesting notion, but for the present, I mean to concentrate on Smythe. He's the bigger hare."

"Here I thought it was Lady Gilham you'd be concentrating on," she said, looking at him archly. "Since she's so very attractive, I mean."

Belami's hand went around her neck, his fingers stroking her throat as he pulled her toward him. She looked into his smoldering black eyes and felt a shiver course through her. His lips touched hers, a brushing touch. A sensation like an electrical charge jolted through her, and suddenly his arms were around her, pulling her mercilessly against him, while he kissed her with passion.

"Why should I be interested in that hussy when I've got you?" he asked, his voice husky.

She pulled reluctantly away and patted her hair, with a prim face from which a pair of excited gray eyes betrayed her tumult. "We'll know more about Lady Gilham tomorrow when Réal gets back from London," she said, trying for an air of calmness.

"It hardly matters who she is. She has the damned letters and enough royal artifacts to open a museum. She must be handled. I'll speak to Prinney or McMahon tomorrow and outline her demands. My own instinct is to break in and steal the lot."

"I worry about your instincts, Dick," she said, shaking her head.

"Well you might! But it's a different instinct you should be concerned with right now," he cautioned, pulling her back into his arms. After a friendly battle, she extricated herself and flew upstairs, tiptoed past her aunt's door to her own room, where the duchess sat on the end of her bed with her arms crossed and a scowl on her face.

"There is no need to inquire where you have been," her aunt said.

"I was just having a—a word with Dick," she said with a convulsive swallow.

"You will have no more words of *that* sort with him. I know what stains your face scarlet, my gel, and it ain't innocent chitchat. Allowing yourself to be bundled like a common pantry maid. I was about to go in and haul you out by the ear, when I heard you running away from him. What was he up to, eh?"

"Just saying good night," Deirdre replied, as red as her aunt had described her color.

Such an infraction of the rules should have been good for an hour's scold and would have been, but at the moment the duchess had a different subject. It was an interest in Smythe that had brought her forth.

"What does Belami feel are Smythe's chances of proving himself?" she asked curtly.

"He thinks Smythe is a scoundrel and means to prove it," Deirdre answered promptly.

"If the prince accepts Smythe and manages to establish him in some sort of position without bringing on a revolution, Smythe would be a good gentleman to know. We shan't alienate him. We shall be polite, just in case. What are your feelings toward Smythe?''

"*My* feelings?'' Deirdre asked, surprised. "I don't have any.''

"What, no feelings about an inordinately handsome young gentleman of royal blood? You're a cold minx, indeed!''

"How should I have any feelings for a perfect stranger?''

"Ninny!'' The duchess's beaked face lunged toward her. "Don't you see the possibilities inherent in this situation? I've been raking it over, and Maria Fitzherbert just might pull the thing off. If this lad is Prinney's son, and if he can get his marriage to Fitzherbert legalized, you're looking at the next king of England! How would you like to be *his* lady, eh? Not bad for a chit that never had a beau to her name till I tricked Belami into offering. Smythe has got an eye for you, Deirdre. Several times this evening I saw him gazing at you most fondly. Oh, discreetly, but fondly. It's a long chance, but when you get to be my age, you'll know long chances can pay off handsomely. Life is full of surprises. That's the only thing I can say for sure after eighty-plus years on this dull old planet. It's the surprises that make it worthwhile.'' Her voice had faded to a wistful tone seldom heard before.

"He hasn't a chance in a thousand.''

"He has scarcely a chance in a million. I'm not a fool. I don't intend to turn Belami off, but that's not to say you can't roll your eyes a little at Smythe at the same time. Lord, most girls can juggle half a dozen men at a time. Why must I get stuck with a slowtop like you? What we shall do is remove from Belami's house. In a perfectly friendly way, but we shall move and hire an apartment for the next month or so. It is clear as glass the excitement will be in Brighton this winter, and I don't know that I want to be worried night and day that Belami is sneaking you off to dark corners to misbehave.'' This was actually a part of her reason, but only a small part.

"Think of the expense, Auntie,'' Deirdre said, knowing this would be a strong inducement to remain where they were.

"I have thought of it! It's been bothering me greatly, but, by God, it's worth the expense. I shall contact Mr. Nailer, the real estate agent, and see what he has up for hire.''

She went to her room and scanned the local paper that same night, to have an idea what price was reasonable or at least being demanded. It must be a handsome apartment, and hang the expense. Spend a sprat to catch a mackerel, for after all the future queen of England could not hang her hat in just any old pair of rooms to let.

Belami knew McMahon would precede the prince to Brighton to have everything ready for him. He went to the Pavilion right after breakfast the next morning to meet McMahon in private. And with nothing to hamper her activities, the duchess went trotting down to Nailer to be shown possible places to let. There was no difficulty in the off season. The duchess, a famous haggler, struck an excellent bargain on a tidy little cottage. It was a coincidence, and a stroke of luck, that the place formerly hired by Mrs. Fitzherbert herself should be vacant. It was a cottage practically at the back door of the Royal Pavilion, behind the Castle Inn. Two servants were living in and included in the lease. She darted back to Marine Parade and had her bags packed that instant.

"Where are we going? Auntie, what will Dick think?'' Deirdre asked, astonished at the speed of the removal.

"Let him think what he likes,'' the duchess said recklessly. "Of more importance is to notify Mr. Smythe of our change of address. Naturally we must let Belami know as well—you take care of it, Deirdre. So fortunate I haven't sent in the betrothal notice to any of the papers yet. I shall leave my card at the Pavilion this very day. Prinney will doubtless be entertaining on a grand scale. I have decided to support him, Deirdre. Even if he doesn't succeed, he'll never forget our loyalty. This is the chance of a lifetime.'' There was a blaze of fire in her faded eyes and something strangely resembling a grin on her cadaverous countenance.

Deirdre ranted against the scheme, but in vain. She worried about what Dick would think of this infamous insult, running away from his home as if he were a monster. He was proud, and worse, he was susceptible to other women. Lady Gilham, for instance, might yet ensnare him. On the other hand, she could hardly remain unchaperoned in a bachelor's house. She left a note of apology and jumbled explanation, but she knew he had been insulted in a way that wouldn't be easy to forgive. The duchess knew it, too, and fully expected a stony silence from the troublesome baron who had managed to gain her approval. She counted on his infatuation with Deirdre to bring him back to heel if the prince failed to legitimize George Smythe.

The cottage she hired had fallen into a little disrepair, and bringing it to rights took up the remainder of her morning. Her only other occupation was to drop her card off at the Royal Pavilion.

While all this was going forth, Belami, all unaware, paid his call on Colonel McMahon and laid before him his findings and suspicions.

"Is it possible this Captain Stack might be instrumental? What do you know of his history?" Belami asked.

"Damn all," McMahon said bluntly. "I hadn't clapped an eye on him for twenty or thirty years. I didn't recognize him till he approached me at the Old Ship. He spoke with some familiarity of other officers I do know, so I had no reason to suspect him. I'll have the army trace him for us. I'm more interested in this ring with the lock of hair in it. I didn't notice any such ring on young Smythe. He must have worn it the last evening when he was alone with the Prince. But where did he *get* it? Even to have it made, he'd have to know the story," McMahon said, frowning.

"It wasn't a new ring; it was worn smooth around the edges."

"Not by Fitzherbert, if she lost it shortly after it was given to her," McMahon pointed out. "You said Smythe had been in London. I seem to recall Stack was also there last autumn. He was complaining of the price of accommodations. They didn't speak as if they had known each other long when I met them at the Old Ship," he added doubtfully.

"They wouldn't, would they, if they meant to conceal they were in league?" Belami pointed out.

"How would he know about the private doings of the prince and Mrs. Fitzherbert? No, if an older person is behind it, it would more likely be a woman who knew all the gossip. I wonder if Stack has a wife," he added, rubbing his chin. "I'll have that looked into from his army records."

"My friend Pilgrim is in London inquiring into Smythe's alleged background with a friend from Ottery," Belami mentioned.

"*Pronto* Pilgrim?" the colonel asked, aghast. "That's risky business. I wouldn't have taken him into my confidence for all the tea in China."

"I didn't know he was coming to Brighton, but he had registered at the Old Ship and has been helpful," Belami said.

"Did you hear we've found Fitzherbert?" McMahon asked.

"No, where was she?"

"She's gone to Bath visiting friends. The Prince Regent has posted off another missive—God knows whether she'll heed it, but I sent a man I trust as well, with orders to see her in person if he has to climb in her bedroom window at night to accomplish it. And even then we may be hopping from the frying pan into the fire if she supports Smythe's story. The brouhaha in the House of Parliament will be something for the history books if she does. They'll be debating the Royal Marriage Act and the Act of Settlement and probably the Prince Regent's sanity as well. A pity there isn't an act prohibiting such folly as we see here. We live in interesting times, Belami.''

''Yes, and will reap the rewards of the old Chinese curse, I fear.''

''He's invited Smythe to the Pavilion for a private dinner this evening. God only knows what new nonsense will come of it. I never took young Smythe for a rogue. Not that he'll look one after all, as he never made any claims of any sort.''

''He makes no claims, but every detail he lets out confirms the story. That broad, frank smile conceals a sly character.''

''Well, I'll be skulking around corners and trying to waylay Smythe on the way out to see what's transpired. Prinney scarcely speaks to me nowadays since I have no good to say for his scheme,'' McMahon said.

''Keep an eye on him. I mean to take advantage of this short lull to finish with Lady Gilham. She demands five thousand and threatens to open up her museum to the public if she doesn't get it. No one told me the prince had given her so much domestic stuff. Dishes, silver—and God only knows what in the boudoir.''

McMahon blinked at him. ''What the deuce are you talking about? He gave her nothing but a few trinkets, bits and pieces of jewelry and a little money.''

''That's not her story! No crass lucre sullied her lily white hands. She has her dining table set up with royal china and silverplate. I saw it myself,'' Belami insisted.

''By God if she has anything of the sort, she stole it! We'll have her put into Bridewell,'' McMahon declared, his voice rising dangerously.

''She's got it,'' Belami said simply. ''And not stolen either, to hear her tell it. What's to do? It almost seems easiest to pay her off and have done. The other business is more important and needs more time.''

''But if someone can walk out of the Pavilion with anything he cares to hide under his jacket, we must know about it! Good God, is there no end to our troubles? A black-mailing hussy, a fool of a Prince Regent bent on destroying himself and the country, and now a thief," McMahon said, weary with so much trouble.

"She claims the prince brought it to her. I doubt she'd lie about it, when she knows I'm representing his interests. It might be worthwhile to have someone watch her house in case she's enlarging her royal collection all the same," Belami suggested.

"One of your people?"

"I can spare a footman. Meanwhile, what do I tell her about the money? She's hellbent on making mischief. It's not wise to turn her down flat. Why don't I say I'm pressing her case, let her hope for the five thousand till we get a better line on her?" Belami said.

"Yes, you can tell her the prince is coming to Brighton and that you'll urge him to be generous. That might hold her hand for a few days and give us time to think of something," McMahon agreed.

"If all else fails, we can steal the loot back," Belami added, looking sharply to see if this was out of line.

"The prince could not be involved in such a caper," McMahon said sternly, but there was a smile lurking behind the frown. "Which is not to say Lord Belami need cavil at stealing from a thief," he added. "I'm eager to see the affair finished."

"It's an easy ken to bite—er . . ."

"I'm familiar with thieves' cant," McMahon said with a lazy smile. "How easy?"

"A front door I could open with a piece of wire myself. The objects don't present a real problem. It's the letters that concern me. I'm not sure where she keeps them—in her boudoir, I imagine."

"That shouldn't prove impenetrable to a gentleman like yourself," McMahon suggested.

"I'd prefer to get them by some other method," Belami said reluctantly.

"Is it true you're on the edge of an engagement to Charney's young niece then?" McMahon asked.

"Over the edge, but it hasn't been announced publicly yet. The old aunt is a high stickler for the proprieties," Belami said, then frowned. "I have a man in London looking into the history Gilham gave me. No doubt it's a bag of moonshine, but it had to be checked into."

"Have we decided what course to follow for the present at least? You'll return to Gilham's place today and hold out some hope of getting the sum she demands, and I'll see what I can learn of Captain Stack in London. Meanwhile, you can plan to bite the ken."

"Right, I'll call on her as soon as I get word from London about her past," Belami agreed.

He went straight home to Marine Parade. His groom was back from London, waiting for him in the stable. Réal's first concern, as always, was for milord's grays. After being away from these beauties for a day, Réal had to inspect them to ensure the stand-in groom hadn't lamed them. He ran his hands carefully over their joints, loudly imagining a slight swelling in the left knee.

"I'd better give 'em a good rubdown," the groom said. He knew well that Belami was on thorns to hear his report and always enjoyed discomfiting his master in any way he could.

"Are you too simple-minded to do two things at once? Talk, dammit," Belami scolded. "I suppose there was no Mrs. Lehman at Upper Grosvenor Square, no one who'd ever heard of Lady Gilham."

"*Au contraire*," Réal said, his black eyes snapping. A jerk of his head brought his underling forward to brush down the grays, and he turned his full attention to Belami.

"You mean there actually *is* a Mrs. Lehman?"

Réal sat on the mounting block, folded his arms, and cast a dark, accusing eye on his master. "This was the very difficult assignment," he said grandly. "I, Pierre Réal, used the wits, as you are recommending constantly. I h'assumed the disguise of Bow Street and presented myself at the door, with talking of difficulties in Brighton with Lady Gilham. The strong torrents of abuses were coming forth immediately. Mrs. Lehman, she says Lady Gilham will end up dancing on the gibbet. She is the no-good, marries the old man, Sir John Gilham, and soon drives him into his grave. Next she is selling his excellent property in Cornwall and runs off to London for the flirtations. She is refusing to live in the decent house of Mrs. Lehman, but drops her daughter there. When the money is nearly gone, she trots down to Brighton to become the trollop of the Prince Regent. When this is known, Mrs. Lehman says the invitation to live with her is no longer extending. *Voilà, c'est tout.*"

"That's a surprise. I see at least some relation to what Lady Gilham told me," Belami said, pacing the stable. "I was sure Gilham made up the whole thing."

"Me, I, too, would not care to inhabit the very decent house of Mrs. Lehman with the cold saloon and no offer of wine. Regarding the daughter, her I do not see, but in the hallway there is the child's sleigh and a small pair of mittens drying. Speeds being of the h'essence, I do not dally to see with my own eyes the child. We *deduce* she is there," he said, with emphasis on the effectual word.

"You did well, Réal," Belami congratulated, clapping him on the shoulder. "How's everything at the house?"

"Uggams and his wife are returned from the honeymoon. The missus, she is a *boule de suif,*" he added disparagingly.

"What, fat, is she? I'm shocked at Uggams's taste. It was always the slender maids he chased in the past."

"The thin ones, they are fast. They escaped him," Réal said. "You have more assignments for me, milord?"

"Yes, it's such a relief to have you back, Réal. I'm lost without you," Belami said. He found praise even more effective than money in getting good performance from his employees. "I want you to set up a schedule with a couple of the footmen to watch Lady Gilham's residence. Let me know who comes and goes, and if she goes out herself, follow her. She had a male caller the first night I saw her. If he's a suitor of respectable inclinations, we might be able to threaten her with disclosing her seamy past. You'll get to know how she goes on after a day or two. It's a busy street with coach houses nearby. I'm sure you can manage to make yourself invisible.''

"It is done,'' Réal said with a grandiose bow.

Belami looked around the stable and said, "Where's the duchess's carriage? I didn't know she was going out.''

"*Je ne sais pas.* It is gone when I arrive from London.''

Belami entertained some hope that Deirdre had remained home alone. He might actually have five minutes with his betrothed without the hovering presence of her chaperone. He turned eagerly toward the house and stopped. If she was alone, she'd want to accompany him to Lady Gilham's place. He wanted to go there immediately and much preferred to go alone. He straightened his shoulders, nobly putting business before pleasure, and got back into his carriage. He'd go to Gilham now. There'd be time for privacy with Deirdre soon, after the wedding.

Chapter Eight

As Belami was driven to Lady Gilham's address, he thought over what Réal had told him. The coloring of the lady's story had been lighter than Mrs. Lehman's, but the facts certainly coincided. The only real lie was that the prince himself had revealed their liaison. Obviously the story had reached Lehman via the grapevine of gossip. He assumed Lady Gilham's plight was indeed desperate and fought an emotional battle with himself.

To be perfectly reasonable, though it was always hard to be reasonable with a charming lady, Gilham had permitted herself to be seduced. Mrs. Lehman implied it was not the first time. A lady who took that path didn't customarily revert to the straight and narrow. She went from lover to lover, and to reveal herself as a grasping schemer was poor policy. Other men would be afraid to go near her. What hardened his attitude was the purloined china and silver. He could not in good conscience pity a woman who planned to set up a sideshow. His job was to "handle" her, and he'd do it. But he hoped she wouldn't cry. He hated being hard with sobbing women.

The servant at the door recognized him by now and admitted him immediately. He was shown into the saloon where Lady Gilham sat alone. She did not arise to meet him, but extended her hand to bring him to her. She looked quite lovely today with her hair pinned up, revealing a pair of cameo ear buckles on two ears as dainty as furled rosebuds. She looked innocent and dignified in a dark dress that fitted rather snugly over her curvaceous body.

"You don't waste any time, Lord Belami," she said and gave an approving smile. "I wasn't looking for you before tomorrow. I hope you bring me good news?"

"I don't really bring any news at all," he admitted, then watched as her lips drooped forlornly. "That means, however, that I don't bring *bad* news at least," he pointed out. She motioned to a striped satin chair beside the sofa, and he went to it.

"No news? I don't understand. Will the prince give me my money or not? You know the situation is urgent."

"The prince is coming to Brighton today. I mean to speak to him in person and try to advance your cause."

She cast a doubtful eye on him. "How that news would have thrilled me a few months ago. The prince coming to Brighton! It was like hearing spring had just arrived. Now it only brings heartache. I suppose Lady Hertford comes with him?"

"I believe not," Belami said briefly.

"Has *she* been replaced in his fickle affections as well?" There was a bitter twist to her lovely lips.

"I know nothing of that, and it's irrelevant in any case."

"So you have nothing to tell me? I begin to wonder why you bothered to come at all, milord," she said, a curious little smile slanted at him through her lashes. Coquetry was much easier to handle than tears. He was relieved and returned the smile.

"As you complained of a lack of callers, I thought you might be happy to see me," he bantered.

"Is it the boudoir you wish to see now that Miss Gower is not with you?" she asked archly. The hot glances she bestowed on him suggested some ambiguity regarding the boudoir.

He felt a sense of danger. This woman would be hard, perhaps impossible, to handle in a boudoir. He thought of

Deirdre and resisted the natural impulse to accept her offer. "I'll take your word for it that you have further items belonging to the prince along with the letters," he parried.

"What a shocking lack of interest!" Her smile assumed the aroma of mocking laughter. "Shall I enumerate the items for you? One Sevres shaving mug, with matching razor, the handle decorated with Venus *au naturel*. A set of gold-backed brushes bearing the prince's three plumes—quite distinctive, don't you agree? One dressing gown of violet silk with a crested pocket and a pair of matching violet kidskin slippers. Oh, and a very fine snuffbox. I use it as a paperweight for the billets-doux," she added to remind him of the most damning evidence of all.

What Belami paid most interest to was the location of the letters. But he wouldn't have an affair with Gilham to get them. He'd lure her away and have Réal break in one evening. The most obvious and credible way to remove her was by making an assignation. To do this, he must make up to her a little.

"I see the prince was very much at home here. I'm surprised he didn't supply you with a carriage and pair of matched cream ponies from the Hanoverian stud," he said lightly.

"That would have been much too public. He wished to keep me very much out of the public eye in case his friends went tattling back to Lady Hertford. None of the items I mentioned was intended as a gift. The plate in particular he wished to have back. Did I ever tell you how I acquired it?" she asked.

"You mentioned Carème bringing some food here, I believe," he answered blandly.

"He cooked us dinner here a few times, but on my birthday the prince had dinner prepared in his own kitchen, as special equipment was required. There were six footmen in my house that night. They were supposed to wash and pack up the china and plate afterwards, but the prince was called back to the Pavilion in a great rush. Some ministers had arrived from London on urgent business. He was so eager to get away and hide any evidence that he'd been here that he rushed all the servants off, forgetting the plate. He didn't want his carts to be seen outside of my house. Lady Hertford arrived in Brighton the next day, and I never saw the prince again. He sent servants over to collect the forgotten items later, and I refused to give them up. That was very shocking of me, was it not?" she asked playfully.

"Understandable, given the circumstances," Belami said.

"I sent a message that if His Highness wished the return of his belongings, he had only to come in person for them. You may tell him that that offer still applies. I'll give them up to the prince, but to no one else."

"All the same, that course could land you in Bridewell," he cautioned.

"It could also land me—and the prince—on the front page of every newspaper in the country," she answered, and patted her hair. "*Point non plus*, I believe is what you gentlemen call it."

"Do you know, Lady Gilham, this vindictive course you choose to follow is enough to frighten other potential suitors away?" he said in an avuncular way.

"Other patrons, you mean. But I do not intend to find myself in *that* unenviable position again."

"I said suitors, not patrons," he pointed out.

"Yes, you *said* suitors," she agreed with a knowing glance, "but no decent gentleman would offer me marriage now."

"Society is not so straitlaced as that. You are a widow after all, not a deb."

"Widows are considered fair game, I believe. I've had a few other bids of that sort. I'm not interested."

"Pity," Belami murmured, an appreciative eye trailing over her face and slowly downward, then back up.

Their eyes met and held for a long, pregnant moment. Neither spoke, but there was a tacit question in the air. At length, Lady Gilham backed down. "I'm certainly not interested in a weekend in Paris or anything of that sort. Of course, if some *honorable* gentleman made an exceedingly generous offer . . . Well, I am but flesh and blood after all, and must provide for myself and my daughter. I would prefer England to Ireland actually," she admitted, while a flush of pink rose up her creamy throat.

Belami gave her a soft smile. He felt a twinge of conscience, but when you came down to it, the woman was a conniving hussy, and, to compound the matter, she was a hypocrite, claiming respectability when what she wanted was an ironclad contract. "Perhaps we could meet one evening and discuss possibilities," he suggested.

"Why not *this* evening, Belami, since Miss Gower has jilted you?" she replied. "I hope *I* am not instrumental in the affair. Truth to tell, I thought her much too insipid for you."

He blinked, not understanding this speech. "Jilted me?" he asked. "What on earth are you talking about? Where did you hear that?"

She gave him a quick, guilty look. "I heard it somewhere or other. Mrs. Morton told me not an hour ago. She said the duchess had removed herself and her niece from your house. Is it not true?"

"Of course it's not true!" he answered, shocked.

"In that case I withdraw my comment on Miss Gower. She will suit you admirably. So admirably that you are already looking about for a mistress."

He laughed a debonair laugh. "Gentlemen like a little variety in their lives. About this evening, as I mentioned, the prince will be in town. He might wish to see me. Shall we say—tomorrow evening? You can tell Mrs. Morton you are engaged to see a play. I'll drive into the country and find a discreet inn for us."

Her utterly calm demeanor suggested she had some familiarity with these goings-on. "There will be no need to return. Just send a note telling me the time and I shall be ready. Will it be convenient for you to pick me up, or shall I meet you there?''

"I wouldn't want you out alone on the roads at night. I shall call here for you. Till tomorrow evening then." He bestowed a caressing glance that was not very difficult to simulate.

They arose, and she advanced toward him, her hips moving from side to side in a seductive manner not formerly employed. Oh, yes, she was an experienced strumpet. Her eyelids drooped, and she placed one dainty white hand on his arm. He lifted it to his lips and placed a kiss on it.

When he lowered it, she was gazing at him with those great, dark, doe eyes. "Kiss me, Belami," she said in a throaty voice.

He knew it was impossible to refuse. He put his arms around her and drew her against his chest. She pressed herself against him, her lips warm and yielding on his while her fingers entwined themselves in his hair.

"Oh, I've been so lonely," she gasped when he stopped kissing her. "You have no idea how lonely it is for me here."

He held her two hands and tried to read the expression in her eyes, but all he could see was passion. She was a hot-blooded woman. "Mrs. Morton might come in at any moment," he cautioned, desperate for an excuse to extricate himself.

"She's lying down upstairs. She is discreet—she wouldn't come barging in unannounced."

He marked this revealing statement. "Lady Gilham . . ."

"Call me Moira," she crooned softly. "And what shall I call you?"

"My name is Richard."

"Richard," she repeated softly. "It suits you. Richard the Lion-Hearted! I knew the first time I saw you that it would come to this. You felt it, too, didn't you?" She smiled.

"I had hopes."

"You won't regret this, dear Richard."

He was deeply regretting the whole thing already, but he assumed an ardent countenance, kissed her again, and fled from the house as if it were on fire. Lady Gilham watched his departure from behind the curtains. All traces of passion had faded from her face to be replaced by a wily grin of victory.

Belami drove straight to the Royal Pavilion to report to Colonel McMahon. "She's an accomplished lightskirt," he said after revealing the general tenor of the latest visit. "I'll have her out of the house tomorrow night. So far as I can discover, there's the manservant, a cook, and Mrs. Morton residing with her. They should be asleep by midnight. I'll have my men go in and nab the stuff. The trickiest part will be the boudoir. It shouldn't be locked, but it will be close to Mrs. Morton's room."

"Do you want any help from this end?"

"No, no, we'll leave the prince out of it, as you suggested. By the way, I discovered how she got the china and silver," he added and relayed that story. "Is it true, do you suppose?" he asked when he had finished.

"It's entirely possible," McMahon told him. "He was there on her birthday, took a whole caravan with him, and had to come darting back early. He never admitted to anyone that she refused to return his belongings. Carème could tell us. I'll go and have a word with him now. Can you wait? I daren't ask him to come to me. I am only the Prince Regent's private secretary. His chef is a more important personage altogether," he said with an ironical smile.

Belami poured himself a glass of wine and waited. Inside of ten minutes, McMahon was back. "Yes, it's true. They all scrambled off in a mad rush to avoid the carriages being seen by the London crew. Carème himself went back the next day to pick up the effects and was given the message. The prince simply ignored it, so far as he knows. We could get an injunction from a judge . . ."

"And a deal of bad publicity. Believe me, Colonel, my

way is better. The lady obviously believes possession is nine points of the law. When we have the goods in our possession, she hasn't a leg to stand on.''

"By Jove, we won't have to give her a penny," McMahon crowed.

"I'm inclined to give her the thousand pounds," Belami said. "She has been wronged, to some extent. It won't break the prince to let her have the payment agreed on."

"Well, well, this is an unexpected bout of gallantry, my friend!" McMahon charged, his eyes widened in surprise. "Quite pretty, Lady Gilham, of course. Is that why the old duchess ducked out on you, taking her charge with her?"

"What do you mean?" Belami asked, his muscles tensing at this second statement of that story.

"Why, she left a card off at the Pavilion today. She's hired the little cottage Mrs. Fitzherbert used to use in the old days."

Belami was bewildered, but he smiled and tried to put a good face on it. "Oh, that—she is merely trying to help me with the Smythe business. She hopes to learn something there in the house—the neighbors and so on," he said matter-of-factly.

"A shot in the dark, but then I don't suppose you tried very hard to stop her. She must be impossible to live with."

Belami got away as soon as he politely could, promising to keep in touch with McMahon and the prince, who was expected to arrive at any moment. He bolted his horses back to Marine Parade, remembering the duchess's carriage had been gone when he was there over an hour ago. It still wasn't back, which filled him with foreboding. He rushed into the saloon and was handed Deirdre's note.

As he already more or less knew they had left, he was able to make some sense out of it. Mostly he read how very sorry Deirdre was and that she was eager to see him at her new residence. There was no denying it was a relief to enter his own house without having to deal with the duchess. Deirdre was always welcome, but he had more than once regretted having brought her and the duchess to Brighton with him. The present arrangement offered the benefit of having Deirdre close at hand without the inconvenience of the duchess under his roof.

He would be freer to come and go as he pleased, as he must at this time. All in all, he was satisfied with the arrangement, but he would go immediately to visit the ladies and confirm that the engagement was still intact.

Chapter Nine

Belami made a fresh toilette before driving around to the little cottage behind Castle Inn. He didn't recognize the butler who admitted him, but he was assured that Miss Gower was within. Unfortunately, the duchess sat with her before a flaming grate in the Blue Saloon. He perceived no more venom than usual on the duchess's dour face. She greeted him with her customary grim smile and allowed him to pay his respects, with a civil grunt of reply. It was only Deirdre who looked conscious of having given offense, and he was swift to reassure her of his continued regard.

Deirdre had spent an awful day of suspense, imagining the most scandalous reaction from her beloved. She was very much gratified, but also highly curious at his mild, indeed benevolent, reaction to the insult perpetrated against him.

"I hope it was no laxity on my part that caused you to leave Marine Parade," he was saying to the duchess.

"I do not hold you entirely responsible for my niece's misbehavior," she told him. "I refer, of course, to her habit of returning below stairs at night after she had ostensibly retired to her bed. That cannot all be laid in your dish, Belami, though I make no doubt you egged her on to it."

"No, truly he didn't!" Deirdre interjected.

"An engaged couple is generally allowed a little privacy,

101

your grace,'' Belami said, not defensively but only stating an obvious fact.

"*Hmpf*," her grace snorted, a little disappointed at Belami's mild behavior, but not wanting to annoy him further. "There were half a dozen reasons for our leaving. One likes the privacy of her own establishment, and you were so much away on business that we decided to snap up this cottage when we heard of it to let.''

These excuses made no sense at all, of course. His being away so much allowed her a good deal of privacy. What did make sense, or was at least of interest, was that the cottage hired had once housed Maria Fitzherbert. Belami assumed the real reason for moving was to look around for anything Fitzherbert might have left behind. A misguided move, after so many years, but well-intentioned.

"I notice the servants came with the house," he said. "Were any of them here when Mrs. Fitzherbert occupied the house?''

"No such luck. The first thing I did was to quiz them," the duchess replied. "They're slovenly and likely overpaid, but good enough for our brief visit. How is the case progressing, Belami?''

When the duchess said "the case," she referred to Mr. Smythe, and Belami knew it. "I'm awaiting Pronto's return from London. He should be here soon. I'll keep you posted. Deirdre,'' he continued, turning to her, "did you remember to ask your aunt about old acquaintances of Mrs. Fitzherbert, ones who might still be living in Brighton?''

"I didn't know that ramshackle set at all," the duchess answered. "I've told you so three times.''

Dick cast a resigned look at Deirdre. The duchess was conscious of having offended a very prime *parti*, even if she might in the end dump him, and became lenient. "I see you two wish a moment's privacy. I shall be in the study across the hallway with the door open if you need me. I am writing a note to my London house asking some staff to come down to Brighton at once. It will take five minutes.'' This was an oblique statement that she was permitting five minutes of semiprivacy. She limped across the hall and arranged her chair to allow a good view of the Blue Saloon.

"Are you very angry?'' Deirdre asked in a low voice, gazing at him doubtfully. "I think it was horrid of Auntie to run from your house and not even tell you.''

"Of course I'm not angry,'' he answered, smiling to reassure her. "To tell the truth, I'm half glad, though of course I miss *you*. It was like coming home to an empty barn to find you had gone.''

"I thought your pride at least would be hurt,'' she exclaimed, surprised at his easy acceptance of the deed.

"No, no, it's much too hardy a plant to be battered by every breeze. My pride always survives intact. It's not as though I'm barred the door. I'll see you every day,'' he pointed out.

"And the evenings?'' she asked eagerly.

"We'll go dancing at the Old Ship one of these evenings. I expect Prinney will have a do as well now that he's here. I may have a party myself, if time permits.'' He arose and moved to sit beside her on the sofa, with a peek into the next room, to intercept a glance from the duchess, who hadn't set pen to paper but sat like a spy, staring. It was enough to cool the hottest blood. The only familiarity Belami could contrive under such strict supervision was to hold Deirdre's fingers and squeeze them.

"What are you doing tonight?'' she asked.

"Snooping around. I'll wait at the Old Ship for Pronto's return and see if I can learn anything new of Smythe. There's Captain Stack, too, who bears scrutiny.''

"What about Lady Gilham?'' she asked suspiciously, wondering why he didn't mention going to her that night.

"I have no reason to call on her this evening,'' he said with perfect honesty. It wasn't till the next night that he had his assignation with her.

"Perhaps you and Pronto will find time to come by here after dinner," she mentioned hopefully.

"I'll certainly let you know the minute we learn anything," he promised, which was not what she wanted to hear at all.

"I liked being at Marine Parade much better than being here," she said. Her little pout demanded to be kissed away.

"If you don't stop puckering your lips, Deirdre, I shall ravage you on the spot, duchess or not," he cautioned. His head inclined purposefully toward hers.

"I'm glad you're not angry," she said, finally easy in her mind. "I was afraid you'd fly into the boughs and cancel our engagement."

"You don't get rid of me that easily, my girl," he said, smiling.

The duchess set down her unused pen, glanced at the clock and arose with a grimace of pain for the ache in her knees. Five minutes were up, or three and a half minutes anyway, which was plenty long enough. As she strode through the hallway, she noticed a shadow at the window and hollered for the butler. Soon Mr. Smythe was being shown into the Blue Saloon.

His cheeks were rosy from the cool weather, and his blue eyes were flashing, to enhance his natural good looks.

"Ah, Mr. Smythe, you had my note informing you of my change of address," the duchess said, greeting him with a smile that revealed her yellowing teeth and made her look so terribly like a skeleton. Belami was annoyed to hear she had written to Smythe when she hadn't even left a note at the house for him.

"I was extremely gratified you took the bother to inform me, ma'am, and came right around to thank you." Smythe made a tolerably fashionable bow. His eyes veered toward Deirdre as he spoke, but she was looking at Belami and didn't even notice.

Belami had been on the point of leaving, but he settled in

for a longer visit, always eager to study Smythe in hopes that he would betray himself.

"Have you been to the Royal Pavilion yet?" was the duchess's first question for Smythe.

"My invitation is for dinner," he replied. "I shall change and go there as soon as I leave here."

"Be sure to give him my kindest regards. I left a card to notify him I am here," she said. "And it is a smallish party this evening, is it?" she asked.

"He mentioned the word intimate. I hope there's someone other than myself there," Smythe said uneasily. "I'm afraid he'll start up on that business of my being his son again."

"It must be resolved one way or the other," the duchess said calmly. "In your own interest, Mr. Smythe, you must give him every assistance in the way of childhood memories and so on."

"What would be the point of it?" he asked simply. "What is to be gained by being proven his son? Royal by-blows are not of much account in the world and anything more is impossible."

"One trembles to consider the upheaval if he tries to legitimize you," the duchess said, "but you are quite mistaken in the perquisites bestowed on royal by-blows. Your being the only male one of the Prince Regent, soon to be king, might give you any position you care to think of. Remember that the Duke of Clarence, *not* the heir apparent, but only a younger son, has ten children and each of them is being settled. Army, navy—but that is not for the only son of the heir apparent."

Smythe listened intently. Belami saw, or imagined, an avaricious gleam in his blue eyes. "What do you think would be a reasonable settlement? I am not at all interested in the army or navy," Smythe said.

"I have no idea, but it would be something powerful, don't you think, Belami?" the duchess asked.

"I expect doors would be opened; how far one advances would depend a great deal on his ability," Belami answered.

"I might make a few discreet inquiries this evening," Smythe said thoughtfully, stroking his chin.

The duchess served a glass of wine, and as she was too newly installed in the house to have watered it yet, it was enjoyed. Though Belami was eager to get away, he remained till Smythe took his leave and went with him, offering him a drive back to the inn.

"Do you think the old girl knows that she's talking about? Is it worth my while to play along with the prince?" Smythe asked, speaking more frankly to a gentleman of the world than to a lady.

"He'll try to talk you into taking a commission in his own regiment, the Tenth Light Dragoons, but you mentioned disliking military life. He might assign you to some diplomatic post. Are you interested in foreign travels?"

"What you're saying is that a job is the best I can expect," Smythe translated.

"A position, Mr. Smythe. There is a difference. You have to work harder at a job."

"I don't mind hard work, but if the fellow really wants to do something for me, I wish he'd just give me some blunt and let me find my own niche. I don't enjoy hobnobbing with the aristocracy, Belami. Present company excepted, of course. And it would avoid all the talk and trouble as well, if he'd just let me fade away quietly with a little blunt in my pocket."

"You have no aspirations at all to be instituted as a legal son?" Belami asked, and listened closely for the answer.

Smythe emitted a barking laugh, slapped his knee, and said, "I wouldn't be king, even for a day. I can't think of anything more appalling than to fritter away my life signing papers and dressing up like a monkey at a circus to prance in public. No, thank you, but if there's a purse of cash in it, I shan't try to dissuade Papa. After all, he's in a better position than I to know whether I'm his son, and if *he* thinks so, I'll abide by his decision.''

"And what do you think, Mr. Smythe? Do you think you're his son?''

Smythe drew a long sigh. After a pause he said, "I honestly don't know, but I think I *might* be, and if I am, I deserve something. That's my feeling on the matter.'' He gave a wide-eyed, innocent look. Belami could have sworn he was telling the truth.

When he left Smythe off at the inn, he drove into the stable yard to see if Pronto's carriage had arrived. It wasn't there, but he was told that Mr. Pilgrim had returned half an hour before and gone out again. It was four pence to a groat he had gone to Marine Parade, and that was where Belami found him a quarter of an hour later. Pronto was passing his time by reading Plutarch.

"Damme, it's about time you got here. I've been reading for half an hour,'' he complained when Belami entered.

"I'm very sorry. Your lips must be tired,'' Belami apologized in his most mellifluous voice, which caused instant suspicion in his guest's breast, but he could find no slur in the remark.

"They are, and my throat's as dry as a desert. I expected to see a bottle on the table now that you've got old Charney blasted off. Or so the servants say. How'd you do it?''

"She did it herself and good riddance,'' Belami said.

"Aye, fish and company stink after three days, so Smythe tells me. Likely got it from this book,'' Pronto said, and gave a fatuous little smile. He concluded this hasty departure meant the engagement was over. His hopes rose, and he smiled more broadly. "That's a pity, Dick, a real pity, but I never thought the two of you suited in the least. Pretty cut up by it, is she? Maybe I ought to nip over and console her,'' he said, reaching for his book.

"What are you talking about?'' Belami demanded, but

soon had it figured out. "It's not a jilting, so you can wipe off your smirk and tell me what you learned in London."

"What I learned there will put a smile on yours," Pilgrim told him.

"Were the Wyckertons familiar with Alex Smythe?" he asked eagerly.

"The old lady knew him from the cradle. He never took any lad to America with him at all. And as for the sister, Ann, she never had any kid either. What happened is that some old pelter died on the boat crossing the ocean and Smythe adopted her boy. He was a couple of months old. That's where George Smythe came from. All a hum, letting on he had an aristocratic father, the liar. I could tell by those hands he was no gentleman. Had a pair of hands on him like a sodbuster."

"That's wonderful news, Pronto! Well done!" Belami beamed, slapping his friend's back for joy. "You've earned a glass of France's finest."

"Wine will do just as well."

"Of course," Belami said, biting his tongue. "I'll get some Burgundy brought up from the cellar." He rang for a servant and asked Pronto for more details after the servant had left.

"There's nothing more to tell. That's it," Pronto said.

The wine arrived, and two glasses were poured. "Ah, that takes the wrinkles out of my throat," Pronto said, licking his lips.

"She didn't know the name of the woman who died on the boat?" Belami queried.

"She never heard who it was, and it don't matter neither, for it wasn't Maria Fitzherbert and that much we do know."

The first bout of euphoria was beginning to wane as a few doubts crept into Belami's mind. "That could have been the story Mrs. Fitzherbert and Alex Smythe decided to send back home," he said, after a frowning pause.

"Use your head, Dick," Pronto said with an impatient

shake. "How could they talk some poor old woman into dying on the boat? No amount of money would make that worthwhile."

"Who is to say there ever was such a woman? Mrs. Fitzherbert could have had the child put aboard with a nursemaid, with Alex Smythe to claim him after the ship left or after it landed or whatever. It would be a good ruse to conceal the boy's true identity."

"Well, if that ain't just like you to go making more trouble after I've got to the vital core of it and straightened it all out!" Pronto ranted. "I'll tell you, Mrs. Wyckerly don't deal in rumors. She knows everything."

"She wasn't on the boat, and she wasn't in America. She only knows what Smythe told his sister via letters," Belami pointed out.

"You mean to say you sent me trotting over to London in the dead of winter when you knew all along it wasn't worth the trip?" Pronto demanded, his fierce blue eyes glittering. "The most important part of the whole case, you said. Deirdre heard you. I see you've managed to turn her off as well with your two-facedness."

"Have another glass of wine, Pronto. You did well, very well. In fact, you did a superb job, and so swiftly too. I'm the fool for not having thought of this sooner."

"There's something in that," Pronto agreed swiftly, somewhat mollified by the excellent Burgundy. "Besides, we've known all along Smythe ain't an American at all—the English clothes, the accent. . . . Or were they faked, too, to fool us?" he asked, sinking deep into confusion.

"I don't know. Lately I begin to wonder if his tale isn't true. I'm so confused, Pronto. I was never so bethumped with doubts in my life. Gilham's story was true—well, more or less at any rate."

"I didn't mean to rip up at you, Dick," Pronto said, his soft heart touched at the unusual sight of Belami admitting to a doubt. "So what's afoot here, other than the duchess and Deirdre shabbing off on you?"

"Not too much. Prinney's in town, and he's invited Smythe for an intimate dinner. He's been to call on Charney—Smythe, I mean, not the prince. I'm taking Lady Gilham to an inn tomorrow night. I really must . . ."

Pronto put down his glass with a bang. "Not much! Oh, no, not much! I should have stayed here and kept a watch over you. Upon my word, Dick, it won't do, you setting up assignations with Gilham right under Deirdre's nose. She's bound to hear all about it. I'm sure Gilham's a taking little thing, but you promised me you'd lay off the lightskirts. Don't expect me to cover up for you, for I won't do it."

"Business, Pronto. It's all business. Gilham wouldn't accept the money, so I have arranged to get her out of the house and have Réal go in and pilfer the letters and crockery and other stuff."

"Seems to me you could arrange a better spot to take her to than an inn," Pronto insisted.

"Where do you suggest, in the middle of winter, when I can't be seen with her in public?"

"Bring her here," Pronto said at once.

"My own house! You're mad! If Charney ever got wind of it she'd have me put through a meat grinder. I plan to cut straight north up Queen's Road and stop just outside of Lewes, at the Red Herring probably. In that way I won't be seen with her. I should go to the Herring now and arrange it. I don't suppose you . . ." He looked hopefully at his friend.

"Good. I'm glad you don't suppose I plan to make the booking for you. Fagged to death. On the road nearly seven hours. Got saddled with a winded old pair at Croydon. Couldn't get a private parlor at Horley, and at Cuckfield I left Plutarch behind and had to drive back a mile to get him." A remembrance of this litany of woes put him in a pucker.

"Plutarch?"

Pronto hefted the book. "It's all about old Romans, Dick. Very interesting."

Belami stared, bemused. "If you won't do it for me, then I'd better nip up there myself and arrange it now. I'll hire a private room, order a dinner and wine . . . ."

Pronto's eyes diminished into slits of suspicion. "Just how long do you plan to be there? It won't take Réal two minutes to get in and nab the stuff."

"I have to make it look good," Belami complained.

"Well, you ain't, my friend. You're making it look about as black as the ace of spades."

"Lady Gilham's staff have to have time to go to sleep. We can't leave at midnight. We'll leave around nine and Réal will bust in after eleven, or an hour after all lights are extinguished."

"Why not leave at ten or even eleven?" Pronto demanded.

"I'm taking her out for *dinner*, Pronto," he explained patiently, though as the difficulty of getting in several hours without compromising himself began to strike him, he thought ten o'clock would not be too late to call on her.

"How are you going to explain this to Deirdre?"

"I'm not going to explain anything. And don't you attempt it either. I think I better be feeling poorly tomorrow night. I'll drop by in the afternoon and have a coughing fit."

"You're skating on thin ice," Pronto said doubtfully. "Don't count on not being seen at the Herring. No matter where you go, when you especially don't want to be seen, you are. Somebody will see you and go trotting to the duchess with the news. I'd make a clean breast of it beforehand if I was you."

"I'll risk it," Belami said rashly, for he hated being told what to do. "Are you coming with me now or not?"

"Believe I'll stay here and read my book. I've just gotten to Mark Antony. Devilish man, spoiled rotten by bad company, just like me," he muttered, leveling an accusing eye at his host. Then he sat down to read, poured out another glass of Burgundy, and put his booted feet up on the fender.

Belami made his arrangements at the Red Herring with no difficulty, unseen by a single soul he knew. He booked a private parlor under the name of Mr. Harcourt and left a note at Gilham's telling her he would call for her around ten the next evening, though he intended to be half an hour late. He had some misgivings about his scheme, but as he was innocent he saw no need to upset Deirdre unnecessarily. Of course she must begin to learn that the nature of his work required an occasional escapade of this sort, but somehow this didn't seem the time or the escapade to begin her indoctrination.

He dined at home with Pronto, after which they paid a brief visit to the duchess and Deirdre. With the chaperone riding bobbin throughout, nothing was accomplished but a universal state of vexation. Belami and Pronto soon left and went to the Old Ship, to allow Belami to make Captain Stack's acquaintance. He was discreetly sounded out on the subject of George Smythe, but he claimed he had only met him a few weeks ago at this same inn.

"Have you been in Brighton long?" Belami asked civilly.

"I hired a little cottage north of town and raise a bit of livestock. Been there a year, since I retired from the army," he answered. "I live alone, so I come in here to pass the time of an evening."

"A bachelor, I take it?" Belami asked.

"Aye, they say women are fools, but I never found one fool enough to have me." Stack laughed.

"Must be lonesome," Pronto said, rolling blue, suspicious eyes. "Seems to me a man ought to get himself a wife."

"I was born in bed with a lady, Mr. Pilgrim, and that has

been my sole experience with the fair sex," he said, and gave a wink aside to Belami.

When Stack suggested a hand of cards, they soon found an excuse to leave his table as there seemed little to be learned from him. A chance acquaintance of Pronto's stopped them on their way to the door. It was the local gossip, a retired judge named Humphreys. Pronto presented him to Belami, and they sat together for a glass of ale.

"I'm happy to make your acquaintance, Belami. I am a little acquainted with your mama," Humphreys said. "I understand you have the Duchess of Charney staying with you. I shall pay her a call one of these days."

"No, she was only with me till she found a place to hire," Belami said to avoid gossip. He told Humphreys the address.

"I hadn't heard that!" Humphreys exclaimed, all eager interest. "And the Prince Regent arrived today too, they say. We don't usually have many visitors during the winter months. Usually I pass my evenings here with whatever company the hotel offers or drive up to Devil's Dyke for a game of cards with Captain Stack, but his play is a bit deep for me."

Humphreys spotted some cronies entering the room and took his leave. Belami sat silently staring at the wall, his fingers beating a tattoo on the table.

"Want a game of écarté?" Pronto asked.

"No, thanks."

"I noticed Humphreys was quick to avoid Stack's table. The old boy's getting himself a reputation for a cheat."

"I got a look at his deck. You notice he brings his own cards? He uses a system of filling in certain spaces on the patterned back of the deck. When a man produces his own cards, and the backs are highly embellished, you can expect to be rooked, but that's not what I was thinking about."

"I'll bear it in mind—the marked cards. Must have been small marks. *I* never noticed them."

"Humphreys seems well up on local doings, does he not?"

"A regular Intelligencer."

"But he didn't know the duchess had moved from my house. She hasn't gone out to meet anyone, and to move from my place to the cottage behind Castle Inn is only a couple of blocks. Up around the Steyne, up Pavilion Parade, and a left turn. She didn't have any furniture to take, to call attention to the trip. Just two cases that would have gone in the carriage with her," Belami said musingly.

"Explains why Humphreys didn't know," Pronto answered, stifling a yawn.

"Yes, but it doesn't explain how Lady Gilham *did* know."

"Maybe she don't know," Pronto suggested.

"She knew all right. She twitted me about it this morning before I knew myself. If the word had gotten around town, Humphreys would have known. Gilham claims to have virtually no callers," Belami said, frowning at the wall.

"Who would have known outside of yourself?" Pronto asked, sensing some importance attached to this detail. No doubt there would be some deducing going on before long.

"George Smythe," Belami said, a little smile curving his lips.

"Aye, the duchess must have let him know; you mentioned he called on her this afternoon."

"She sent him a note. Is it possible Smythe knows Lady Gilham?" he asked, his eyes alight with curiosity.

"Don't see how he could if she never has any callers."

"Oh, she has callers. She had one the first evening I visited her. She shuffled him out the front door while her servant kept me busy. He wore York tan gloves with the finger out and a curled beaver with a well-worn nap. Not Smythe's—his English-made gloves are in good repair, also his hat."

"Lots of men have gloves with a finger out. I have myself. Must get a new pair," Pronto said. "Matter of fact, old Captain Stack's gloves are out at the tips."

"So I noticed. I suppose the same can be said for twenty percent of the population, but I shall bear it in mind *quand-même*."

"Eh?"

"I'll bear it in mind all the same."

"Oh. Well, I'm for a blood and thunder and the feather tick. How about you?"

"I'll go home. I have to speak to Réal and see who Lady Gilham entertained this evening."

"Wasn't Smythe—he's at the prince's Pavilion. And it wasn't Stack. He was here."

"Réal will inform me. He is an excellent spy," Belami said confidently, and unfolded his lithe body from the chair.

Réal came from Lower Canada and claimed a great fondness for snow and cold. As there was a brisk breeze blowing a flurry of flakes through the black night air, Belami wasn't surprised to spot Réal out for a stroll. He stopped the carriage and got out to accompany his henchman.

"Is anyone minding the house on North Street, Réal?" he asked, falling into step beside Réal.

"Darby, from ten tonight to one in the morning. Me, I took the importanter daylight shift, for not to be seen."

"I thought you'd prefer the chillier temperatures of the nightwatch," Belami said, joking him.

"I go for the stroll along the beach to cool off," Réal explained, undoing his coat buttons to let the wind whip against his jacket. "The spying, she is very dull. Madame has no visitors all the day long excepting yourself and Twitch, with a letter."

Twitch was Belami's own servant, who had delivered the note setting up the assignation for the next night. "What's the setup on the back door?"

"There is the fence in back, with an alley from the front. To use the back door, it is necessary to trespass across her rear neighbor's yard. I was happy to see the large dog in that neighbor's backyard. There is no one using the back door, except he goes in by the alley, visible from the front. I, Pierre Réal, am keeping the sharp eyes on these things for you, milord.''

"You're a pearl beyond price, Pierre. Now do up that jacket before you come down with pneumonia.''

Pierre removed his gloves and fanned his face. When Belami hastened up the walk to his own house, Réal turned his frozen toes toward the beach, but scooted into the stable as soon as he saw Belami was safely beyond watching him.

Chapter Ten

Even in winter, Brighton blossomed into gaiety when the Prince Regent was in residence at his Pavilion. The next morning his liveried footman was delivering gold-edged cards of invitation to an impromptu little soirée arranged for that same evening. The duchess was *aux anges* to receive hers. Deirdre was also pleasantly excited to anticipate a party. She had visions of dancing with Belami in that elaborate fairy castle thus far seen only from the outside.

"The dear man, he's acknowledged my card with a handwritten note," the duchess crooned. "I shall put this away with my mementos—my insurance policy and the rental agreements for the London apartment houses. This soirée is certainly in our honor, Deirdre. I wonder if his wind band is here. I do hope His Highness can be persuaded to sing a little for us—so much easier on a body than a dancing party."

Deirdre hoped her chaperone would be disappointed. To submit unwitting guests to Prinney's indifferent serenading seemed a hard fate. She was eager to learn whether Dick had received a card, but felt fairly sure he must have, as indeed he had.

He felt more concern than joy at the honor as it conflicted with his assignation with Lady Gilham. Within the space of an hour, Belami received another card. It was an invitation from the duchess summoning him to dinner before the party.

That she had bothered to send around a formal card suggested that he was not to be the only guest. He drove over that morning to deliver his acceptance in person and found Pronto already ensconced, looking as guilty as a fox in the chicken coop to be caught in his illicit wooing.

"Just came to answer the invitation in person," he explained to Dick. "You know how I hate to set pen to paper. Tried it—made a terrible blotch. Fell into a passion with the pen and smashed it to smithereens. Can't answer an invitation without a pen."

"All is forgiven," Belami said, patting his hand gently while he smiled at Deirdre across the room.

"Everyone is coming," the duchess crowed. "Mr. Smythe, too, has accepted. I've asked Lady Donwin to fill in the table. You recall asking me for an old friend of Mrs. Fitzherbert, Belami. I have come up with Lady Donwin, an old Brighton resident. She might be able to give you some help with that ring business tonight."

This news took the edge from Belami's ire at learning Mr. Smythe was being put forward so noticeably. He gave Pronto a commanding eye, which meant Pronto was to engage the hostess in conversation, thereby allowing him a moment with Deirdre.

"I've been studying up on Mark Antony," Pronto said, shifting his head toward the duchess.

Deirdre turned to Belami. "Isn't it exciting, a party at the Royal Pavilion? I hope there's some dancing this evening."

"There'll be plenty to see at least. Your maiden trip to Xanadu, isn't it?" he asked, then remembered to cough into his handkerchief.

"Xanadu?" she asked in perplexity. It was really shocking how even a well-educated girl like Deirdre knew so little of poetry.

He explained the allusion to her, again coughing when he had finished. She took more note of the cough than of the talk about Mr. Coleridge's poem. "I do hope you aren't coming down with something, Dick," she said, worried.

"I'll be all right. It's these winter sea breezes that are to blame."

"Oh, please, don't get sick, not today!" she pleaded. He saw that the party meant a great deal to her and felt miserable at the deception he was perpetrating. He considered putting Lady Gilham off till tomorrow, but time was pressing at his back. He could postpone the meeting with Gilham till eleven, and at least attend the duchess's party and leave the Royal Pavilion a little early.

"I'll be there if I have to come on a litter," he promised.

"No, not if you're truly feeling unwell," she told him with a look that begged to be assured.

Later she asked, "Have you settled with Lady Gilham? Have you seen her again?"

This touchy issue was sidestepped. "We're putting her off for the moment, hoping she lowers her price."

"You haven't been back to see her?" she asked pointedly, her clear gray eyes holding his.

"I had to deliver the message that the prince wouldn't meet her price," he explained defensively.

"You could have written her a note."

"It was better to go in person," he said. The lift of his chin implied that the matter was closed, but he *did* hate the deception.

"I see," she answered curtly and looked away. After a prolonged silence, she turned back and found him staring at her.

"You've got to trust me," he said simply. "It's difficult enough never being able to talk to you alone without having you think I'm doing something I oughtn't to when I'm not with you, Deirdre."

"She's very pretty" was her answer.

"She's nothing to me. I wouldn't give her a moment's thought if it weren't for getting back the letters from Prinney. She's just a nuisance, that's all," he said impatiently.

Oh, but she had once been only a nuisance to him too. She knew well what could develop from an enforced proximity.

She looked at his arrogant, handsome face and was amazed, as she always was, that Belami could be attracted to her. He was known for his high flyers, always the prettiest, wildest, most expensive women. But here he was, with her, knuckling under to her aunt's impossibly strict code.

"I know. I trust you, Dick," she said shyly.

He felt like a slayer of infants. While Pronto explained the shenanigans of Mark Antony and Cleopatra to the duchess, he lifted Deirdre's hand to his lips and kissed her fingers. They discussed Pronto's trip to London to see the Wyckertons for a few moments.

"All it proved is that George Smythe didn't leave England with Alex Smythe, but that doesn't mean the deal wasn't arranged in England before they left," he explained.

"Practically a wasted trip for Pronto," she said.

"The more facts we know, the better. You can't deduce without facts. My usual method of working hardly applies in this case. The motive we know—money. The opportunity seems to exist well enough, so it is the method that preoccupies me. McMahon has sent a messenger off to Mrs. Fitzherbert, but it will take an age for him to get back. I hope something breaks before then."

Deirdre nodded, and into the silence the mumbling voice of Pronto was heard. "And then she dumped Caesar and took up with Mark Antony. A regular dasher, by Jove. As bad as the Wilsons," he finished.

"I hardly think that that is a story to repeat in polite company, Mr. Pilgrim!" the duchess exclaimed. "As for Harriet Wilson, I'm sure I don't know what all the gentlemen see in that ugly piece of goods. Who has got her under his protection these days?" she went on to ask, more interested in a live courtesan than in a dead queen.

Belami turned back to Deirdre. "Since Smythe hasn't got a carriage, I'll deliver him here this evening," he told her.

"Why?" she asked, instantly suspicious. "Pronto could do it."

"To please your aunt, my dear," he answered reasonably. "And because I want an excuse to get into his room at the inn. Maybe it will put your aunt in a happy enough mood to let you drive out with me now."

"What's that you say, Belami?" the duchess called to him. "Go out with Deirdre and leave me here all alone?"

"Pronto will remain with you," Belami told her without daring to look at his friend. The puff of annoyance that greeted this suggestion made that gentleman's feelings clear enough without looking.

"I suppose we can give them half an hour, eh, Mr. Pilgrim? What do you say? Shall we pass the time with a hand of écarté?" she asked, reaching for the deck.

Pronto grasped it and checked the backs. They were not elaborately embellished. Not that it mattered. The duchess's trick was to keep a few face cards up her sleeve.

When Deirdre was handed into Belami's carriage, she felt happily excited to be alone with him. "Where shall we go? Let's go down to the sea and walk along the Esplanade," she suggested.

"Wouldn't you prefer to go over to Russell Square?" he asked, some mischief gleaming in his dark eyes.

"I didn't know there was a Russell Square in Brighton. Where is it?" she asked, suspecting some trick or treat had been arranged for her amusement.

"It's not far, and if I'm not mistaken it was the address on Lady Donwin's card, which was on the table," he answered.

"We'll be seeing her this evening. Is she a special friend of yours?"

"Not at all, but my mama knows her. Bertie knows everybody. I wish she were here—she could tell me all the details about Fitzherbert and Prinney. I'm hoping Lady Donwin can fill in some gaps."

"You mean it's business," Deirdre said accusingly.

"Business before pleasure," he said conciliatingly, but took the precaution of indulging mostly in pleasure as the carriage was driven west to Russell Square. Lady Donwin was at home, and after Belami introduced himself, she received him with pleasure. She was fiftyish and fashionable with dark hair tipped with silver wings at the temples.

"How is your mama, dear Bertie?" she asked.

"The same as ever. Ramshackle and bubble-brained and utterly captivating," he answered.

"It runs in the family," the lady replied, running a practiced eye over Bertie's son. Odd how he had got the dark looks of his papa and Bertie's charm to alleviate that Belami dourness. She welcomed Deirdre and mentioned her joy at the unexpectedness of being called to dinner that evening.

She served coffee and biscuits, and before the first cup was half empty, Belami had steered the talk around to Mrs. Fitzherbert. "She was a good friend of your ours in those old days, I believe I've heard Bertie say," he mentioned after the infamous name had been introduced.

"Not in London. I'd as soon lose the last tooth in my head as live in London, but when she moved down to be near the prince, we became quite close."

She went on to recount some anecdotes about various outings she had had with Maria and her beau.

"I suppose he was very generous to her," he mentioned.

"If you call six thousand a year generous," Lady Donwin said curtly.

"I wasn't speaking about her settlement. Before they broke up, was my meaning," he corrected.

"She had her fair share of jewelry, but the half of it had to be returned, you must know. It was official stuff, not truly belonging to him."

"The prince was mentioning some little gold-domed ring he had given her—a sort of preengagement ring, I believe. It held a lock of his hair," Belami said, as though it were a mere passing thought.

"Yes, indeed! He remembers it, does he? It was the merest bauble, not even a stone in it, but it had great sentimental value for Maria. She was so sorry to lose it," she said, shaking her head in sad memory.

Belami jerked forward, but Deirdre spoke on to distract Lady Donwin's attention. "Isn't that always the way!" she exclaimed quickly. "We manage to lose or displace what is most precious. A ring in particular is so small and easy to lose. How did it happen, do you know?"

"Not really. It happened eons ago, but I still remember Maria's lamentations. It was inscribed on the back—love me true—so romantic, from a poem or song that was popular then. She insisted she didn't lose it at all, but that someone stole it to make mischief. She didn't breathe a word to the prince and made us all promise not to tell him either. He never noticed, for he had given her showier pieces by then."

"Who did she think took it?" Deirdre asked, her heart racing. Belami sat holding his breath for the answer.

"She never knew for certain. She always kept it in a little brass box on her dressing table, and all her friends were in and out, but *I* don't think a *lady* would sink to stealing."

"Perhaps one of her servants did it," Deirdre said, hoping to jog her memory.

"That's what I told her! Help was in short supply, and everyone was stealing servants from everyone else and hiring anyone who came along. Maria required more than most because of the entertaining she had to do, though she eventually got a regular crew."

"When did she lose the ring? Was it before she got her staff regularized?" Deirdre asked doggedly.

If Lady Donwin found this keen interest in history peculiar, she was too polite to say so. "Yes, it was early on. I seem to remember we all thought it was her newest upstairs maid. A saucy chit who gave herself great airs. I saw her with my own eyes trying on one of Maria's bonnets one day when she didn't know anyone was around. She looked so very like Maria I thought it was her—just at a quick glance, you know."

"You wouldn't remember her name?" Deirdre asked, and directed a questioning look to Dick, wondering if she was pressing too hard. He nodded his encouragement.

"Bless me, I haven't a notion. I think she was an Irish girl. No, it comes back to me now. She was *engaged* to an Irishman, a lieutenant, which is why she was so above herself. Pretty good for a maid, nabbing an officer, but he was no one we had ever heard of,'' she said dismissingly.

"Do you remember the officer's name?'' Deirdre asked.

"No, I only heard him mentioned once. He was a nobody, a career soldier. I remember that girl's face so plainly and can't put my finger on the name. It will come back to me. I remember someone saying that mean—somebody—stole the ring, and it was three M's in a row. Now how did I ever remember that after thirty years? But I'm boring you silly with all these old reminiscences. I must be getting old to be harking back to the past. When is Bertie coming to Brighton, Belami?''

There seemed no point in questioning Lady Donwin further. They finished their coffee and their conversation and soon left.

"Was it worth the trip?'' Deirdre asked when they were alone.

"It certainly was! We know that if Smythe's mother did, in fact, leave him that ring, she hadn't received it from Prinney. And she knew Prinney didn't know it was stolen, so it was safe for him to produce it.''

"His mother must be that 'mean M. M.' maid,'' Deirdre said.

"That's the obvious thing, though Smythe might have got it elsewhere. The mean M. M. might have pawned it, for instance,'' he suggested.

"At least we know Mrs. Fitzherbert didn't give it to him,'' she said.

"And he's *not* who the prince thinks he is. All we have to do is have Lady Donwin tell Prinney about the ring and he'll stop thinking Smythe is his son. I'm going to nip over and tell McMahon about this right away, Deirdre. I'll deliver you home first, then go to the Pavilion.'' She sensed the urgency in him and didn't try to prolong his visit. "You're a great little questioner," he complimented. She glowed with pleasure at this faint praise and went home happy.

He met McMahon at the stables, looking at his bays. "I don't like these damp breezes," McMahon said. "What's the point of setting up a stable as fine as any drawing room you might enter when the poor horses have to brave the outdoor winds. Foolishness," he said, grouchily, revealing he was in a bad mood.

"Can we talk in private?" Belami asked, ignoring the mood.

"Aye, we've got a deal to discuss," the colonel replied, his temper worsening. "Our friend, Smythe, is playing off more tricks." They walked into the garden where they were quite alone.

"What is he up to now?" Belami asked in alarm.

"I've just come from the prince. He's smiling from ear to ear and positively *gloating* over 'dear Georgie.' I wouldn't be a whit surprised if he makes his announcement this very night."

"What convinced him?" Belami demanded.

"It seems *Georgie*, as he's now called, was reading his Bible last night and discovered a letter tucked into the pages. Damme, he *showed* me the letter today, and it is unquestionably written in the prince's own hand, all aged and yellowing. It's to Maria Fitzherbert, a silly love note, but where did Smythe get it if he's not Fitzherbert's son? I think we must begin to accept that he is. The prince is drooling over it this minute."

"Think again. It was stolen by the same woman who stole the gold ring, if I know anything," Belami replied and, of course, went on to reveal what Lady Donwin had told him.

McMahon's face broke into a broad grin. "Well, that's a weight off my mind. I'll go and tell him your story this minute. I've told him a dozen times the ring could be a forgery, but I never thought it might have been stolen. He says Maria treasured it as though it were a crown."

"She never admitted losing it and coached her friends to say nothing as well. No word from Bath?"

"No, but my man should have spoken to Fitzherbert by now. I hope to God she doesn't refute this story you've just told me."

"Lady Donwin has no reason to lie. She knows nothing of Smythe and his claims," Belami pointed out.

"At least I hope this prevents the prince from making any announcement tonight, but his behavior is so erratic there's no saying what he'll do."

"And if he doesn't do it early, I won't even be there to see it," Belami said, rather disappointed. "I must leave early to keep my date with La Gilham."

"Hard to worry about a flea when we have a tiger raging at us," McMahon said, but his temper had improved.

Belami didn't mention his theory that Gilham and Smythe knew each other. The only clue that they did was Gilham's knowing of Charney's move so early in the day, and he was loath to draw attention to that move. So he kept it to himself, but he didn't forget it. He stopped at the Old Ship before going home to change for the evening. Pronto was there, fortifying himself for the night ahead with a few drinks.

"Charney will have got the wine watered by tonight. It's my plan to kill this bottle before I go." He smiled a cagey smile at the wine bottle.

"Don't kill it yet," Belami said, removing it from his fingers. "I need your help, Pronto."

"Aye, aye, sir," Pronto said, and saluted.

"Here's what I want you to do. I've inquired at the desk, and Smythe isn't in his room. I want you to go down to the lobby and waylay him if he comes in."

"Why?" Pronto asked, screwing up his eyes in suspicion.

"Because I've got to get into his room and search it, and I would prefer not to be caught in the act."

"How will you get in? Oh, I suppose you have that *passepartout* key thing with you."

"Yes, I have my magic key right here," Belami answered, dangling it from his fingers. "I want to do it now, this instant. Pull yourself together and run downstairs."

"What are you looking for?"

"A Bible, amongst other things."

"A Bible? Damme, you've got one at home in your library."

"A different Bible."

"They're all the same. Full of 'begats.' Now if you want a real book . . ." His eyes strayed to Plutarch's *Lives of the Noble Romans.*

"Which is Smythe's room?"

"Three down from mine, on the left. Never let it be said that Pronto Pilgrim stood in the way of a man getting religion."

He babbled on as Belami led him to the door and headed him in the direction of the staircase. Then, with a quick look up and down the hall, Belami hastened to Smythe's door and let himself in with his passkey. The room was neat and tidy, with none of the clutter generally accumulated when a person makes his home in one room. Belami went first to the dresser and quickly rifled the drawers. They held nothing but an assortment of linen, all of it of an English make.

Next he went to the clothespress and sorted through the jackets, pantaloons, and waistcoats hanging there, discovering nothing of interest. He went quickly through the pockets, finding a clasp knife, a few gentlemen's cards with Brighton addresses, a deck of marked cards similar to Stack's, a small comb, and a slightly bent farthing.

He shook out the few pairs of boots standing in the corner and again found nothing. The washstand held Smythe's shaving equipment; the dressing table his brushes and comb, a bottle of lavender scent, and a bottle of hair oil. There wasn't a Bible to be found anywhere.

It was incredible that a man should carry so little of a personal nature with him. He had no other residence; this room held his worldly goods. How was it possible for a man of twenty-five years to have accumulated nothing save his clothing and personal toilet articles? Not a letter, not a miniature likeness of a parent or sibling or loved one, not a book of addresses, not one single memento from America. The very absence of any cherished object was incriminating. Nobody was this detached from his past, unless it was a past he was anxious to conceal. This wasn't Smythe's home; it was just a room he had hired to perpetrate this hoax on the prince. Belami looked around a little more into nooks and crannies, under pillows and mattress, under the faded carpet, then slipped out, locking the door behind him. It flitted through his mind that Lady Gilham's saloon was similarly bare of personal mementos. No picture of the late Sir John, of the daughter, of anything that reeked of Cornwall. It was a hired, furnished house.

From the top of the stairway he beckoned to Pronto, who came back upstairs to hear what had been found.

"He's a liar all right," Pronto agreed, when Belami told him his feelings. "I know he has one book he likes, for he's always quoting Ben Franklin. And there's those books he took out of the library. Where are they? He said his papa gave him that book on Franklin, and he cherishes it. Know how he feels. That Plutarch, Belami—great stuff. Mean to buy myself a copy when I have to take this one back to Donaldson's."

Belami nodded. "I'll leave a note for Smythe at the desk that I'm picking him up for the duchess's party tonight. I told Charney I would."

"Good, then you can give me a lift as well. Not worth harnessing up a pair for such a short jog."

"You forget I also have a jog to the Red Herring. Take your carriage and you can deliver the ladies home for me."

"I will then, but I won't promise to bring Smythe along. Liar, letting on he had a copy of Ben Franklin's book."

"I'll leave you to Plutarch and go home to change."

"I haven't got time for Plutarch now. I've got to finish

that bottle. Suggest you do the same, my lad. It'll be a dry night at Charney's.''

"And a hot one at the Pavilion," Belami said.

"A hotter one at the Red Herring I'll warrant," Pronto said with a sapient look, and lifted his glass.

Belami was struck with a fear that Lady Donwin might notice Smythe's gold ring and mention it, thus alerting him to the investigation. Should he alert her and warn her off? No, it would be best to ignore it and hope it would be overlooked. And if the subject arose, he'd be quick to divert the conversation. It was going to be an uneasy night, on many points.

Chapter Eleven

The duchess was not famous for her table. She was an excellent eater, but her best efforts were put forth at tables other than her own. With the ready-made excuse of a new cook, she spared all efforts at elegance and served a leathery leg of mutton, eked out with a beef stew that she decided to call a *ragoût*. After being served small glasses of watered wine, her guests went in formal state to the dining room, where her one male servant stood prepared to tend six persons.

"We are informal this evening," she said. "You will not mind helping yourselves, country style."

At the first sip from his wineglass, Pronto nodded knowingly to Belami. Watered, of course. Belami had unwittingly come up a notch in the duchess's estimation when she learned he had taken Deirdre to call on Lady Donwin. He would have sunk lower if she had guessed the nature of the visit, but Deirdre had kept it from her. Her grace, with great condescension, invited Belami to carve the roast.

It was a task requiring all his strength, for the knife was as dull as the meat was tough. It left him no energy for speaking. A sluggish mood hovered over the table, and Pronto took it upon himself to get the conversational ball rolling.

"Too bad about Cleopatra," he said to his companion, Lady Donwin.

"I beg your pardon?" she said, leaning closer.

"I say, too bad about Cleopatra. Dead, you know. An asp."

"Ah—yes, I believe I heard something about it," the confused lady replied. "You are referring to *Queen* Cleopatra, I take it?" She wore a confused frown.

"The same. Charming lady, if you have a taste for chicanery."

"Is there a new book or play out about her?" Lady Donwin inquired, assuming there must be some reason for so obscure a subject to have arisen.

"Haven't heard if there is. Did you hear about Rome?" was his next conversational gambit.

"Rome," Lady Donwin said weakly, and looked around the table for assistance. She was met by a sea of perfectly blank faces.

"Named after a kid that was reared up by a wolf. Shocking," Pronto said, shaking his head. "Next thing you know they'll be naming London after a chimney sweep. I hope this notion don't catch on."

"I wonder what London *was* named after," Lady Donwin said, as she felt some comment was called for.

"Believe we stole it from the Frenchies. They call it *Londres*," Pronto told her. "Don't see why we must let the Frenchies be naming our cities. We borrow everything from them. Would you mind handing along that *ragoût*, ma'am, while Dick chops up the meat for us. As we're serving ourselves, I'll just tipple out a bit of that Burgundy. Yessir, it's a caution how we ape the Frenchies in everything. No use for them myself. You don't see them calling their gels miss after us. It's mam'selle every time."

"We're having petits fours for dessert, Pronto," Deirdre said, biting back a little smile, but he saw no mischief in it.

"Oh, good," he said and splashed a blob of gravy on the linen tablecloth.

Belami had finished his carving and took pity on the guests. He entertained them with a short discourse on the various possible origins of the name London, favoring the opinion that its name derived from King Lud, who built the old walls around the city.

Dinner passed in this amiable fashion, and after the petits fours, the duchess led the ladies to the Blue Saloon, leaving the gentlemen to their port. At least no one had mentioned Smythe's ring.

Pronto, deciding to get on with the case, turned a belligerent eye on Smythe. "What has old Ben Franklin got to say today, Smythe?" he asked.

" 'Beware of meat twice boil'd and an old foe reconcil'd,' " Smythe said and laughed.

"Twice boil'd or thrice baked," Belami added with feeling.

Pronto considered this unhelpful interchange a moment, but could find no vice or sense in it. "I wouldn't mind having a look at that almanac of Ben's when you're through with it. Where do you keep it anyway?"

"Buy your own, my friend. I never part company with Ben Franklin," Smythe answered easily.

Before Pronto could utter any revealing secrets, Belami jumped into the conversation. "How did the party at the Pavilion go last night, Mr. Smythe?" he asked.

"About as usual," Smythe answered blandly. Not a word about the letter, about "Georgie," or anything else. "It should be a good deal livelier tonight with a larger company. The duchess was telling me an interesting story at dinner, something about her losing a diamond necklace and your recovering it," George went on, rather hurriedly. It served to change the topic, and Smythe was such an enthusiastic listener that the telling of that tale took up the remainder of their isolation from the ladies.

In a benign mood, the duchess allowed Belami to transport Deirdre the few steps to the Royal Pavilion with no other escort, while she and the others went in her carriage, except for Pronto, who had orders to take his own. They all met under the domed porch of the Royal Pavilion, where lights blazed everywhere, beckoning them into the vestibule. They left off their outer garments in the entrance hall. While the ladies adjusted their toilettes in front of the mantelpiece mirror, Belami gave their names to be announced. They were called and went in a troupe into the Chinese Gallery.

The Prince Regent stood in the center, welcoming his guests. They were a motley crew for this hasty party—such society as Brighton had to offer, along with a few guests down from London. Most notable amongst these was the Countess de Lieven, the Russian ambassador's wife, who always reminded Deirdre of a long-necked waterfowl with a dark crest of hair. The Marchioness of Hertford was noticeable by her absence.

Poor Prinney, the duchess noticed, was becoming fatter by the day. His ever-spreading girth was covered in magnificent apparel, plastered with ribbons and medals. She looked from him to George Smythe and shook her head sadly. At this moment, she discerned no real resemblance between them. She had to wonder, for the first time, if fond memory had led her astray. Had Prinney *ever* looked as much like Mr. Smythe as she thought? The pouches and sagging flesh he wore now made it difficult to remember his youthful visage, as listening to one tune will prevent a person from remembering another. Those bright and evanescent days had become a forgotten melody.

Then the prince turned to her, advanced with his hands out and a smile on his face, and all else was forgotten. So very proper of him to come to her first, for a special greeting.

"You have been too kind to my dear little George," he said, smiling widely. "I appreciate your taking note of him. If only the rest of society would follow your lead, the thing would be done in the twinkling of a bedpost. You always knew how to lead them, your most charming grace," he finished, lifting her gnarled hand to his lips.

She was flattered to death and assured His Highness of her continued support in any project he might undertake.

"It is such circumstances as this that show us who our *real* friends are." He cast an extremely meaningful and long look into her eyes.

While he welcomed the other guests individually, Deirdre took the opportunity to gaze around at the splendor that surrounded her. The long Chinese Gallery was divided into sections by decorative iron bamboo. Overhead in this central portion hung a highly decorated Chinese canopy. There was much evidence of oriental finery—cabinets built into yellow marble niches, a brass and metal fireplace, a porcelain pagoda and glass lanterns everywhere, some of them fashioned into tulips and lotus flowers. On the painted canvas portion of the walls, images of more flowers and birds flaunted their beauty. The lights, the heat, and the overpowering opulence of it all were difficult to assimilate.

"By jingo, I haven't seen anything to equal this, not even the Pantheon in London," Pronto said, craning his short neck at awkward angles to take it all in.

"Quite a Chinese bazaar," Belami opined, but even he was impressed at the display.

"I never saw anything so gorgeous in my life," Deirdre breathed, her eyes as big as saucers. "My, and to think I was impressed with your place at New Year's," she added artlessly to her fiancé. She even knew why her aunt had urged George Smythe on her. But as she looked from Belami to Smythe, she knew she'd rather live in a shoe with Dick than in a mansion with George.

A servant passed by with a tray of drinks, and the duchess's party moved on to make way for other arrivals. They walked north toward mirrored doors that stood open.

"Excellent! His Highness is going to entertain us with a little music," the duchess declared, as these doors led to the music room where all manner of lights blazed. Red and gold were the predominant colors of the room, with more Chinese splendor of columns and canopies, dragons and flowers, another marble fireplace, topped by an outrageous clock, featuring Cupids and Venus and other Roman deities.

"They may rant about bad taste all they like, you must own this is very *good* poor taste," Pronto said.

"The very best poor taste I've ever seen," Belami agreed.

As the prince made his way toward the mirrored doors, every heart younger than forty years sank. "We're in for it now; he's going to play for us or sing," Pronto said, groaning. Even as he spoke, the orchestra was filing into place on the platform, where the prince's violoncello rested against a stand.

"Worse, he's going to do both," Belami said.

The duchess and a few older people smiled approval, and the others resigned themselves to the concert. The Prince Regent first played for them, then was kind enough to sing as well. His opening selection was "Sleep You or Wake You." The younger guests were much inclined to accept the former, but livelier glees and catches followed. There was a general stirring of excitement when the prince announced that one of the guests had agreed to join him in a duet. Heads turned this way and that till Mr. Smythe was seen to rise to his feet and join the prince.

It had all been prearranged, obviously. Excitement was high amongst the London guests. "Who is he?" the Countess de Lieven was heard to inquire. "He looks familiar—something in the shape of the forehead."

Standing side by side with the prince, one *could* see some sort of resemblance, but Belami thought it was only a resemblance of types. He searched around the room for McMahon, wondering that the news from Lady Donwin hadn't quenched the prince's ardor, but McMahon hunched his shoulders. "I've told him and this is the result," that despairing face said.

The pair sang "When Laura Smiles," an uninspired choice, and executed it without much vigor. The prince's eyes, with tears standing in them, never left George's face. George was clearly embarrassed and looked at a point on the rear wall.

After the one duet, the prince apologized most humbly and proclaimed that his throat was a little rough from the weather. The band would continue without him. This was good news as it meant the guests could leave without giving offense to His Highness.

"We are informal this evening," he announced to the throng. "The youngsters might want to dance. The Crimson Saloon is at your disposal. We oldsters shall soon retire to the card room."

As he spoke, he put a fatherly arm around George Smythe's shoulder and herded this one youngster off with him, to present him informally to his London guests. He withheld the words "my son," but his outstanding condescension and his singular kindness throughout the evening had a very paternal air to it. When he went on to the card room later, he had Smythe at his table.

Deirdre had been looking forward to the evening, but even when she finally got to dance with Belami, the mood was not what she had anticipated. His talk was all of Smythe and the prince, and worries about what was going forth in the card room. Dick was complaining of a nagging headache as well. She suspected nothing as his eyes did have a feverish glaze. At ten, Mr. Smythe escaped the card game and found his way to the Crimson Saloon. Colonel McMahon, looking daggers, was close behind him.

Belami led Deirdre from the dance floor and approached the colonel. "Was any announcement made in the card room?" he asked.

"His every word and gesture was an announcement, but nothing was said formally. I'm afraid the reaction of the friends present tonight will only egg him on to a more public demonstration, though. Too genial by half."

"Didn't you tell him what Lady Donwin told me about the ring?" Belami asked, startled.

"He doesn't believe a word of it. He knows I have been against this scheme from the start, and he thinks I've invented it. He all but cut Lady Donwin dead."

"Was there ever such an impossible man!" Belami exclaimed impatiently.

"Not to my knowledge," McMahon said grimly.

"Deirdre, why don't you have the next dance with Smythe? You might learn something, and the colonel and I have a few things to discuss," Belami said.

She went, eager to hear what Smythe might have to say about the evening, and Belami turned to McMahon. "The prince knows I have to leave early?"

"Yes, yes, he puts up no stumbling blocks when it's Gilham who is the target of our schemes. Does Miss Gower know?"

"No, I didn't tell her. Perhaps you could explain that I had a slight headache and went home quietly to avoid disturbing her pleasure," he suggested.

"Everything is arranged for North Street?" the colonel asked with a slight smile curling his lips.

"All set. The goods will be taken to my place for the night. I'll bring them here tomorrow. Or should I just burn the letters?"

"The prince will want to be present at their incineration. No slur on your integrity, but to check their authenticity and for the sheer pleasure of it. This was well done of you, Belami."

"It's not done yet," Belami pointed out.

"A good effort at least, and we shan't forget it."

The gentlemen parted, but before Dick got away, the dance was finished and he saw Deirdre approaching him. He rubbed his temples and managed a wan smile.

"Are the lights and heat getting to you too?" she asked.

"A little. I believe I'll go in search of a headache powder, but don't worry about me," he said. Her face was the very picture of concern. He felt a pang, to be deceiving her.

"Of course I shall worry," she answered simply.

"Did Smythe say anything of interest?" he asked to divert her thoughts.

"He talked mostly about you and your work, asking what

sorts of cases you've done in the past. He's becoming suspicious, Dick," she said. "He wondered how you found time for the research you came here to do and twitted me that I wouldn't get a very good idea of your summer home when I am living elsewhere. That was the excuse I gave him for being here when I first met him, you recall. He also asked when we were leaving."

"Did you get an opportunity to quiz him about the way the prince is singling him out?"

"Yes, but he only laughed and made foolish jokes about it. Something about having a foolish friend being like going to bed with a razor," she said.

"Back to Ben Franklin, I expect, for that quote."

Pronto ambled up to claim the next dance, and Belami took the opportunity to escape. He hastened to Marine Parade to rehearse the night's job with Réal. "You've got the *passe-partout*?"

"She is here in the pocket," Réal assured him.

"And you know exactly what to do?"

"*Mais parfaitement!* I attend till the lights are out for an hour; go softly into the hall, turn right into the dining room, pass the crockery out to Chubb, who is at the front door with his bag. Chubb hastens it to the carriage—the borrowed carriage that has not your crest on it. I have arranged all these details, me," he said in a tone that inspired absolute confidence. "Next I ascend to the boudoir, where the letters will be on a table under a snuffbox. If I see a man's shaving set, housecoat, and slippers, they, too, are included. Take *le tout* back to your stable, transfer it to your carriage, and guard it with my life till your return," he said, and stood waiting for praise.

"And if you're caught by Mrs. Morton or a servant?"

"Then I say nothings, in case they have the large ears and imagine an accent in my voice. I h'escape *à toute vitesse*. If I am followed, I do not go to Marine Parade, but lose myself in the coaching yards of North Street. If I am captured—which will not occur—I say nothings."

"That's right. And if you're not home when I get back, I'll nip over to the constable's office and rescue you."

"This will not be necessary, however," Réal assured him.

"I know it well. You're top of the trees, Réal. There'll be a *grande récompense* in it for you."

"*Pas nécessaire*," Réal said with a shrug of indifference, while he suppressed the urge to inquire: "*Combien?*"

Undeceived by this show, Belami told him the price, which brought a reluctant smile to Réal's saturnine countenance. "I'll tell Chubb," he said.

Belami wished him luck, gave his shoulder a tap, and called to his groom to leave. Réal's only regret in the otherwise savory affair was that he had to entrust his grays to the second groom. But he had jawed his stand-in driver so mercilessly that no harm could come to the team at the Red Herring. It was a heavy responsibility, being Belami's first lieutenant, and a delightful one.

Chapter Twelve

A light showed at the front window of the little house on North Street. Belami left his carriage in the road and went to tap lightly at the door. Lady Gilham waited alone for him with her cape on the chair beside her.

"I sent the servants to bed early," she whispered. "I must be home before seven, when they usually arise."

"Sorry I'm a little late. The prince held an impromptu party."

"Did anything interesting happen?" she asked with so casual an air that he suspected her keen interest.

"We were subjected to half an hour's royal caterwauling, but that is hardly unusual. Mrs. Morton is asleep, too, is she?" he asked.

"Hours ago," she assured him as he held her cape for her. It was an elegant affair in blue velvet, with a fur-lined hood.

"I hope she's not a light sleeper?" he asked, mindful of Réal.

"She doses herself with laudanum three nights out of four. She had a megrim tonight and has been out like a candle since nine o'clock," she answered. The tension eased insensibly out of his shoulders. With Morton asleep and the servants in the attic, he foresaw no trouble for Réal.

"How convenient." He smiled and felt the occasion called for at least a kiss on the cheek, which he hastened to bestow. Her arms went around his neck, and she pulled his head down to hers.

A tantalizing fragrance of musk perfume emanated from her throat, her hair, her wrists. Her soft white hands stroked his neck, and her lips were soft and warm beneath his. She let her head fall back and said softly, "I can hardly wait. Let's go, darling."

She extinguished the lamps and locked the door on the way out. He helped her into the carriage and sat beside her on the banquette. Without a moment's hesitation, she climbed onto his lap and began kissing him passionately, with low moans of desire and crooning words of pleasure.

"I've been so lonesome, Richard. You have no idea what it's like after you're used to being loved. Oh, but Sir John wasn't like you. He was old and horrid. You're so handsome, so manly. Kiss me again," she breathed into his ear. "I'm on fire with wanting you."

The fire proved contagious. He wrapped his arms around her, and she molded her soft femininity against his harder masculine body. He felt her seductive curves with his hands, admiring the sharp inclination where her waist diminished to swell below in a graceful billow. The perfume and her rapturous cooings went to his head, inciting him to wild imaginings. Guilt mixed with it, to give her a nearly irresistible aura of sinful pleasure.

"It's not far. We better wait till we get there," he said reluctantly, holding her hands to prevent them from further invasions of his privacy.

"I didn't take you for such a patient man, Richard!" Her laugh was intimate. She had an adorable laugh, throaty and low. He found himself kissing her white throat again, inhaling her heady perfume.

"You'll be well worth waiting for," he said huskily.

They continued this bantering lovemaking till the carriage pulled in at the Red Herring, a half-timbered inn, low and sprawling. There was no one outside to see them, he noticed with relief. The host was waiting inside and bowed them into the chosen parlor, where the table was laid for dinner.

"Are you planning to eat first?" Lady Gilham asked, adopting a moue of disappointment. "Let us go right upstairs."

"I haven't had a bite since tea, and it was only a bite then. I'm ravenous," he said, taking her wrap and feeling like a fool.

"I'm ravenous, too—for *you*," she said, turning in his arms and lifting her hungry lips to his.

What could a man do? He kissed her for an unconscionably long time and enjoyed it in a painful sort of way. "I won't be any good to you till I've eaten," he said in a wooden voice that reeked of insincerity, even to himself.

With a glance at the clock on the wall, he realized this had to be a very long meal. It was only eleven o'clock. "They have a marvelous raised pigeon pie here," he said heartily.

"They have marvelous feathered ticks too," she murmured temptingly, tilting her head a little to one side. She strolled off to the window and pulled back the curtain to look into the yard. Fearful of being seen, he twitched it away.

"I've ordered champagne. Come, let us drink to each other," he suggested.

She was coaxed to the table, where a glass of champagne was pressed into her fingers. She was much inclined to share a chair with him, but the waiter knocked at the door, and Belami darted to it. For a long time he discussed dinner— was the mutton good, not too dry or not underdone? Would the lady care for some ham or perhaps a little *ragoût*? A fish dish to start with would be nice.

"Whatever pleases you, Belami," she said sulkily. He frowned at her use of his own name.

"Let's start with a turbot then," he said. He hated turbot. The only fish worse than turbot was cod.

When the servant departed ten minutes later, Lady Gilham had taken her own chair at the table. "I didn't realize it was a *dinner* partner you wanted," she snipped.

"Confucius says the preliminaries are often more enjoyable than the main event," he said in a rare moment of tactlessness.

"Confucius has never shared the main event with me," she said, lifting her glass and directing a long, sultry gaze down the table.

"Then he is to be pitied," Belami answered, getting back into stride. "I only meant I want this evening to last as long as possible and to be enjoyed in more than one way. I want to *know* you, Moira, before I make love to you. My eyes tell me you are a beautiful, desirable woman, and my heart craves to know what cruel twists of fate have . . ."

"Brought me so low?" she asked, her expression sardonic.

"No, brought you to me, to be cherished," he said with a yearning eye.

She gave one quick, suspicious look, but was lured into fabricating an exciting background for herself, encouraged by much champagne and much admiration till the turbot arrived.

Back at North Street, Pierre Réal donned a black face mask, removed the *passe-partout* from his pocket, and inserted it into the door without a sound. The lock twisted and the door pushed inward. He waited, heard no sound from within, and entered on cautious feet. The dining room was on the right, with a pale moonbeam lighting the table, which was set with china and silver. He silently lifted the settings from the table and placed them carefully, one by one, in a canvas bag. The cups felt heavy for fine china, but in the darkness and with an eye frequently turned to the door, he took little notice. When the table was stripped, he took the bag to the front door. A dark arm reached out from the shadows and removed it without saying a word.

Réal went to the staircase and climbed stealthily, listening for the betraying squeak of dry boards. Belami hadn't informed him which chamber was milady's, but there was only one door open and he walked stealthily to it. The elegance of the chamber indicated that he had guessed right. The dressing table was adorned with containers that glinted in the moonlight—glass and silver. He felt around with his fingers in the shadows till he felt a snuffbox and lifted the papers from beneath it. The top one was all he glanced at. It began with the words "My dearest Moira." He shoved the lot into his jacket and looked around for the shaving equipment. It was on another stand across the room. These items went into another bag. He could not find the dressing gown or slippers.

Réal was a perfectionist. It stung him to have to leave without all the items mentioned. He stood still, listening for sounds from the sleeping house. It was perfectly silent. Only his own breath hung on the air. His eyes had adjusted to the darkness, and the furnishings had taken on a more visible form. There was a chair with some light clothing on it in one corner. He tiptoed forward and lifted a silken garment of some sort. On the pocket, he felt heavy gold threads. On the floor sat a pair of slippers. He picked them up, stuffed garment and slippers into his bag, and uttered a silent prayer of thanksgiving to God, for Réal was a devout Catholic. His heart was bursting with joy and pride as he crept quietly down the stairs and out the front door, locking it behind him. He sped through the night to the carriage, waiting half a block away.

He took the ribbons himself and whipped the team into swift motion. His orders were to leave the goods in Belami's other carriage in the stable, then return the hired carriage and team. He placed the letters in the canvas bag with the bedroom items and dispatched Chubb to the coaching house, while he sat in triumph in the driver's seat of the carriage that held the goods.

"A good job, Chubb, if I say so myself," he admitted when Chubb returned from his errand. "We've earned a wet, *n'est-ce-pas*?"

It was no ale or inferior brew that was awaiting them, but a bottle of milord's finest claret. Belami would be very angry if they didn't reward themselves.

The Prince Regent was encouraged by his initial introduction of dear George into society. He knew forces were building against his scheme. That Banbury tale about Maria having had her ring stolen, for instance. His enemies wouldn't have invented that unless they feared he would succeed. The thing to do was to take George to London and let the world see what a fine son he had produced and what a future king was theirs, if only they had the fortitude to *demand* him. He could count on the support of the Duchess of Charney, the Countess de Lieven, and all of Lady Hertford's many enemies.

Simultaneously, he would arrange wide coverage of Princess Caroline's exploits abroad, let the world see that neither she nor any offspring of hers merited the throne of England. A bright, golden future spread like a mirage before him, where he was once again the dashing Florizel, beloved by his people. With a contented smile at his party of well-wishers, he bowed himself out of the chamber. His guests could now depart or remain partying till they were surfeited.

He blew the Duchess of Charney a kiss, bowed to the Countess de Lieven, gazed one last time on dear Georgie, who didn't happen to be looking at him, looked straight past that upstart Lady Donwin, and retired to his private chambers.

Lady Donwin was unaware of the latest snub. She was looking around for Deirdre Gower, and found her behind a pillar, yawning into her fist.

"Lovely party, Miss Gower, but where is your fiancé? I haven't seen him around this last hour," Lady Donwin said.

"He had a headache, and Colonel McMahon told me he went home. I hope he's feeling better," Deirdre said. "I fear he's catching cold."

"It's only the heat and noise. I feel like a loaf in an oven myself. Do you know, Miss Gower, my coming here to-night has jogged my memory about that ring business we were discussing this afternoon. I remembered the name of the saucy servant who *I* think stole it. It was Moira Morton—that's who it was. I remember someone saying 'that mean Moira Morton has stolen it!' I think it was the Duchess of Devonshire, for the voice had a lilting accent.''

"Moira Morton," Deirdre repeated, while a little frisson scuttled down her spine.

"The name would mean nothing to you, of course. Maria never did like her, perhaps because she was rather pretty in the same style as Maria herself. A blond, blue-eyed hussy. Not that I mean to say Maria was a hussy!" she exclaimed. "Belami seemed interested in it. I can't imagine why," she finished vaguely.

"I'll tell him. Thank you so much," Deirdre said, and walked to the edge of the room and sat down. The name Moira had first sent that ripple of significance down her spine. It was Lady Gilham's name, Dick said, but obviously Lady Gilham hadn't even been born at that time. And she wasn't either blue-eyed or blond. Moira Morton would be an older woman by now. The name Morton was also floating around in her mind, but it took her a moment to attach it to Lady Gilham's companion. But Morton was her married name—unless she took the mature woman's prerogative of calling herself Mrs. without benefit of a husband. She was the right age and coloring, which was a coincidence. And was her name Moira as well? Another coincidence. Dick would find this highly interesting. He had the utmost suspicion of coincidences. She'd write him a note first thing to-morrow morning.

While she sat pondering, a page boy came up and said, "Miss Gower?" She nodded, and he handed her a note, unsealed but twisted into a bow. She unfolded it and read, "Mrs. Fitzherbert has just arrived at the Red Herring Inn. She will be departing early tomorrow morning. If Belami wishes to speak to her, he must do so tonight." It had no signature and no salutation, but the message was enough to send Deirdre into a flutter. Her heart raced painfully fast. She must get this note to Belami at once, but something inside her wanted more than that. She had been left too much out of this case. She wanted to go with Dick. Her aunt, of course, was the stumbling block. As she sat racking her brain, Pronto ambled up to her.

"Sitting all alone, eh, Miss Gower? How would you like to stand up and jig it with me?"

Instead of answering, she handed him the note. He read it, pursed his lips into whistling form and emitted a breath of air, while his eyes bulged to an enormous size. "Where did you get this?" he asked.

"From a page boy. I expect Colonel McMahon gave it to him. And there's more news, Pronto," she added, and told him about Moira Morton. "It's a pity to have to get Dick out of bed at this hour when he has a headache, but he will want to see Mrs. Fitzherbert," she said.

"Headache? Dash it, he . . . Of course he'll want to go," he said, pulling himself up short.

"I mean to go with him," she said very firmly.

No amount of deducing showed him the proper way out of this tight corner. He had to fly free and invent his own course. "Well, you're too late, for he's already gone," he told her.

"How did he know Mrs. Fitzherbert was there?" she asked, disappointed that Dick had bested her again.

"He didn't . . . That is, he wasn't sure," he said, his cheeks coloring up in that telltale fashion that announced as clearly as a sign that he was lying.

"If he didn't know she was there, why did he go to the inn?" she asked sharply.

"Because of the rumor. I already told you," he declared, turning rosier by the minute. "He just wasn't sure which inn," he invented recklessly.

"You're a terrible liar, Pronto," she said bluntly. "He didn't know Mrs. Fitzherbert was there at all. Why did he go? And letting on to me that he had a headache, the wretch!'' Her paramount emotion was anger that Dick had tricked her. She did n't suspect anything worse yet.

"You may be sure it was for a very good reason,'' he answered defiantly.

"What *is* the reason?''

"It's—it's private. That's why he needed a private parlor. He hasn't got a woman with him, Deirdre, so you can stop narrowing your eyes like your aunt.'' He experienced a definite diminution of his love for Deirdre. A bit of a bad-tempered girl and suspicious beyond all reason, even if she was dead right.

"He doesn't know anything about this, does he?'' she asked, showing him the note.

"No matter, m'dear. He's bound to see Fitz while he's there, and there's an end to it,'' he said, taking the note and tearing it in two.

She grabbed the pieces and shoved them into her reticule. "I disagree. He won't think to inquire if Mrs. Fitzherbert is there at all. Why should he? She'll go off to London or Paris, and we'll never know whether she is George's mother. I'm going to see her myself.''

"No, you're not!'' he shouted, in accents much too loud and desperate for a prince's party.

"Indeed I am, and I'm taking my aunt with me,'' she told him as she knew that dame would insist on going along. The frightened, staring look in his eyes told her that Belami was up to something outrageous.

"Not the duchess! Deirdre, if you have a hope in the world of ever marrying Dick, you can't take the duchess,'' he said, weak with confusion and a terrible sensation that he had botched it.

"Why not? I can't very well go alone.''

"I'll take you,'' he offered wildly, for anything was better than exposing Charney to such a scene of wild debauchery as would greet her eyes.

"I'll have to tell her I'm going. I can't rush off at such an hour without letting her know."

"Write her a letter," he suggested, incoherent.

"And post it after I get back?"

"She wouldn't want to go. We'll just nip out, the two of us."

"You mean you don't want her to go. In other words, Belami would dislike it," she translated, becoming more curious.

"That too," he admitted. Since she insisted on going, it seemed best to give her an inkling that what she might see was not what she might think she was seeing. "Truth to tell, it has to do with Gilham," he said, wearing a frown to hide his shame for Dick.

"I knew it!" she exclaimed. "I had a feeling in my bones that hussy was wound up in it somehow. A private parlor too!"

"It's not what you think. Not a tryst at all," he insisted.

"No, I suppose they drove all the way to the Red Herring and hired a private parlor for her to receive a package of money from him!"

"That's it exactly! You've hit it on the head," he said, grasping at a straw.

"Do you think I'm an idiot? You talk like one yourself!"

"And you're getting to sound mighty like Charney. By Jove, I pity poor Dick, getting stuck with you."

It was unfortunate that the duchess chose that moment to join her niece. She raked Pronto with a scathing grin. "What's this, Belami wanting to call off the match?" she asked. "He won't find any opposition in this quarter, and you may tell him so." 'Getting stuck' with Deirdre, indeed! We'd see about that. George Smythe as close to a throne as made no difference!

"We shall go home now, Deirdre, and write up Belami's dismissal," she said.

"No, no, Dick doesn't want to call it off. You misunderstand," Deirdre said. "It all has to do with this note." She didn't want to show her aunt the note, but to have her dismiss Dick was even worse.

"Where did you get this?" the duchess asked after piecing it together and reading it.

"McMahon sent it to Deirdre," Pronto told her.

"We must leave at once," she declared.

Pronto made a distracted effort to dissuade her, but she hardly listened. "Rubbish, I shan't mind a short drive in a well-sprung carriage. I have a fur rug in mine. Kind of you to be concerned, Mr. Pilgrim. You will accompany us, of course, as Belami is gone home with a megrim."

"I'll go in my own rig. Faster," Pronto said. With luck he might get to London and hide where Dick could never find him.

"Very well, we'll all go in yours," the duchess decided. "Pray send word to the stable to deliver Lady Donwin home in my carriage and have your rig sent around immediately."

It was done. There was never any point arguing with Charney. Pronto's next concern was to see to it that Belami didn't show his nose while the duchess was there. He had some hope of pulling it off if only Belami didn't decide to cart Gilham home at the same time the duchess was arriving. Much depended on Deirdre's discretion, and he was at pains to get her alone for a minute.

"If you say a word about Belami being there, you can say good-bye to any chance of marrying him" was what he whispered into her ear. She had come to realize it, and while she was almost too angry to care, she hadn't positively decided to reveal his presence to her aunt. If she could just take a look around for herself and see that he was innocently employed, she might even forgive him. It was possible, for instance, that Gilham was on her way out of town forever—lovely thought!—and had ordered Dick to bring her payment to the inn.

The duchess chattered on about the prince's party during the trip, occasionally wondering aloud why Mrs. Fitzherbert had stopped at the Red Herring when she knew dozens of people in Brighton who would have been happy to give her rack and manger. "No doubt she learned Prinny is there and wishes to avoid him," she decided.

Pronto was out of the carriage almost before it stopped and helped the duchess and Deirdre down. He spoke to his groom before entering the inn. "If Belami's rig is gone from the stable, let me know," he said, hoping against hope that Belami had left.

The duchess strode purposefully up to the front desk and said, "I wish to see Mrs. Fitzherbert at once. You may tell her it is the Duchess of Charney here on a most important matter. Most important," she repeated, nodding her feathered turban at him.

The innkeeper, a jovial, country soul, was intimidated but helpful. "I don't have a Mrs. Fitzherbert here, ma'am," he said.

"Idiot! Of course you have. I received written notice of her visit half an hour ago. Give me her room number, and I'll go up unannounced. Come now, my good man, don't trifle with me."

"I ain't trifling, your grace. Mrs. Fitzherbert isn't here. She's *never* been here," he maintained stoutly.

The duchess considered this a moment and said in an aside to Pronto, "She isn't using her own name in case someone slips the Prince Regent the word she is here. She wouldn't satisfy him to arrive when he needs her." She pulled the register around and squinted at it.

Mr. Harcourt was the last entry. "Who is this Harcourt person? Mr. Harcourt and friend, it says. No, that couldn't be her. It will be two women, I should think," she decided, looking higher on the page. Deirdre saw Pronto's face turning a dangerous purple shade and had a fair idea who Mr. Harcourt might be.

"Harcourt—that's a young lad and his, er, wife," the innkeeper said.

"*Wife*, is it? So that's the sort of establishment you're running here. I'm very much surprised Mrs. Fitzherbert chose your place. Ramshackle, I call it. It ought to be closed down.'' She read the day's entries, but there wasn't a pair of women registered, just couples.

"Maybe she'll be along later,'' the innkeeper suggested helpfully.

"My note said she is here,'' the duchess informed him, tapping her foot in impatience. "We require a little organization here. Mr. Pilgrim, you nip out to the stable and see if her carriage is here.''

"I wouldn't know it to see it,'' he said, reluctant to leave.

"Idiot! Ask the stable boys if her rig is stabled. Someone will know her. She's a byword in this town. I'm surrounded by incompetents.''

Pronto didn't know how to refuse her and decided to leave and make a stealthy search of the premises for Dick. He met his groom in the hall and learned that Belami was still here. The groom had no idea whether Mrs. Fitzherbert was or not, but hadn't heard it mentioned.

"We will have a private parlor and await her arrival,'' the duchess decided. She was tired, she was cold, and, most of all, she was hungry. "Send along a bottle of wine—unwatered, mind!—and a plate of mutton,'' she told the innkeeper. "Deirdre, come along.''

The innkeeper took them to his only free private parlor, closed the door and left. "Open that door,'' the duchess told Deirdre at once. "I must keep a sharp eye on the hall to see when Fitzherbert arrives. I'll have a short rest here on the sofa if you will go fetch me a blanket.''

Deirdre was delighted to have an excuse to get away. She had a good idea that Pronto was looking for Dick, and she went after Pronto. She spotted his ungainly form slouching around a corner at the end of the hall and darted quickly after him. As she rounded the turn, he was scratching at a door.

Inside the chamber, Belami heard the sound and was happy for the interruption. Lady Gilham was bent on seducing him. He had dragged the dinner out as long as he could, but it was finally finished before he felt it safe to return the lady to North Street. He had told Réal to wait for an hour after the lights were out, and if the servants decided to amuse themselves once the mistress left, he wouldn't be surprised. At the time of Pronto's arrival, Lady Gilham had got Belami cornered on the sofa, pulled off his cravat, helped him out of his jacket, and had thrown her own gown aside, revealing an elegant and provocative set of undergarments.

She sat on his lap with her two arms around his neck. "Tell them to go away," she said softly in his ear.

"Wouldn't you like some more champagne?" he asked, a desperate note creeping into his voice.

"No, I want *you*," she answered.

The scratching increased in intensity and Belami's agitation along with it. The servants hadn't scratched before. They'd knocked. Who would be fool enough to *scratch* at a door? Pronto was the only one . . . "Dick, it's me!" Pronto whispered as loudly as he dared.

"Oh, my God!" Belami exclaimed. He opened his lips to answer, and Lady Gilham smothered him with a kiss. Pronto opened the door an inch and peeked in. The lights had been extinguished. The only illumination was the orange glow from the grate, which bathed the protagonists in its eerie, flickering light, lending an unreal touch to the scene. It was a scene to make Bacchus blush and even Pronto colored up. He opened the door wide and took one step inside. "Damme, Belami, get up out of there! You promised you wouldn't!"

Deirdre saw him disappear and raced to the open doorway.

The stifled gasp that issued from Belami's throat went unheard by them all. It was overridden by the scream coming from Lady Gilham, mingling with the heavy thud of Pronto's advance, and the strangled "Ohhh!" from the doorway. Soon a harsher sound was added to the medley as the duchess thrust her gaunt, forbidding anatomy into the room.

"So this is what you are up to the minute our backs are turned!" the duchess exclaimed in accents of venomous delight. It was so fortunate she had decided to go after the servant to light her grate.

"You get out of here!" Pronto demanded. "Deirdre, didn't I tell you to keep her out of here?" He didn't know what he was saying, but he knew that in some fatalistic way it was all his fault. He'd botched it again.

Lady Gilham hopped to her feet and held her hands over her bosom, screaming louder and louder, loud enough to bring the innkeeper running. Belami struggled up and for once was speechless. He just glared at Pronto, and at the duchess, because he was afraid to look at Deirdre. Not till she had pulled her engagement ring from her finger and thrown it at him, hitting him on the chin, did his head spin in her direction. "Pig!" Deirdre said, loudly and coldly, then she turned on her heel and bolted out the door.

"Swine!" the duchess added, agreeing entirely with the sentiment, but using a more ladylike expression of it. "I need hardly say, Belami, the engagement is terminated."

He gave her one short, fierce stare that would have frozen fire. She didn't flinch, but she did feel a quiver of fear at the murderous expression in those black eyes. She inched closer to Pronto, watching Belami as a rabbit watches a snake. "The hell it is," he said through clenched teeth, then he stalked out the door after Deirdre.

The duchess breathed a sigh of relief, but had soon recovered her composure. "Who is this trollop?" she asked Pronto, while her close-set, sharp eyes turned to examine Lady Gilham.

"All a misunderstanding," Pronto muttered.

"Ladies, gentlemen, please!" the innkeeper implored. "You are disturbing my other guests."

"I think I'm going to faint," Lady Gilham whispered and slid daintily to the sofa. Pronto picked up the water jug and poured it over her white face, bringing her to sputtering consciousness, while the duchess nodded in approval.

The room was so cozy and the wine on the table of such a good quality that the duchess decided her first duty was to interrogate the damp lady, which she did, as soon as she had sent Pronto after Deirdre to bring her back. She then informed the innkeeper that she wouldn't be needing her private parlor after all and didn't intend to pay for it either, if *that* was what he had in his mind. She thought she had covered every base, but Lady Gilham was a jump ahead of her. She had slid her hand along the sofa and palmed Deirdre's diamond engagement ring while the duchess was speaking to Pronto.

Deirdre found herself stumbling along strange corridors that never seemed to end but only met other crossing corridors, all lined with doors. She knew that hell had fire and brimstone, but she thought purgatory must be like this, endless corridors of misery, with no exit, and nowhere to go if you could find a way out. Tears pricked at the back of her eyes like a hundred sharp pins, but pride held them in. Another corner loomed ahead, and she hastened toward it.

As she rounded the bend, she recognized the jacketless man advancing toward her as Belami and stopped in her tracks for an instant. When she recovered her wits, she turned and fled back the way she had come.

Belami didn't bother calling. He just ran after her and had soon overtaken her. She felt his strong hands on her shoulders, stopping her, turning her roughly around to face him. Incredible though it was, he looked angry. She had thought he would be humble, imploring, apologizing, but he glared at her as though he hated her.

It was his unfortunate custom to shout when he was wrong and knew he was wrong. "You couldn't trust me, could you?" he shouted now in a voice that could be heard through every door in the corridor.

"Trust you!" she said in a slightly lower voice. "I'd as soon trust Jack Ketch with a rope! You'd best go in search of your jacket, Belami. That cough you've been practicing all week will catch up with you. You've been planning this for days. Don't deny it!"

"I'm not denying anything," he said proudly. "You know my work takes precedence."

"Yes, especially when it involves such dashers as Lady Gilham! I don't see you working so hard on the more important case, however! The prince may set a crown on Smythe's head tomorrow for all you care."

"That would please your aunt!" he said swiftly.

"You leave my aunt out of this. This has nothing to do with her! You're the one who was caught red-handed. Nothing you can say will convince me this night's work was necessary. If this is the nature of your *work*, then I want nothing to do with it or with you." She lifted her chin and glared at him.

He knew her pride, and her intransigence, and began trying to calm her. "Deirdre, I can explain everything."

"Not to my satisfaction," she said, unmoved.

"Réal is at her house this minute, stealing the letters. I *had* to bring her here," he said, reaching to put his hands on her upper arms in a rather tentative way.

"Did you have to take her dress off?" she asked, but she allowed the hands to remain on her arms, where they soon began moving carefully around to her back. She was weakening. He knew she was caving in and pulled her into his arms while he had the chance. His lips came down on hers, hot, hard, insistent and much too soon. She struggled to escape, but the harder she pushed, the harder he held her, forcing her to comply, confident that his masterly kisses would have the desired effect. He felt the fight go out of her, sensed a great wave of relief when her lips stirred and she put her arms around him.

I can't lose him. I can't! Her blood warmed as his lips pressed on hers and his hands stroked her back. But just two minutes ago he was doing this with *her*! She pushed him off with a sob. "You're a devil!" she said, her voice a hoarse whisper. "A devil, and I hate you."

"Darling, you know perfectly well you love me," he said

with his reckless, confident smile in place as he pulled her back to him.

And it was true. She did love him. In frustration, she raised her open hand and struck him across the lips, a hard, stinging slap. While he blinked in astonishment, she gathered up her skirts and fled. Ran and ran and ran till she saw the open door with her aunt framed within, lifting the champagne glass.

"Ah, there you are. It is high time we were leaving," the duchess said. "Mrs. Fitzherbert would never stay at this bordello. Come along, Mr. Pilgrim. Belami will see that his lightskirt gets home, I daresay," she added as she hauled herself up from the table.

Chapter Thirteen

"What did I tell you?" the duchess crowed as the carriage sped back to her hired cottage through the night. "A confirmed rake. A lecher. Leaving the Royal Pavilion for a rendezvous with a lightskirt. You described Lady Gilham very inaccurately, Deirde. Ladylike, you called her, and pretty. She is a hoyden, but deuced attractive. I hope this opens your eyes to Belami's true nature, my girl. I don't know whatever possessed me to give the match my approval." All these thoughts whirled around in her mind, which was giddy from having to drink up the half bottle of champagne so quickly.

"It ain't what you think at all," Pronto defended weakly, aiming his pleas at Deirdre.

"My niece has no thoughts on the matter," the duchess told him comprehensively.

Deirdre's febrile, glittering eyes refuted this statement, but in the darkness of the carriage she remained silent and still, save for an occasional shiver. How *could* he? She had known from the first time she had laid eyes on Lady Gilham she would be trouble, and she had been right. Dick must have been seeing her regularly, all the time he let on that he wasn't or that it was only business. The affair hadn't leapt from "business" to what she had seen without some working up to it. Stolen kisses in the lady's saloon, secret visits clandestinely arranged when Mrs. Morton was away. It was a betrayal, a planned, thought-out treachery. No wonder he put up no fuss when the duchess removed them from his house. It suited him right down to his heels.

The drive seemed endless. Her jaws ached from holding back the tears. She entered the house without even saying good night to Pronto, but the duchess more than made up for her silence.

"We owe you an eternal debt of gratitude, Mr. Pilgrim. If you hadn't taken us to the inn, my niece might have made the dreadful error of marrying that creature. Buck up, Deirdre. There are better fish in the sea than that tiger shark. I'll find you another match, never fear. You may call on us tomorrow morning, Mr. Pilgrim," she informed him with grand condescension.

"Don't know that I will," he muttered unhappily.

"Rubbish! Of course you will. Meanwhile you ought to dart around to the other local inns and see if Mrs. Fitzherbert is putting up somewhere else."

Pronto left, but he didn't bother going to any other inns. He went straight to Belami's house and stabled his rig to await his friend's arrival. He was shaking like a blancmange and made a deal with God that if Belami didn't kill him, he'd swear off trying to steal Deirdre from him. He was surprised to see Réal sitting in the box of the traveling carriage with a pistol cocked and aiming straight at him. He naturally assumed he was there at Dick's orders for the purpose of putting a bullet through himself.

That evening had held many surprises, the greatest of which was that Pronto discovered he wasn't a coward at all, as he'd always thought. A magnificent calm descended on him as he peered through the shadows at the muzzle of that pistol, knowing a flash of fire would soon issue from it to terminate his mortal existence. He was half relieved, as it would obviate having to face Dick. "Tell him I'm sorry," he called in a firm, loud voice.

"Comment?" Réal called, setting down the pistol.

Pronto realized he had misconstrued the situation, but no

wonderful wave of relief washed over him. "Belami ain't back?" he asked.

"*Non, monsieur.*"

"Whole world's gone mad tonight," he mumbled, and went in the back door, through the kitchen, and up to the saloon, where he felt justified in resorting to the brandy bottle. He also took a poker and concealed it cunningly beside his chair, for in the aftermath of his brush with death, he realized he wasn't quite ready to quit this world or even to be knocked senseless. Dick had a wicked left.

It was less than half an hour later when Belami entered the saloon. The dejected droop of his head was a reassuring sign. Dick never used his nabs when he was in this mood.

"Suppose you're wondering why I took the ladies to the inn," he said apologetically.

"No, I've figured it out from the things the innkeeper said. Someone told you or the duchess that Mrs. Fitzherbert was there?"

"That's dashed clever deducing, Dick," Pronto complimented, knowing his friend's love of praise for his work.

"And of course she wasn't, so that means it was a deliberate ruse to lure the ladies to the inn and catch me with Gilham."

"Who'd do such a wicked thing?" Pronto demanded, astonished.

"No one knew but you, Gilham, McMahon, and my servants. Of that lot, I'd have to select . . ."

"On my word of honor, it wasn't me, Dick. I've given up all thought of Deirdre."

A weak smile showed on Belami's face. "No, it was Gilham herself. She set me up, Pronto. I never felt such an egregious ass in my life."

"Buck up. At least you snaffled the letters and loot from her house. She's outsmarted herself this time," he pointed out.

With an embarrassed shake of his head, Belami enlightened him. "No, she outsmarted me entirely. I just had a look at what Réal brought back from her house. Ordinary, cheap crockery and tin tableware—in the darkness he couldn't distinguish what it was. It was exactly where she formerly had the prince's stuff. As for the letters . . ." He held out a handful of papers, comprised of bills from milliners and butchers and his own note to her. "Here I thought *I* was clever. She's been a jump ahead of me all the way. She knew exactly what I was up to and outwitted me, plain and simple."

"But she's only a woman!" Pronto said.

"No, she's half fiend. I'll get that she-devil if it costs me my soul," he said, his dark eyes flashing with determination.

"Seemed to me you already got her. Certainly looked like it."

"A blow to my vanity as well. All her seducing was only to put me in a compromising position when the company arrived. Her swoons and shrieks were playacting. But why did you bring *Charney,* of all people?"

"Might as well try to stop the tide, Dick. Once she sets her cap for anything, there's no holding her," Pronto said, hiding his shame behind the brandy glass. He poured one for his friend, who gulped it and shook his head.

"I needed that," Belami declared vehemently.

"Have another."

"One's enough. That stuff is slow death."

"You ain't in that big a hurry, are you?"

Belami pulled the cord to summon a servant and ordered coffee. "It's going to be a late night, my friend. Will you stay and help me?"

"You can always count on me, Dick," Pronto said humbly. He didn't say a word when he received a scathing shot from the obsidian eyes of his host.

"What did Deirdre say?" Belami asked when the servant had left.

"Not a word. You're off to a fine finish there, I fear. She just sat as if she was frozen stiff, except for shaking a little."

This heartbreaking image burned itself into Belami's brain. "I'd give every penny I own if I could undo this night's work," he said, his voice husky.

"Me, too," Pronto seconded and applied himself again to his glass.

"Don't overdo it. We'll need all our wits to wiggle out of this one," Dick said, removing the glass from Pronto's hands.

"There's such a thing as knowing when you're licked, Dick. This is it."

"I haven't begun to fight yet."

"Licked like a spoon," Pronto said dolefully.

"Faint heart never won fair lady," he replied, as some of his customary jauntiness seeped back to replace the drooping shoulders. The coffee soon arrived, and the gentlemen settled in to lay plans.

"Looks pretty demmed hopeless to me," Pronto began. "Gilham knows you're after the goods, and she's hidden them. You'll never find them. Could be anywhere."

"They're not in China or Peru. She plans to sell the letters to the papers and must have them close by."

"We'll go over the town with a fine-tooth nail. And comb," he added when Dick looked at him askance.

"I've had her place watched. She doesn't have many callers, but a tall, elderly, unidentified gentleman has been to see her two evenings, very late," he said. "He comes in at the front door after looking around carefully. Réal followed him as far as the north edge of town, but didn't want to leave the house long enough to follow him farther. Last night he took a large parcel away with him. I even knew that, Pronto, and didn't put two and two together that it was the crockery. I never for a moment suspected that *she* suspected *me*. I only thought she was giving some old clothes away to the poor. My damnable conceit is to blame. I thought Mrs. Morton was the one the man was actually visiting."

"Deirdre used to say *act*-ually. Remember, Dick, till you joked her out of it?"

"I remember," he said with a wistful little smile, easily detoured to this subject.

"Mrs. Morton!" Pronto exclaimed suddenly, starting up from his chair. "I knew there was something I had to tell you. Not that it matters much, but old Lady Donwin remembered who stole Fitz's ring. It was Moira Morton, a servant. She was blond and blue-eyed," he added. "Deirdre thought you'd want to know."

"Moira Morton," Belami said, massaging his chin. "I wonder if Mrs. Morton's name is Moira. It's Lady Gilham's Christian name—an odd coincidence." This, of course, was entirely suspect and they discussed it for a few minutes.

"If old Mrs. Morton stole the ring, it's more than coincidence," Pronto said. "Have I got this all mixed up, Dick, or ain't the ring involved in the George Smythe business? It ain't Lady Gilham who's mixed up with the ring affair. Is it?" he asked doubtfully.

A pleased smile creased Belami's face. "It begins to seem that there are a few points of intersection between the two cases. I've figured out how Gilham knew the duchess had left my house—knew it before I did myself. Smythe was the only other person the duchess had told of it, barring leaving her card at the Royal Pavilion. Smythe hasn't been to call on Gilham since Réal has been watching her, but he only started spying *after* that morning. The elderly man, whoever he is, could be the go-between, carrying messages and so on."

"I don't quite see what difference it makes if the two *are* in league," Pronto said.

"The prime difference it will make is that Prinney despises Gilham and won't be eager to call her friend and cohort his son. Then, too, we haven't determined the relationship between the pair of them."

"Haven't determined there *is* a relationship actually," Pronto reminded him.

"Let us assume, for the purpose of conjecture, that there is. Now what could the connection be? Relatives? Brother and sister? They don't have a single feature in common, including their accents.''

"Cousins?" Pronto asked. "I don't look a thing like that ugly turnip, Andrew Patton. They're too young to be each other's mother or father.''

"Husband and wife, perhaps?" Belami suggested with a flash of amusement.

"Smythe will kill you if he finds out what you was up to tonight, Dick,'' Pronto exclaimed, taking the suggestion for fact.

"He doesn't seem to be an Othello in that direction. He must have condoned Gilham's arrangement with the prince. Wouldn't it quench Prinney's ardor for his *soi-disant* son if it were only true? It's obvious Gilham has helpers. That note Deirdre was handed at the party for instance . . ." he said musingly.

"You're never saying McMahon is in on it?" Pronto gasped.

"Lord, no. Was it McMahon who handed her the note?"

"It was a page boy, but we thought it must have come from McMahon. We didn't ask him, though.''

"I'll do that tomorrow. Smythe was at the party as well. It was certainly Gilham who put him up to it if Smythe is the one who wrote that note. She did it for spite, to make a fool of me. Do you have the note on you?" Belami asked.

"Deirdre has the pieces in her purse. It got ripped.''

"Begin writing your list, Pronto. Number one, retrieve that note from Deirdre. Number two, get a sample of Smythe's writing to compare with the note. Next we have to discover who the elderly gentleman is who calls at milady's back door and where he took the loot. Any suggestions who he could be?"

"Elderly—could be some friend of Mrs. Morton. Moira Morton was said to have married an officer. Are you sure you can trust McMahon, Dick? He could have slipped the page that note.''

"I consider him above reproach. He's the one who asked me to stop Smythe."

"Red herring," Pronto said. "Not the inn, McMahon's asking you to help. Of course, if Moira Morton was married to McMahon, she'd be Moira McMahon."

"And his wife, his *real* wife, would have something to say about it as well. He's a solid family man," Belami told him.

"We're a pair of cloth heads, Dick. Moira Morton ain't married at all or she wouldn't be Moira Morton still. Have to take her husband's name."

"We can disregard the names they're using. Professionals have a dozen aliases."

"Why would Gilham's chaperone let on she was a thieving maid? Furthermore, you can't disregard Lady Gilham's name, for that Lehman woman in London vouched for her story. I don't know how it is, Dick, but this coffee seems to be making me very sharp," Pronto added, and took another cup.

"I wish it had the same effect on me. My mind is all awry. I underestimated the adversary earlier. I wouldn't be surprised now if Mrs. Lehman isn't a part of their organization. A hasty note to her would tell her what to say. In fact, add another number to the list. We'll have to send someone to London to double-check Lehman."

"We'll have to get a bigger paper for the list as well," Pronto complained, writing along the edge.

"So what have we got?" Belami said, pacing the room to aid concentration. "We have Gilham blackmailing the prince, Smythe trying to gouge some cash out of him. He has no more desire to actually *be* a royal son and heir than I have. He only wants money. We have an elderly gentleman calling on Morton or Gilham. We have a possible tie-in with the woman who stole Fitzherbert's ring. Possibly Mrs. Morton is that same Moira Morton, using her maiden name. But she was said to have married an officer. He could be the elderly man who calls at the back door and hauls away evidence."

"Except we don't know if Mrs. Morton's name is Moira. Lady Gilham is Moira."

"Mothers have given their daughters the same name as themselves before. Could Gilham be Mrs. Morton's daughter? The age is right . . ." He stopped talking and conjured with all these jumbled thoughts.

"You mentioned Smythe must have some place he keeps stuff, too, since he don't have Ben Franklin's book in his hotel room," Pronto said. When Belami gave him an approving smile, Pronto blushed and said, "It's the coffee, Dick. Wonderful stuff."

"If they're all in league, Smythe, too, could have his effects stashed with the elderly gentleman. Since he called two days in a row on Gilham, I assume he lives nearby."

"That includes a lot of old men. There's old Humphreys, there's the Captain Sharp who diddled me at cars . . ."

"Captain Stack!" Belami exclaimed with a eureka look. "Did I happen to mention that Smythe had a similarly marked deck in his pockets?"

"No! Dick, you should have told me! I might have been skinned alive. I wouldn't put it an inch past that old bird, Stack."

"An army man, of the right age . . ." Belami said, his expression a calculating smile. "I wonder where he lives. He mentioned a cottage north of town. Didn't Humphreys say Devil's Dyke? He'd be staggering out of the card room at the Old Ship right about now."

Belami drew out his watch and glanced at it, put down his cup of coffee, and headed for the door.

"Wait for me!" Pronto hollered and darted after him.

They took Pronto's carriage and alit outside the inn, but had the carriage drive ahead fifty yards, ready to follow when necessary. A peep through the hotel window showed them that Captain Stack was still at the table. It was a cold wait in the damp night air.

"I wish I'd brought the brandy," Belami said, slapping his hands against his arms.

"We could go in and have a wee drop," Pronto suggested at once.

"No, we'll wait for him out here. We need clear heads."

It was twenty minutes before the captain arose from the table, patted his pockets with satisfaction, and left the room.

"He drives a broken-down old whiskey," Pronto said out of the side of his mouth, his customary manner of speaking when he was doing spy duty.

When the rig issued from the stable, they darted swiftly to their carriage and followed it at a safe distance. It took the Queen's Road north toward Devil's Dyke and stopped at a little thatched cottage in a secluded area.

"Do we go in now and snaffle the goods?" Pronto asked, not at all liking the notion of doing it, but feeling he owed his friend some extraordinary support.

"Not now. We know where to find it. I mean to confirm that he *is* the elderly caller," Belami said pensively.

"How can you find out for sure?"

"Need you ask? By deduction, of course. We'll go back to town and lay our plans. Plans that won't go awry this time," he added, still angry with his own gullibility.

"Just thought of something," Pronto said as the carriage jogged along.

"Me too. The gloves—you mentioned the captain's were out at the thumb. Lady Gilham's caller, the first time I went to see her, sported the same style. Also she mentioned Mrs. Morton was always away on Wednesday—she visited a friend out by Devil's Dyke. She had no reason to lie to me at that time. She didn't know I was investigating Smythe. I think we'll call that confirmation," Belami decided.

"Must be—too much coincidence," Pronto agreed, happy to have the matter settled. "Does this mean I can go home to bed?"

"No, it means we can have that brandy now. I'll stop off at the Old Ship with you and walk the rest of the way home."

They went to Pronto's room for privacy and ordered a

bottle of brandy. "Why do I feel so miserable?" Belami asked Pronto as he swished the amber liquid around in his glass. "The investigation is going well."

"Both know dashed well what ails you. Deirdre," Pronto answered, and tipped his glass.

"And the duchess," Belami added. "She's never liked me. I'll be stapped if I know why she ever accepted me in the first place."

"Best thing to do is forget Deirdre."

"How can I? She's become a part of me, the better part. I've treated her badly, Pronto. I've excluded her from the investigation. How could I do otherwise, dealing with such rakes and rattles as Gilham and Smythe?"

"You can't suck and blow at the same time, Dick. Finish up the case, then go after her," Pronto advised.

"Every minute we're at odds, Charney will be feeding her stories against me. If it comes to a choice, I'll drop the case. Yet, we're so close to having it solved."

"Then you'll have to include Deirdre in the rest of it. If you'd told her what was afoot, this could all have been avoided," Pronto said.

"But I didn't do anything wrong! That's the injustice of it."

"I'll tell her you said so if I happen to meet her around."

"You'll have to go and see her," Belami said.

"I promised I wouldn't, Dick. Like to give you a hand, but I promised."

"You didn't promise *me*. Who did you promise?"

"God," Pronto told him. "Made a deal. He kept his end of the bargain—you didn't kill me. Mind you, I only promised I'd let up on courting her."

"This won't be a courting call. Old Charney can be talked around with Prinney's help," Belami said, throwing himself into solving his other major problem.

"True, she fair dotes on him. Disgusting to see her bearing her yellow fangs at the old blister. Don't worry, I'll patch it up with Deirdre for you."

This promise gave Belami all the reassurance of a scream in the night. "But wait till I invent a plan first, Pronto."

"You'll think of something. Always do. Talked them both around before. Pity old Bessler ain't out of Newgate and you could have him mesmerize the pair of them. Think I might know how to do it myself, in a pinch. Bessler used his monocle, remember?"

"I remember," Dick said sadly, staring into space. "But I'll need a fresh trick this time. Deirdre's onto that one. Give me the night to sleep on it. Some of my best ideas come in bed."

A smirking "heh, heh" into his collar earned Pronto a slap on the shoulder and a command to lift his mind above the gutter.

"I will then, but just before I scramble out, how was Gilham?" he asked, then waited impatiently to hear.

"The most forward wench who ever called herself a lady. She damned near pulled the clothes off my back. I had uphill work of it keeping her from raping me," Belami said, trying to hide his approval.

"Preventing?" Pronto inquired, his eyes narrowed.

"You heard me. I'm an engaged man, whether my fiancée knows it or not. I'm going home now, Pronto. You'll have to get Deirdre's note and a sample of Smythe's handwriting, but don't see Deirdre till we've discussed it further."

"Can get Smythe's handwriting at the registration desk."

"By God, I must be disguised! Why didn't *I* think of that?"

Pronto gave a cavalier toss of his head. "Can't be deducing all the time. Stands to reason you'll slip up on the odd thing. Like not getting the goods from Gilham, and swallowing that story of Lehman's from London, and not twigging to it that Captain Stack's in on it. Quite a botch you've made of it, one way and the other."

"Thank you for that crushing assessment of my abilities. And good night to you."

"By jingo, your upper story's to let, Dick. What good will it do *you* to have a look at Smythe's John Bull? *You* didn't see Deirdre's note. *I'm* the one who can verify if it's Smythe's writing or not. I'll take care of it for you, *as usual*," he added with a satisfied sniff as he pulled himself up from the chair.

Belami held in all his bile and waited for Pronto to swagger down to the desk. He examined Smythe's signature for a long time, tracing his finger around loops and circles. "Same writing," he finally decided. "Not a doubt of it. A bold, broad hand—the 't' crossed crooked."

"And nothing like McMahon's. His is like a lady's penmanship, neat and small."

"That really proves it then," Pronto said.

"The whole band of them are acting together. That makes things much easier," Belami said, always happy to have his thoughts confirmed.

"You've got a plan, Dick. I can tell by the way your shoulders are swaggering, and you ain't even walking. A dead giveaway. Let's hear it."

"I have some details to work out tonight in bed, but I can tell you one thing, my best of friends," Belami said, gripping Pronto's arm. "Your services will be absolutely essential—*as usual*."

"Of course," Pronto agreed magnanimously. "Just give me the word."

"Don't worry, I will."

With a wave of his hand, Belami was off, whistling himself out the door in a way that Pronto felt ill-befitted a man who had just lost the sweetest girl in the kingdom.

Chapter Fourteen

Belami lay in his great canopied bed, surrounded by blazing tapers, with no thought in the world of sleeping. He had a problem of an extremely complex and delightful magnitude to consider. Some weaker part of his mind wanted to worry about Deirdre, but he knew well enough her face would float before his eyes once the candles were out and he was alone in the dark. In this artificial daylight, he would solve the more immediate problem and allow himself the luxury of undisturbed repining later. Some poetic streak in him decreed that the punishment of the various miscreants in the case ought to fit the crime. They had been universally guilty of unconscionable greed, and their greed would be turned against them. He thought and thought till he came up with a scheme that would have made Machiavelli green with envy.

Lady Gilham's price was five thousand pounds—that would do for a start. Smythe, he felt, had stumbled into his scheme quite by accident. The traveling band of rogues had come to Brighton with the plan of compromising His Highness. Their housing arrangements suggested it, setting Lady Gilham up in town with an obliging chaperone who disappeared at the proper moment. The others, he thought, were only hanging around on the periphery waiting for her trap to spring.

No actual, overt effort had been made by Stack to attract

the prince's attention. McMahon had just happened upon him at the inn and invited him to the Pavilion. It was the merest chance that the whimsical prince had developed a fondness for Smythe. The ring, he believed, was an afterthought. Smythe hadn't worn it the first few times, but when he was to be alone with the prince, it had been brought forth. It must have been sitting idle for years, then its original source was recalled. It must have seemed worth a try. Being professional con men all, they had seen the possibility for an extra bit of blunt and had played the second trick simultaneously with the first. It loomed large in McMahon's eyes, but, in fact, George had no intention of putting himself forth publicly as the prince's son. All he wanted was some money.

So they must all be led to believe that they had a chance to get what they wanted. Greed would blind them, as fear had blinded McMahon and himself to the true nature of Smythe's game. He would use Lady Gilham's trick of time pressure as well, rushing them ahead before they had time for deep consideration.

Before he extinguished his tapers, he brought out his writing box and wrote two notes on his most expensive embossed paper. The first was addressed to Mr. George Smythe and requested him to step around to Marine Parade the next morning at eleven. Lord Belami had a matter of extreme importance and urgency to discuss with him. The second note was to Lady Gilham, requesting permission to call on her at eleven forty-five the next morning to discuss a pecuniary matter of royal importance. His lip curled sardonically as he composed this missive, and his mobile eyebrow lifted high on his forehead. To an onlooker, had there been one, he would have appeared slightly diabolical.

The delivery of the notes must be timed carefully. He preferred that Smythe not have time to contact Lady Gilham before coming to Marine Parade. There would inevitably be some brief exchange of news between them at Devil's Dyke, but it would be only a few words. Réal would be entrusted with the carrying of the notes before he jaunted off to

London for further investigation of a certain Mrs. Lehman on Upper Grosvenor Square.

Réal arrived at the Old Ship at ten the next morning, but when he learned Mr. Smythe had not come down yet, he didn't go up to his room. He let him finish his coffee in the common room, only putting the letter into Smythe's hand at ten-forty-five, just leaving him time to go on foot to Marine Parade and arrive at eleven.

Belami greeted him at the doorway of the Blue Saloon.

"George! May I call you George? It was so kind of you to come," he said, offering his hand.

"Not at all," George replied very civilly. "I must confess I'm very curious to hear what you have to say."

"And I am very eager to say it. Do have a seat. A cup of coffee? Tea, perhaps?" How *common* the man looked today with the magic aura of the royal family dissipated. He looked exactly like what he was: an adventurer in an ill-cut jacket, and with a shifty eye to boot.

"I've just had breakfast, thank you, but I'll have a seat at least."

They sat looking at each other for a moment. At length, Belami said, "I hardly know where to begin. The fact is, George, I have been an utter and complete fool." There was a polite murmur of disagreement, soon overridden by Belami. "You'll agree with me when you hear what I've done," Belami said humbly. He saw the curiosity on his guest's face grow stronger and began reeling him in.

"There is a delicate matter I was entrusted to handle for the Prince Regent—having to do with a conniving woman. You wouldn't know her and her name is of no importance to us. Let us call her Madame X. I was chosen to—now how shall I put it?—to retrieve some delicate letters and bric-a-brac she planned to use to get money. I failed quite miserably. The hussy outwitted me plain and simple. She's obviously a very experienced lightskirt of the worst sort." Not a muscle twitched on his listener's face, though the eyes were becoming feverish and a certain telltale movement of the fingers revealed his disquiet.

"He who dances must expect to pay the piper," Smythe said, a trifle stiffly.

"True."

"Well, go on," Smythe urged impatiently.

"Now comes the really difficult part. Are you sure you won't have something to drink?"

"No, no, get on with it!"

"I shall. This is where you come in, George."

"I don't see what it can have to do with me," he said swiftly.

"You will. You might think a prince has a bottomless purse, but it is not the case. Money is tight just now. The prince is so terribly fond of you. He asked me to keep a brotherly eye on you, to sound you out on what career interested you and so on. You may recall we discussed the matter one day, seemingly by chance?" Smythe nodded. There was some unnecessary delay while Belami helped himself to snuff and offered the box to his guest.

"It's only Spanish Bran, I fear," Belami said blandly. Smythe waved it away and sat on thorns while Belami inhaled and sneezed. Eventually, he resumed.

"I relayed your feeling that a little cash would suit you better than anything else. His Highness was disappointed, but began amassing what funds he could lay his hands on."

"How much?" George asked eagerly.

"Only five thousand pounds, but he meant to see you settled in a career as well. He had that money set aside, George, and *I*, fool that I am, lost it. What I mean to say is that I failed in my mission with Madame X. By coincidence, five thousand pounds is the sum she is extorting from the prince. His advisers now feel he must give her the money or a certain scandalous matter will be made public."

"I see," Smythe said, biting his lip, while his face betrayed rampant calculating. "Plans to give her the lot, does he?"

"Much as it goes against the pluck, I think he must."

George considered this for a moment in silence. "I am in no hurry," he said reluctantly. "Let him give the money to this Madame X, and I shall wait till he gets hold of more."

"That is what I hoped you would say," Belami said, warmly approving. "I would feel derelict in my duty, however, if I didn't warn you of one other circumstance. Mrs. Fitzherbert's arrival could just change the picture for you. Of course, we know pretty well she *is* your mother, but she is so cross with the prince that she might deny it."

"You mean she's here?" he asked as a jerking motion partially lifted him from his chair.

"Did you not hear the rumor at the party last night?"

"Yes, but . . . That is—I seem to have heard later it was all a hum," he said in confusion.

"She was said to have already arrived, but it was premature. The Duchess of Charney had a letter from her this very morning. She left Bath the day it was posted and shouldn't be more than a day behind her letter. If she takes it into her head to refute your story, then I cannot promise that mere friendship will lead the prince to be open-handed with you."

"But it wasn't *my* story!" Smythe was swift to point out. "I never claimed to even *know* the woman."

"But there is the matter of the ring . . ."

"Oh, damme, Belami, there are dozen of rings just like it around. It means nothing."

"McMahon mentioned something about a letter as well . . ." Belami said with a questioning look.

"Why, to tell the truth, I came across that letter in an old Bible I bought in a used goods store right here in Brighton. I only showed it to the prince as a curiosity and *he* took the notion I had had it forever. It gave him such pleasure, I didn't like to disillusion him," Smythe said, coloring up in embarrassment.

"Then what *is* your kinship to the prince based on, if not the ring and not the letter?" Belami asked, acting bewildered.

"On a whim. Nothing more."

"Well, it will all come out in the wash when Mrs. Fitzherbert arrives. We'll never convince the prince otherwise without some real proof."

"But in the meanwhile, Madame X will be given the five thousand?" George asked, trying to temper his interest.

"He's sitting on the money like a broody hen on her nest, wanting to give it to you, but afraid Madame X will create a scandal if he doesn't give it to her. McMahon has spoken to a judge about getting an injunction against her, and something may come of that," he added calmly.

"An injunction? How long would that take?"

"I have no idea. Perhaps Madame X will beat him to it and get her letters published before the judge makes up his mind. It would certainly be easier to just give her the money, but . . ."

"If I am the stumbling block, Belami . . ."

"It's an unkind description, but that's exactly what you are, I fear. If it weren't for your claims on the prince's generosity, he'd give her the money and be done with it."

"Let him give her the money then. I don't want to make any trouble," Smythe said nobly. "If I am not his son, then I deserve nothing."

"And if you are, then there will be plenty of time to arrange your future, but as I mentioned, the prince keeps procrastinating. If there were some way we could convince him to take action—if we could find out, for instance, who you *really* are, that would be an end to it."

"I never wanted to be his son! I never wanted that sort of notoriety. I myself wish I could prove I am not, but how can I do it?"

"Did your father not leave anything in the way of documents? No birth certificates, no parish records, not even a letter to anyone with the details of your birth?"

"He left me a box of papers. Truth to tell, I only glanced at them once. Dull stuff about purchasing the plantation . . ." He stopped and sat staring into space, frowning.

"Do you still have the box?" Belami asked quietly.

"Yes, it's in a safety box at a bank."

"Here or in London?"

"Here, in Brighton."

"Why don't we go and retrieve it?" Belami suggested.

"Why should I help you prove I am *not* his son?" he asked, suspicious.

"Would a thousand pounds persuade you?" Belami asked softly. "Better an egg today than a hen tomorrow, as your countryman Ben Franklin said."

"Where would this money come from? You said he only had five thousand and all of it is for—for Madame X," he said, pulling himself up short on the name.

"It comes from my own pocket, George. Not out of the goodness of my heart, I promise you. The fact is, there is an advancement in it for me if I pull us out of this quagmire with honor. An earldom," he added bluntly.

"So *I* will get one thousand and Madame X the five thousand?" he asked and observed Belami closely.

"Only if it is proven you are *not* his son. If you are, then Parliament will have to sit down and discuss your future."

"Very well then, I'll go to the bank," Smythe said, his decision made.

"Shall I accompany you?" Belami asked.

"No, I'll meet you back here in, say, two hours?"

"Surely it won't take so long!"

"I have to sort through the papers. It's a large box," George said.

"Very well, we'll meet here at . . . ." He glanced at his watch. "At one-thirty."

"Right, and you'll have the thousand pounds?"

"In case," Belami answered, "you find you're not the prince's son."

Smythe left, and Belami removed the bag of gold given to him by McMahon from the drawer of a desk. He removed one hundred pounds from the bag, the *douceur* for Lady Gilham's locket. He rubbed his hands and smiled. His plan was proceeding satisfactorily. Greed had done its job well. The rogues saw a hope of six thousand in solid cash and had taken the bait. He put on his curled beaver and cape and called his carriage.

He had no fear of meeting Smythe at the bank, where he had to arrange to receive five thousand pounds in cash and transfer it to a pigskin case with his own initials engraved on the flap. Smythe kept his papers, of whatever sort, at Captain Stack's cottage, of course, which was why he needed two hours to retrieve them. Next Belami stopped at the constable's office to arrange for some assistance. A mention of Colonel McMahon's name sufficed. There was no need to drop such an elevated name as the Prince Regent.

This done, he proceeded to call on Lady Gilham. He had had no reply to his note, but assumed her curiosity would make him welcome or would, at least, admit him into her saloon. He didn't have to wait a minute. She sat on her sofa waiting for him, and she looked like a cat who has just had her fill of cream. He almost expected her to purr when she spoke.

"Milord, I had a notion I might hear from you after last night," she said, biting back her smile.

He cocked his head to one side and smiled. "You win, madame. I have met my match. A crushing blow to my pride, that all your advances were only to lead me on."

"Not all!" she objected, working a pretty pearl-handled fan. "May I conclude you are here to take me seriously at last?"

"Precisely," he agreed, taking up a chair opposite her.

"Excellent, but I don't see any package large enough to hold my asking price," she pointed out.

"I don't see the letters, nor the crockery and locket," he countered with a playful look around the room.

"Let us agree on a time and place for the exchange," she suggested. "Bring the money here . . ."

He silently wagged a shapely finger. "The victim more usually is permitted to choose the venue. Let me see, not my place. Miss Gower, who has taken an unaccountable aversion to me, would dislike it.''

She batted her fan innocently. "Why not here?" she asked.

"Because it is your lair, madame. Who knows what masked men might be lurking behind a door or a sofa?''

"Why, milord, you sound as though you don't trust me!'' she exclaimed in mock surprise.

"I trusted you once and have the knife in my back to prove it. Let us make it a public spot. Say, the Old Ship Inn.''

"But who knows what henchmen of yours might not be lurking there? I shall take a footman with me.''

"Bring as many as you like. I don't plan to either kill or ravage you in a public spot, I promise you. Strong as the temptation might be.''

"You had your temptation under excellent control last night, milord,'' she reminded him.

"Only the urge to ravage. I would happily have wrung your neck, could I have gotten you alone after my fiancée's arrival,'' he responded with a dangerous glitter in his eye.

"You are a poor loser, milord,'' she said, aiming a coquettish smile over her fan.

"I have had little experience at losing. Were we to do business together more often, no doubt I would become better at it,'' he admitted.

"No doubt,'' she agreed complacently. "At what hour shall we meet at the inn?''

"Will two o'clock give you sufficient time to retrieve the letters and crockery?''

She glanced at the clock. "If I move swiftly it will. I'll want cash, not a check.''

"Of course. Would you mind telling me where you hid the things?''

"I would mind very much, milord.''

"I may be a poor loser, but for an experienced winner, you do it with a poor grace, madame.''

"Fie, you men are all alike. Complaints, complaints! I shall be more agreeable when you bring me the stack of *unmarked* bills. I don't want the denomination too large, yet not too small, or it will be an unwieldy packet. I leave it to your discretion, Belami."

"My discretion can always be counted on. I believe that terminates this delightful discussion," he said, arising.

"I can't tell you when I've enjoyed a little cose more. I look forward to seeing you soon," she replied, remaining seated.

"Remember," he said, lifting a finger, "the silverplate as well as the locket and all the boudoir accoutrements."

"I'm not a welsher, Belami!"

"It's a pleasure doing business with a real gentleman," he said, and bowed himself out, to the tinkling sound of her laughter.

It was twelve o'clock. His next appointment was not till one-thirty with Smythe. He went to the hotel to see Pronto, who was pacing around the common room.

"I did what you told me," Pronto said, advancing to meet his friend.

A look of wild fear possessed Belami's face. "What have you done, Pronto?"

"Nothing. You told me not to do nothing and I did it. I've just been waiting here to hear from you."

"Good, here's what I want you to do. I want to use your room this afternoon at two o'clock. Shortly before that time, I want you to lure Deirdre up to it."

Pronto stared in disbelief for a long minute. "You're sick. That's what it is," he said in a weak voice.

"No, no, I have a plan. You call and take Deirdre out for a drive. Charney will make her go to distract her mind from last night. You make an emergency stop at the inn and get her in here."

"But I can't ask her up to my room!" Pronto objected.

"When you see my carriage arrive, draw her attention to

it. She'll want to disappear and you can suggest she run up-stairs to your room.''

''Do I go with her?''

''No, you stay below—tell her you'll get rid of me, but in fact you must dart off here to the common room. If, by any chance, Smythe shows up, you must at all cost remove him.''

''How? He's bigger than me.''

''Tell him any story you like, but don't let him upstairs.''

''Where are they all now?''

''At Stack's place, up toward Devil's Dyke, if my plan is going as it should. Gilham is retrieving her crockery, Smythe is rooting out evidence that he isn't Prinney's son, and the others are probably packing up the carriage for a quick getaway. They won't want to be here when Mrs. Fitz-herbert arrives. They'll be gloating over having cleared six thousand pounds,'' Belami said, gloating himself at having outwitted them.

''I see by your smirk that you think you've sewed this one up right and tight, but I might just point out, Dick, six thou-sand pounds is a lot of blunt.''

''It's costing the prince one thousand. In my opinion, it's a fair price for his dalliance with Lady Gilham.''

''Who's putting up the other five thousand?''

''I am lending it to the cause. It will be returned shortly if all goes well.''

''And if it don't? If Gilham outsmarts you again . . .''

''We won't think of that—yet. I need a clear head,'' Bel-ami said, but the possibility niggled at the back of his mind.

''Care to give me the details?'' Pronto asked, his blue eyes popping with curiosity.

Belami was happy to oblige as it gave him the opportunity to go over it again himself, double-checking for flaws. ''It's a regular maze,'' Pronto said at the end of the discourse. ''I can see a dozen places it might go wrong.''

''It won't go wrong,'' Belami said calmly. ''Greed blinds

them to any little implausibilities inherent in it. Not that there are many. I think I've covered everything."

"Did you cover Deirdre's engagement ring?"

"I beg your pardon?" Belami asked, frowning.

"Diamond ring. Gilham snaffled it down her bodice last night during the confusion. Caught her out of the corner of my eye. Forgot to mention it."

"Did she, by God? I've been so occupied I didn't give it a moment's notice. But it's no problem. I shall get it back as well. I'm very glad you told me, Pronto. That will make excellent fodder to show Deirdre how much I love her. The *pièce de résistance*, you might say."

"Seems to me it ain't a piece of resistance you want. You've got more than enough of that. What you need's a piece of forgiveness."

"You're right, of course," Belami agreed blandly.

"Glad to straighten you out. Wouldn't want you to be making a fool of yourself in front of the others again," Pronto said generously.

"Quite. Shall we order a beefsteak? I omitted breakfast in my morning rush and don't foresee the likelihood of having any luncheon."

Pronto had by no means missed breakfast, but he was easily convinced to have a one-pound bite of beefsteak, with a little helping of pan-fried potatoes, and a few eggs to wash it down. When their meal was finished, Belami returned to Marine Parade to await the arrival of George Smythe.

Chapter Fifteen

At one-thirty on the dot, the front knocker on Marine Parade sounded and Mr. Smythe was shown in, wearing an expression of eager excitement.

"Upon my word, Belami, you could have knocked me over with a feather!" he exclaimed, tossing a folder of documents on the sofa table at which Belami sat. "I got rooting around in that dusty old box my papa left me and what do you suppose I found?"

"A birth certificate?" Belami asked, arching a brow in well-simulated surprise as he reached for the folder.

"Exactly! There are some other parish papers there as well—copies of baptismal certificates and so on. I can't tell you how *shocked* I was!"

"No need to try, George. I can well imagine."

"Well, you can't, for it's really quite a disgraceful background. My father was a convicted felon. Imagine how shocked the Prince Regent would be to learn it. Must he know?"

"What else did you learn? Something to mitigate the stain, I hope?" Belami asked.

"He was legally married to my mother, so at least I am not a bastard as I feared. I brought the wedding certificate as well. This one," he said, pulling the proper paper forth for Belami's perusal.

" 'Millicent Champers and George Smith,' " Belami

read, frowning. "The spelling is slightly different, yet it is substantially the same name. Was Alex Smythe, your adoptive father, some relation?"

"It doesn't say so in black and white, but I assume they were related—cousins, perhaps. Alex obviously led me to believe I was the illegitimate son of some highborn gentleman to prevent me from learning this," he added.

"Very likely, and the birth certificate? Ah, here we are," Belami said, drawing forth a yellowed paper. He politely omitted to compare the dates aloud, which indicated that the marriage had taken place four months before the birth. The location was not Ottery or just north of it, but Exeter, some miles away. What happened, he deduced, was that the impoverished son of Millicent Champers lived close enough to Ottery at some time—perhaps worked there—to learn the story of Alex Smythe and his adopted son and borrowed the identity when he turned "gentleman." "I don't see the adoption papers here, George," he mentioned, sorting through the folder.

"Did I forget to bring them? How stupid of me!" George exclaimed.

"It is no matter. These will be more than enough. It must be some consolation to you to know for certain who you are after all these years."

"It is, in a way. I could wish my father hadn't been a criminal, of course, but Alex kept it from me, so I never grew up with any sense of shame or any proclivity for such a life myself."

"That was well done of him. May I keep these papers for the present? Just long enough to convince the prince's advisers of your true paternity. There will be no need to relay the details to His Highness."

"I must have them back."

"Of course. I'll drop them off at the inn this afternoon."

"And my money—the thousand pounds?" George asked, trying not to sound too eager.

"Count it, if you wish," Belami said, tossing George the

bag of golden coins. Smythe shook out a handful, bit one, hefted the bag, and considered the time involved in counting.

"That won't be necessary," he decided, arising from his seat.

"Good, then I'll go to the Pavilion at once and speak to Colonel McMahon. He'll release the other funds for Lady—Madame X." Smythe bit his lips to hide the exultant smile that wanted to burst forth. "Where will you go now, George?"

"I believe I'll go and say good-bye to a few friends. I shan't want to be around to embarrass the Prince when Mrs. Fitzherbert lands in town," he said, already hastening toward the door.

There seemed to be no danger that he would intrude on Lady Gilham's transaction at the inn. He didn't want to reveal any association between them. Belami set Réal to follow him all the same and heard with satisfaction that Smythe had been met by Stack in his whisky, and the pair of them had gone up toward Stack's place. Belami donned his hat and cape, and took up the initialed case containing the five thousand pounds from the bank.

While Belami had been dealing with Smythe, Pronto went to call at the little cottage behind the Castle Inn and was greeted by a mutinous Miss Gower, who had not the least desire to face the world while her wounds were still fresh.

"Nonsense, the very thing for you," the duchess decreed, eyeing Mr. Pilgrim with a dangerous eye. He was no replacement for Lord Belami to be sure, but he would do to look like an escort till something better could be found. "You can take my book back to Donaldson's and get me a new one. I haven't taken a look at *Orphan of the Rhine* for an age, or *Midnight Bell* will do."

She pulled the bell cord and sent a servant off for her book. "Why are you wearing that dowdy old round bonnet, Deirdre? Put on the new one you got in London last week. Mr. Pilgrim will be ashamed to be seen with you."

"Devil a bit of it. She looks fine to me," Pronto said.

"Oh, ho, do I sniff a little partiality here?" the duchess joked good-naturedly.

"Eh? Oh, yes, by Jove, I am very fond of round bonnets." Pronto harbored no notion of being less than gallant as he spoke.

"Run along," the duchess said when the book arrived. She was bored with him already and more bored with her niece, who had done nothing but mope from the minute they got home from the Red Herring last night.

"It's a dandy day for a drive," Pronto pointed out as they left the house. "Pity we must waste it at the library."

"That won't take long," she said with absolutely no interest whatsoever. What did it matter *where* she went? Her life was effectively over. She must go through the motions of living, but her heart had shriveled to dust within her. How could dust be so heavy? She felt the weight in her chest, a painful weight.

"I might pick up another book myself. Great stuff, this reading, but scary. Did you know Brutus was bothered by ghosts? Yessir, a great scary ghost used to pop in at his doorway at night and threaten him that his days was numbered. Drove the poor fellow loony. He got so sick and tired of it he plunged himself onto his dagger to have done with it. Your aunt would like *that* book, but I ain't finished with it myself yet."

She sighed and smiled wanly, knowing he was trying to entertain her. She only perked up when they drove past the Royal Pavilion. Her eyes scanned the grounds for a sign of Belami's stylish carriage.

"He ain't there," Pronto informed her.

"Has the prince left? We didn't hear it," she said, daring him to say that she had been looking for anyone else.

"No, he's still here, but Dick ain't going to see him. He's very busy."

"With Lady Gilham, no doubt," she said in a bored voice.

"With all kinds of people. What time is it?"

"A quarter to two. Why do you ask? The library is open all afternoon."

"I just remembered I have to meet a fellow at the Old Ship at ten to two."

"Not Belami?" she asked, instantly suspicious.

"Of course not. It's my man of business. I've run short, and he's brought me down some blunt from London. Won't take a minute."

"I'll wait in the carriage," she said, completely uninterested.

"Suit yourself."

At ten to two they pulled up in front of the Old Ship. Pronto sneaked a look at his notebook, to be sure he had the time right. Deirdre *must* be in his room in five minutes. He had to move fast. He tore into the inn as if the hounds of hell were after him and came puffing out thirty seconds later.

"Deuce take it, he ain't here yet. There's nothing to do but to wait for him," he said crossly. "You'd better come in. You'll catch your death of cold out here."

"I have my fur-lined cape on," she said.

"It may take hours. You'd best come in," he insisted.

"*Hours?* In that case, I'll go on home," she answered, most unhelpfully.

"Heh, heh, just a manner of speaking. Not actually hours. Come along and we'll have a cup of cocoa. You like cocoa," he reminded her. "Just like old times. Come along." He half pulled her from the carriage and hustled her into the inn.

"My aunt won't approve of this," she said, looking around the lobby at the motley assembly of patrons. "We'd better take a private parlor, Pronto."

A private parlor wouldn't do at all, but he passed the few minutes till Belami's arrival in pretending to look into it, signaling to a servant and peering down the hall to see what was available. Suddenly he felt Deirdre stiffen beside him, then a sharp tugging at his sleeve. He looked to the door and saw Belami had just entered.

"No private parlor to be had," he told her merrily, aware of a great sense of relief.

"Oh, what shall I do? I can't see him! He'll make a fuss of some sort. Pronto, help me!" she implored.

He slid his room key into her hand. "Take a nip up to number nine," he said. "My room. I'll stay here and get rid of him."

"Oh, thank you!" She grabbed the key and ran upstairs before Belami looked her way.

She kept the door ajar, which gave her a narrow view of the stairs and a slice of the lobby. When she heard a tread on the stairs, she pulled the door to, with only a crack now. The one-inch view of the man approaching was enough to identify Belami. How could Pronto have let him come up? He couldn't be coming to this room! But he was advancing quickly toward that very door. She looked wildly for someplace to hide and plunged into the clothespress, the only place large enough to hold her unless she wanted to roll under the bed.

She pulled the door shut behind her, but, with no latch inside, it hung open a crack. She looked out and saw with amazement that Belami had sat down on a chair and opened the briefcase he carried with him. It contained a very large sum of money. Thousands and thousands of pounds. The only thing she could think of was that he was going to give it to his mistress. She was furious yet exultant that she should be catching him in the very act. It was warm in her fur-lined cape, but if she tried to slip it off, it might alert Belami to her presence.

While she waited uncomfortably, there was a tap at the door and, before her astonished gaze, Lady Gilham sauntered in. It was a lovers' meeting, so how could she get away? She gasped, but quietly into her cape. She watched transfixed as Belami walked forward. Now what could she do? Must she hide in the cupboard while he seduced Lady

Gilham? No, it would be better to come out at once and bear the shame, for she knew she couldn't endure the alternative without committing murder. She took a breath, gripped the edge of the door, and firmed her resolve to emerge.

"You're punctual," Belami said to Lady Gilham. His voice surprised Deirdre. It was not the dulcet, silken voice he used with her when he had lovemaking in mind. It was a harsh, abrasive sound. She released her grip on the door and listened closely.

"I'm happy to be able to return the compliment," Lady Gilham said coolly and strode boldly into the room. It was difficult to recognize in this self-assured female the timid girl she had first seen at North Street.

"Shall we get on with it?" Belami suggested.

Deirdre's blood curled. Was *this* how gentlemen behaved with their paid lovers?

"Have you got the money?" Lady Gilham countered. She was as cold and mercenary as Dick!

"Have you got the letters?" Dick asked, causing the first dawning knowledge that it was not a love tryst. How quick she had been to accuse him.

Lady Gilham handed him a packet of letters. Dick flipped through them, too quickly to be reading but slowly enough to be counting and verifying their authenticity. "They seem to be in order," he said.

"I take it that's the money?" Lady Gilham said, nodding to the suitcase.

"Examine it, if you wish," Belami offered. She walked forward and ran her gloved hands through the case of bills.

"I can't count it. It would take forever," she said.

"Here's the receipt from the bank," he said, handing her a piece of paper. She looked at it and quickly made her decision.

"You call yourself a gentleman. I'll take your word for it. It's a great deal of money in any case," she said with infinite satisfaction as she closed the lid and took hold of the handle.

"Not yet," Belami said in a dangerously calm voice.

"The other wares are in my carriage in the stable. Your man—that French fellow—is examining them. You can come down with me if you don't trust me," she added.

"Oh, I trust Réal well enough for that job. I refer to something else."

"This, do you mean?" she asked, dangling the golden locket, which she drew from her pocket. "You're thorough, milord."

He went to her and took the locket from her fingers. "I wasn't referring to the locket, but to the other item of jewelry purloined from me at the inn last night," he said, his voice very curt.

"What do you mean?" she asked in astonishment.

"I mean my fiancée's ring," he said harshly. "You have it. I could forgive you all the rest, Lady Gilham. Your holding the prince to ransom is of no importance to me, but for your trick in calling that innocent woman to the inn last night and having her see me in a compromising situation, I will never forgive you as long as I live." His eyes never went within a right angle of the clothespress door, but he angled himself to give the door a view of his face as he spoke. Deirdre watched spellbound as he mouthed these noble sentiments. She felt she was looking at a genuine hero.

"Pshaw," the lady said in disparagement. "Why you worry yourself so over that widgeon is beyond me. You could do much better for yourself, milord."

These words struck his ears most happily. She couldn't have responded better if he'd written her script himself. "How can a man do better than to marry the only woman he ever loved or ever will love?" he asked. "She's worth ten of any other woman on the earth. And she was *mine* till you came along."

"And is that why you resisted me so assiduously last night? I am relieved to hear it. I began to fear my charms were fading," she said mockingly.

"Your charms are intact," he answered carefully. "Most men would have succumbed, no doubt. I happen to have been most deeply and sincerely in love with another woman.''

''If the ninny knows what is best for herself, she'll forgive you one little transgression. Especially a transgression that transgressed nothing but appearances.''

''Yes, and how should Miss Gower ever know that?''

''She doesn't trust you, along with the rest?'' she asked.

''There is no 'rest.' Naturally she believed her eyes.''

''For myself, I wouldn't give a brass farthing for a man who didn't love me enough to trust me and to forgive me an occasional slip. But that is entirely your own affair. Here, have the ring if it means so much to you,'' she said, opening her reticule to hand it to him. ''One would think the ring would lure her back, if not the man,'' she said, taking a last, long look at the diamond.

''She's not lured by baubles. Her mind is of a higher cast,'' he said, and enjoyed the blank look of bewilderment that settled on Lady Gilham's face.

''I personally think it would be extremely tedious to be married to a saint,'' she said. ''Take care you're not both strangled by her halo. I'm off now. Will you accompany me to the stable to see that all is in order?''

''I trust you,'' he said, but walked out behind her, controlling an impulse to look at the clothespress door with a superhuman effort. He went to the stairs, but didn't descend with Lady Gilham.

When they were gone, Deirdre pushed open the door and gasped for air. There was a film of perspiration on her forehead and upper lip from the heat. There were also tears in her eyes, but they had nothing to do with the temperature. ''Oh, what have I done?'' she whispered in a strangled voice. She was unworthy of Dick's constant devotion. She sat on the edge of Pronto's bed, forgetful of where she was and of what she was doing there. She wanted only one thing—to see Dick and to beg humbly for his forgiveness.

How could she have doubted him? All the time he was only seeing Lady Gilham on business, as he had said. Hard as that beautiful woman had thrown herself at him, he had resisted because he was in love with her. His ringing praise sang in her ears, followed by the more worldly denigration of Lady Gilham. Dick had paid no heed to it, but later he might remember and begin to wonder if Lady Gilham was not correct. Her love for Dick had been too weak. She didn't deserve him.

It was a few minutes before she heard a scratching at the door. She looked up, her eyes bright with tears, hoping it would be Dick, but it was only Pronto.

"Lud, what a mixup," he said merrily, deciding that to disregard her state would be the gallant course. "Dick came into the inn in a desperate plight. He had to meet Gilham and didn't want to go to her place or to ask her to his in case you heard about it and disliked it, so he asked if he could use my room. There was no talking him out of it. I hope you didn't mind having to hide."

"Pronto, I shall never be able to thank you enough. It was a—a revelation!" she said with a glowing smile. "There's nothing between Dick and Lady Gilham, you know. Nothing at all."

"*I* knew it all along. Deuce take it, how could he be carrying on with *her* when he's mad as a hatter about *you*?"

"You make me so ashamed for my lack of faith. We'd better go home now," she added reluctantly.

"That's dandy, but don't you want to go to the library first?"

"Yes, of course," she said in a dazed, careless way.

She was very quiet as they drove home from the library. Her dreamy smile dwindled to a frown as they drove up Pavilion Parade. Her mood was light—she loved Dick with all her heart, and he loved her, but between them loomed the gaunt shadow of the duchess. She held Dick in utter contempt and would never sanction the match. She must consult with Dick and arrange some plan to bring the duchess to heel.

"Pronto, where is Dick now?" she asked.

He took a peep at the list in his pocket. "I expect he'd be lurking around outside Gilham's door or possibly picking up the constable. This ain't the minute to be pestering him, m'dear."

"Do you know what he will be doing this evening?"

He only knew the last item on his list was to take Deirdre home. What activities the evening held for them all had not been discussed. "I don't know, but I'm sure *he* does," he told her with a reassuring pat on the hand. "Up to all the rigs, is Dick."

It was not feasible to pass Dick an invitation to call via Pronto. The duchess would bar the door. Pronto knew how she felt and she counted on him to relay her sentiments to Belami. Meanwhile she would go home and do what she could to mend his tattered reputation in that quarter.

Her aunt noticed her changed expression as soon as she entered the saloon and handed her the Gothic novel. "Your outing has done you a world of good. You've put off your Friday face, thank God. Ah, excellent!" she added, glancing at the book. "*Midnight Bell*. I was ever fond of this one."

It proved impossible to whitewash Belami at this moment. She could not explain how she had gone unchaperoned to a man's hotel room, and, without revealing that, the rest of the story could not be told. "What are we doing this evening, Auntie?" she asked instead.

"I have half a mind to pack up and return to London. There is nothing doing here. Nothing at all. No word from the Pavilion, and I cannot give a party when you've just lost Belami. I haven't had a single caller all day—except Mr. Smythe. He dropped in to tell me he is leaving town. Such a charming lad. He has come across some evidence that he is not who the prince believes, Deirdre. It was a blow to us all. Poor Prinney will be in tears. I was moist in the eye myself. He was on thorns to leave—so gentlemanly! He didn't want to embarrass the prince when Mrs. Fitzherbert arrives. He knew she was coming too. I don't believe in squandering money on every worthless charity that comes along, but I was so touched by his proper behavior that I gave him fifty pounds, Deirdre. He was a little short to settle up his account at the inn. Perhaps I shall stick around for a few days and say hello to Maria Fitzherbert. That might bring on a few fireworks and liven up this dull, damp, draughty place.''

"What evidence did Mr. Smythe find?" Deirdre asked, feeling in her bones that Dick had something to do with it.

"I expect Belami forged up a set of papers and diddled the prince out of a son, the son out of his birthright, and you out of an excellent *parti*. We are well rid of that rattle, Belami. If nothing else was accomplished by this expensive trip, it was still worth it." She ran on with a list of her expenses till her eyes fell on the novel awaiting her. Then she dismissed her niece and settled in for a good read.

Chapter Sixteen

Belami wore a tentative smile as he hopped into his carriage and followed Lady Gilham's carriage out of the stable yard. She didn't have her luggage on the rack, so she had to go home and pick it up. He would call on her at North Street.

Réal knew his first stop was the constable's office, and the constable knew his part in the melodrama about to be enacted. Highly irregular, he called it, but when word came from the Prince Regent's own secretary, a mere constable didn't say no. The whole nation knew Colonel McMahon was the prince's private secretary, with wide powers to act for His Highness. He hopped into the carriage with Belami and was hustled along to North Street.

"Make it fierce," Belami told him as the carriage approached its destination. "I want her to hear the clanging of the door at Bridewell. Put the fear of the Lord into her."

"It seems irregular," Perkins asserted, not for the first time.

"It is," Belami answered and laughed, "but this is a highly irregular female."

They alit and went to the front door, where Perkins hammered loudly enough to shake the hinges. "Open in the name of the law!" he shouted, then pushed open the unlocked door and pounced in. Lady Gilham sat with her hands buried to the wrists in money. "I arrest you in the name of the law for stealing that there money from this here lord!'' Perkins said, darting forward to grab her wrists. A pair of manacles jangled from his left hand.

Lady Gilham gasped and shrank back. ''I didn't steal it! He gave it to me! Tell him, Lord Belami!''

''Don't be daft. He's the one what told me you stole it,'' Perkins said. ''Yessir, there's his very initials on the side of the leather case just as he described it. Come along then, miss. Making trouble will only put you behind bars for a longer time.''

''I didn't steal it!'' she repeated, looking at him with great, bewildered eyes, the nature of the trap not yet clear to her.

''Where did you get it then?'' the constable demanded.

''From him, at the Old Ship, not fifteen minutes ago,'' she replied.

''It's true we were there, for an assignation whose nature I would prefer not to go into.'' Belami shared a worldly look with Perkins. ''I assure you the price for the lady's services was *not* five thousand pounds. She stole it while I was still in bed, resting.''

''Oh!'' The gasp that came from Lady Gilham's throat was awful to hear. Her face was frozen into a mask of disbelief, slowly melting to fury. ''You viper! You loathsome snake! You repulsive creature! Officer, I would *never* do what this man has suggested. I insist you arrest him for defamation of character. For libel, for slander!''

''We'll send off for the manger of the Red Herring to clear up that point,'' Belami told her. She was shaken by the triumphant sneer on his face.

''Devil! I'll get you for this!''

''Come along then. I'll just take this with us for evidence,'' Perkins said, shoving the money into the case and snapping it shut.

''Belami! You're not going to let him do this! You've got the letters. You've got all the evidence you wanted. I filled my part of the bargain. I took you for a gentleman.''

"We both erred. I took you for a lady—for about five minutes," he replied, unmoved.

"It's not fair!"

"Were *you* concerned with fairness last night when you had Smythe slip Miss Gower that damned note?" he asked, his voice harsh.

"So that's it. You're after revenge."

"I'm after your neck, milady, and I've got it." She looked at a murderous scowl that turned her blood to ice water. Belami was an excellent performer.

He deemed that her mood was ripe for negotiating, and the constable deemed that the second act of the play was about to begin. He glanced to Belami, noticed the nearly imperceptible nod of his head and said, "It does seem a bit harsh, milord, to hang a lady. Maybe if she just hands back the blunt, you two could come to terms. Once the law gets its hands on her, she'll never go free again."

"There is no contract between lions and lambs," Belami said in a softly menacing voice.

"Take the money. Take it and keep the letters too. I shan't say a word. I give you my word, Belami; just let me go and you'll never see me again," Lady Gilham implored, her white hands out to him in supplication while a tear trembled at the corner of one incomparable eye.

"You tempt me," he said, "but not very strongly."

"What's it to be, sir?" Perkins asked impatiently.

"Give me five minutes alone with her," Belami replied. "Keep a close watch on the front door and have our assistant watch the rear as well."

There was no assistant, but Perkins was clever enough not to remind his lordship of it. "Aye, I'll do that," he said, and went out, carrying the case of money with him.

Lady Gilham's mind was feverish with activity. Five minutes was not enough to bring him around her thumb by her customary means of handling recalcitrant gentlemen. She would only ask for her freedom. George's thousand pounds would see them out of the country, if this human devil hadn't managed to get *that* back as well! She was packed, the horses still harnessed. There was no point trying to get her pistol from the other room with that constable at the door outside. He must have something in mind—*he* was the one who had suggested the five minutes of privacy.

"Here's the bargain," he said with no preamble. "I keep the money and your evidence against the Prince Regent; you get your band of rogues out of the country *today*."

"Agreed!" she said at once.

"I'm not finished yet."

"Anything. Anything you ask. You have the loaf and the knife, Lord Belami. You won't find me hard to deal with."

"That'll be a change. I just want one thing more, and it won't cost you a penny."

"I said anything."

"I want you to satisfy my curiosity. To straighten out the relationship between yourself, Smythe, Stack, Morton, and Mrs. Lehman."

"Five minutes won't begin to do it," she said frankly.

"True. You have four minutes left to satisfy me."

"Very well then. Mrs. Morton is my mother; Captain Stack is my father. When my father—left the army . . ."

"Dishonorable discharge?"

"Yes," she said, her chin high. "But not for cowardice. It was a duel over a card game. After his discharge, we traveled around the country, living by his skill at cards. My mother disliked it excessively. In the larger centers where we planned to stay for some months, she often made Papa live apart, setting herself up with her maiden name, Moira Morton, and pretending to be a widow. The hope was that I might make a good marriage, but as I had to have my own name, for the certificates and so on, she began calling herself my chaperone. In Cornwall, it worked. They married me off to an old slice whose only attraction was his advanced age and his estate. When he died, there wasn't as much money as we hoped. Just enough to bring us here.

Mama knew the prince was susceptible to women and what would please him."

"Where does Smythe come into it?"

"He's another footloose wanderer, like ourselves. His father was a convict, and his mother worked for a country parson who gave George some education. I met him in Cornwall and fell in love with him. When Sir John died, I became pregnant and married George."

"This is the daughter you spoke of?"

"No, the marriage proved unnecessary after all. I lost the child."

"Where does Mrs. Lehman fit into the scheme of things?"

"She's my father's sister. She runs a gambling house in London. I sent her off a note begging her to support the story I told you, in case you checked. She's not a part of our traveling circus," she added grimly, "but she agreed to help and even invented some evidence that I had a daughter with her."

"What about this notion of palming George off as a royal by-blow?"

"That came about by chance. He met this Colonel McMahon at the Old Ship."

"I know that part. You can skip along to the ring."

"Mama remembered that old ring she and Papa had used for a wedding ring eons ago. Mama used to work for Mrs. Fitzherbert for a few weeks. Mrs. Fitzherbert gave her the ring," she said with a bold stare that dared him to deny this unlikely tale. "We thought it was worth a try, but none of us *ever* had any intention of letting that affair go very far. George only hoped for a few thousand pounds to salve the prince's guilty conscience. It was more a joke than anything else, but it started getting out of hand."

"A costly joke," Belami said. "I suggest in future you stick to coursing one hare at a time. Very well, I think that clears up any little questions that were plaguing me. Right on time too," he said, glancing at the clock. "I'll call the constable off, but I want it clearly understood, the lot of you depart today.''

"We're already packed. We're not eager to confront Mrs. Fitzherbert. She might just remember Mama. . . .'' She stopped, and a rosy flush crept up her neck.

"She wouldn't be likely to forget a servant she esteemed highly enough to give the prince's ring to. You're clever, Lady Gilham. You're young and attractive. Why don't you and George use the money he got from me to set up as a decent married couple? You could open a shop or buy a small farm . . .''

The smile she bestowed on him was closer to a sneer than anything else. "I followed the drum for the first fifteen years of my life. Life was never easy, but it was never dull either. I prefer the existence I lead to 'settling down.' You've done your duty to point out to me the error of my ways. Can I go now?''

He tossed up his palms. "The sooner, and the farther, the better,'' he said. With a graceful bow and an eye not entirely bereft of admiration, he left her.

The constable was standing at the front door. "We'd best make our first stop the bank. I wouldn't want to have my money stolen again,'' Belami said with a wink, then hopped into the carriage.

"Could you tell me what that was all about at all?'' Perkins asked hesitantly.

"Just a little misunderstanding, Perkins. It won't even be necessary for you to write up a report on it, but I want you to know that the Prince Regent appreciates your assistance very much.'' As he spoke, he pressed a gold coin into Perkins's hands.

Perkins peered down to ascertain its denomination and smiled broadly. "Any time,'' he said. "Always happy to oblige His Highness.''

After depositing his money in the bank and dropping off the constable, Belami returned to North Street just in time to see Lady Gilham's heavily laden carriage turning up the

Dyke Road. The head on the opposite seat looked remarkably like George Smythe's. He smiled with quiet satisfaction and turned his carriage toward the Royal Pavilion, to inform Colonel McMahon of the case's successful conclusion and to deliver the royal letters, crockery, and other items.

He felt some stirring of sympathy for Lady Gilham, but as he examined his conscience and found none of the same sympathy for the other members of her crew, he concluded it was only sentiment at work on him. He had dealt fairly, even leniently, with the group. Maybe too leniently with Stack, but, on the other hand, Captain Sharps, like the poor, were always with us. Lady Gilham would receive from George some portion of the thousand pounds, which was fair recompense for her dalliance with the prince, and the group would go on to bedevil some other corner of the kingdom. They would find other victims, no doubt, for being a fool wasn't against the law.

He drove past the royal gardens, dead now in winter, with clumps of melting snow nestled between the shrubs and flowers. He had to wait ten minutes to meet McMahon and used the time having the crockery and plate hauled into the Pavilion.

McMahon came hastening into his office where Belami waited. "Belami, what's new with the case? Are you making any headway at all?" he asked.

Belami pointed to the box of wares on the floor. "What's this? You got the prince's belongings? How the devil did you do it?"

The explanation took half an hour. The letters, the documents outlining Smythe's origins, and the golden locket bearing the prince's miniature were handed over.

"You're a caution, Belami! This calls for champagne." McMahon laughed, slapping his thigh. "I'd have given a monkey to see Perkins shaking the cuffs at Lady Gilham. Did you count up how many laws you broke in all?"

"None, so far as I know," Belami answered blandly.

"And, in any case, I persuaded myself it was one of those cases where the end justified the means. I'm no disciple of Machiavelli in general."

"I wouldn't want to run afoul of you," McMahon said and rang for the champagne. When it was opened and poured, he said, "Now there is the matter of your reward to discuss."

"I kept a hundred pounds to cover expenses."

"Bah, a hundred pounds! You've saved the nation thousands in trouble. You've done no less than avert a national scandal, Belami. Let the reward fit the achievement," he advised, nodding his head wisely.

"Oh, I don't know, Colonel. I don't need money, and I already have a handle to my name," Belami answered, his interest waning. "I do it for the excitement and challenge."

"You seem a bit down at the mouth for a lad who has just pulled off a feat of no mean measure. What ails you?"

"Man's second oldest ailment—*crève-coeur*," he admitted. "I enjoyed doing it. Now that it's over, I find it has cost me dear. Not in pounds, but in people. The affair at the Red Herring didn't suit the duchess's notions of propriety."

"I should think not. I should think not, indeed. How about her niece? Would *she* be willing to overlook it, under the circumstances?"

"I believe so," Belami said, though he hadn't recounted Deirdre's presence at the Old Ship.

"Well, then, if it's only Charney who is bedeviling you, we must call in the big gun, *n'est-ce pas*? The prince has her firmly around his thumb. He is always delighted to involve himself in romantic entanglements. He'll have her trimmed into line quick as you can say Jack Robinson. We'll see if his tailor has left and talk it over with him. On second thought," he said, "perhaps I should see him alone first and outline what you've done on his behalf. Can you come back in an hour?"

"My day is empty," Belami said.

"An hour then, and we'll see what we can do."

Belami finished his champagne and let himself out. There was an air of listlessness about him, due in part to the termination of the case, but mainly due to the trouble with Deirdre. He was by no means hopeless on the latter score, but he wanted to be with her *now*. To tell her all the interesting details of the case and to bask in the glow of her approval. It was nice to have your accomplishments appreciated, but more and more it was dawning on him that the only truly satisfying admiration could come from Miss Deirdre Gower. Even the prince's approbation meant little.

He passed the next hour at the inn with Pronto. There were a dozen—nay, a hundred questions to be answered and answered again. Belami was relieved when the hour was up, and he could return to the Pavilion.

Chapter Seventeen

"My dear Belami, too kind of you to come!" the Prince Regent exclaimed, a benign smile decorating his waxen face.

Belami realized it was an honor to be received so intimately in His Highness's dressing room, but it was an honor that made a straight face difficult to maintain. A lilac silk dressing gown of exquisitely embroidered silk encased the large girth of the prince, unhampered by the corset that gave it a form in public. It oozed and rolled like a river.

"The kindness is yours in having me, sir," Belami said, and executed his finest bow.

"Do sit down, and let us have a wee cose," the prince suggested, patting the sofa beside him.

Despite this friendly gesture, Belami knew his proper seat was the chair opposite and went to it.

"Colonel McMahon has told me the whole incredible story," the prince continued. "Ah, I would have given a wilderness of monkeys to have been present, but we must ever be mindful of the dignity owing our position. What an affair it has been—a criminal's son having the impudence to intrude his presence into our home. McMahon isn't too careful who he invites to call, but that is strictly *entre nous*. Of course, I never for an instant believed his wild tales. It was only an amusement to pass the long days. A little respite from affairs of state, signing papers till this poor wrist is worn out,'' he said wearily, shaking his white wrist. ''And the other matter as well was superbly handled. The less said of *that* female, the better.''

''It was my pleasure, sir. It would ill befit yourself to be involved in such goings-on, but I own I enjoyed the encounter. There is the charm of novelty in associating with people of that nature,'' Belami said as he must say something.

''Aye, the charm of novelty! You've hit it dead on. That was the lure they held to me. There is some liveliness in mongrels that no man with blood in his veins can quite ignore, but when it comes to the succession, it is blue blood that is wanted, what? I have appointed Sir Richard Croft to handle my daughter's next *accouchement*. He feels confident he can bring the matter to fruition. Lady Hertford was kind enough to bring Croft to my attention. A sweet note I have had from her today. And now it is time to deal with another matter, I think?'' he asked with a roguish twinkle in his gray eyes.

''If you refer to any sort of reward for myself, sir, I assure it is not necessary.''

A sausage of a finger was waggled before Belami's eyes. ''We have heard from a little bird that whilst you disentangled myself, your own *amours* have not prospered, my dear Belami. We insist on having a hand in the matter.'' As he spoke, the hand pressed a white square card at him.

Glancing at it, Belami saw it was an invitation to a party at the Pavilion that same night. He had not hoped for the royal hand to move so publicly, but he accepted it with every appearance of gratification.

''If it takes a royal decree, Belami, she shall be yours before my little soirée becomes history,'' he promised, with one of his most benevolent smiles.

''You are too kind to involve yourself in such a picayune matter,'' Belami said, embarrassed by the man's coy manner.

"Love is never a picayune matter, Belami. Not to the principals at any rate. What do you think of this jacket my tailor has rigged up for me to wear this evening? Do you think the white satin too farouche for an intimate do?" he asked, almost in the same breath. The jacket was handed to Belami, and the embellishments and decorations explained, while the perspiration trickled down Belami's spine, for the room was an inferno, as usual.

After vivid and mendacious praise of the jacket, Belami escaped the room and went home to sit alone in an armchair and think. The afternoon seemed as long as a Russian night. What if the Prince's interference was taken amiss by the duchess? She had an odd kick in her gallop, never reacting quite as one expected. The matter of Smythe, for instance. She was the last person in the country he thought would support his claim. And if she utterly forbade the match, he couldn't ask Deirdre to bolt for the border. Maybe Bertie could be of some help . . . He thought of his mother and wished that at least *she* were here to comfort him. He missed Bertie so. It was that sort of an afternoon, that kind of a mood he was in: disconsolate, half dreading the night, yet eager to attend and learn the worst.

He was as fussy as a deb in arranging his hair that night, brushing it forward in the stylish Brutus do. He spoiled half a dozen cravats before achieving the perfection of the Oriental and debated two minutes before selecting a diamond stud for it. While he dressed, he wondered who would have the chore of accompanying the duchess and Deirdre to the party. Pronto had dropped in and told Belami he was invited, but he hadn't been asked to escort the ladies.

And in the little cottage behind Castle Inn, the duchess felt honored indeed to consider that the Prince Regent's own carriage would come for her. Prinney would not be inside it, but he had come in person to deliver the card. It must have cost his sensitivities something to reenter those doors once hallowed by Marie Fitzherbert's presence, but he was such a gentleman he showed no sign of it.

"Another party so soon? You are doing us proud, sir," the duchess said. "Is there a special reason for it?" The reason in her mind was that perhaps Lady Hertford had landed in on him, for she knew from Pronto that Fitzherbert was not here after all.

"Indeed there is. I shall be honoring a very special friend," he confided, winking and nodding, but held his secret.

Between pique at Belami, delight at anticipating another party at the Pavilion, and eagerness to get to London and be the first to have hard news of the goings-on in Brighton, the duchess had more than enough to occupy her small mind. But in the usual contrary way of things, just when she didn't need it, another item of some consequence turned up to amuse her. She received a letter from her majordomo at Fernvale, her country home, reminding her that her brother, a very wealthy octogenarian with no heirs of his own, was about to celebrate his eighty-fifth birthday.

She needed no reminding that he might stick his fork into the wall any day, and it was her bounden duty to be in on the death, to encourage him to dispose of his estate in the proper fashion; *viz*, to name herself as the heiress. There was an ominous tone to the vague missive that upset her to no small degree.

While her brother had no sons, he had nephews aplenty, and amongst them was a certain Sir Nevil Ryder who would move heaven and bend earth to steal the estate from her. There was talk of the family planning a celebration for her brother and, worst of all, a hint that "a certain *other* party" had also cropped up of late in her brother's conversation. No name was given, or needed, to tell her this was her brother's ex-mistress, or wife, or whatever she had been. She knew perfectly well "wife" was the proper word but refused to attach it to an actress. A fever began building in her to dart home and take matters in hand. Her mind flew to Belami, who would be an inestimable aid in arranging the affair to her satisfaction, but how to ask him after the little falling-out of last night?

She made the generous decision that she would not cut Belami dead that evening as she had originally intended. No, she would offer very cold congratulations on his successful completion of the task that had brought them here. Given an inch, the encroaching scoundrel would take a league and be at her door the next morning.

It was a perfectly wretched party. In his joy, the prince felt stout enough to sing for an hour. There was no dancing, no decent conversation, and no sit-down dinner. Had the host been anyone other than who he was, the party would have been called bluntly "a crashing bore." As Prinney was the host, it was termed "not one of his livelier do's."

There was some hope for improvement when the champagne glasses were passed around and the guests were urged to form themselves in a circle around the host to hear a joyful announcement. Everyone knew it would not mention the rescue from his latest scrape. That was a secret known only to every soul present, but not to be whispered within hearing of Prinney. The duchess wondered if, by chance, Princess Caroline had come sprinting home from Italy, and poor Prinney was having to smile and pretend to like it. Or perhaps Princess Charlotte was *enceinte* again?

The duchess had cunningly ranged herself alongside Belami, for she had not yet had the opportunity to congratulate him coldly. Belami had no notion what the announcement might be. He only knew that if the damned duchess would step forward one pace, he could get a look at Deirdre. Several looks had passed between them that evening, looks full of unspoken interest, of forgiveness, of continuing passion.

The prince cleared his throat and began to speak. "My dear friends, it gives me great pleasure to announce that Lord Belami's name has been put forward to receive a marquess-ship for his long and enthusiastic endeavors on behalf of England. I have given my personal endorsement to this nomination,'' he added, which was as good as saying the thing was done.

The most stunned person in the room was Belami. He hadn't a wish in the world for this honor. It would raise conjecture of the most lurid sort—that he'd been gambling heavily and had Prinney over a financial barrel, that he'd turned political and become a Tory—or it might even lead to a revelation of the truth. The prince went on with long praise of his father, the late Lord Belami, who had, in fact, involved himself in government matters. That was to be the ignominious excuse then, Belami realized, that he was being elevated for his father's friendship to the prince. Every atom of his body revolted, but he stood like a rock and even managed a stiff, frozen sort of smile.

When the prince had finished speaking the duchess turned to Belami and took his hand. ''Let me be the first to congratulate you, Lord Belami. What title will you choose? Marquess of Beaulac sounds mighty impressive, if you don't mind a suggestion, and is suitable since your country seat is named Beaulac.''

''Well I don't really . . . I haven't thought of it. I had no idea . . .''

''Speechless with delight. It is only to be expected. My heartiest congratulations. Deirdre,'' she said, turning to her niece, ''you haven't congratulated Lord Belami.''

The two lovers exchanged a secret smile. ''Congratulations. I'm very happy for you,'' she said, offering her hand.

''A curtsy will do,'' the duchess told her sharply, and yanked her hand back.

The interlude was over. Other well-wishers pushed forward to congratulate Belami, and the duchess was eased to the rear of the throng.

''There's a fine feather in Dick's cap then,'' Pronto said,

ambling up to them. "Never said a word to me about it. Close as an oyster is our Dick."

More champagne was drunk, and the temperature of the room seemed to rise ten degrees with every glass, till there wasn't a gentleman's collar in the room that wasn't wilted. The duchess found the temperature entirely comfortable. She congratulated the prince for his acumen in advancing Belami's status.

"I thought it might please you," the prince said, giving her a conspiratorial wink. "That lad will be a duke before he's thirty-five."

"Not a doubt about it," the duchess agreed heartily. She began to see that he must on no account be allowed to escape her clutches. Deirdre, the confirmed ninnyhammer, wasn't making up to him in the least, but hung back as if she were no more than a passing acquaintance.

By a kind of filial osmosis, Deirdre knew that her fortunes had changed. Belami had contrived once again to make himself acceptable to her aunt. She longed to tell Dick so, but a crowded party hardly seemed the place for it. If Belami was unattainable, Pronto was the next best thing. He could always be relied on to deliver secrets to his friend, so Deirdre turned to him.

"Does Dick know I was at the inn this afternoon?" she asked, rather shyly.

"You didn't say not to tell him," was his indignant answer.

"No, I didn't. What—what did he say?"

"He said he was sorry to have subjected you to *that woman's* presence again. I believe I was supposed to beg your pardon."

"I don't mind in the least. Actually, I'm happy I was there."

"That's what we figured. Dick is a famous hand at arranging . . ." He came to a guilty stop. "Not to say that he arranged for you to be there." His crimson face told the story. "You must own he handled Madame X pretty cagily."

"Madame X or Miss Gower?" she asked with a scathing glance at Belami, who was unfortunately receiving the congratulations of a stunning blonde at that moment. Her look was intercepted by him. His smile faded, and he knew as surely as he knew he didn't want to be a marquess that Pronto had let the cat out of the bag.

He hurried to Deirdre, deciding the wisest course was to brazen it out in public, where she couldn't hit him and wouldn't cry if she could help it. "Deirdre, I have to talk to you," he said, his voice strained.

The duchess turned her head, baring her teeth in a sly smile. "Ah, Belami, there you are. Congratulations again," she rushed in. "I see the prince is just taking his leave. I'm half glad, for now the rest of us can get home. He sent us in his carriage, you must know, and is having us hauled home the same way. But I see that arrangement doesn't please you," she invented with a laugh of merriment. "Very well then, I shall give in to you this once. You may take Deirdre home, but mind there's no driving out of the way. Straight home, the pair of you. There's a little matter I wish to discuss with you, Belami."

She sailed off, leaving him little choice in the matter unless he planned to make Deirdre walk home. Charney was in fear of hearing Deirdre's footsteps hurrying after her and literally ran the last few yards to summon the prince's carriage.

"Would you like to go home now?" Belami asked Deirdre.

"Yes, if *Pronto* would be so kind as to take me," she replied, giving Pronto a commanding look.

"Charney didn't give *me* permission. *I* ain't the one's going to be a marquess," he said, trumpeting the awful truth.

"Neither am I," Belami said angrily.

"Not accept it!" Deirdre exclaimed, shocked out of her anger. "You must!"

Pronto concluded from the surreptitious nudges Belami was aiming at his elbow that his job now was to disappear with his carriage. He took a last bored look around the party and said he guessed he'd be toddling along.

"I haven't done anything to earn the title," Belami pointed out. "I'll look a jackass when it comes up for discussion."

"Suit yourself. I'm sure it has nothing to do with me," she replied, and scanned the room for a different ride home.

"We'll discuss it in the carriage," he told her, and took a firm grip on her arm. She resisted till it became clear she was going to be dragged forth, at which time she walked swiftly on her own power to the door.

She was as stiff as a snowman when she was seated in the carriage opposite Belami. "Deirdre, what's the matter now?" he asked in exasperation, though of course he knew perfectly well.

"Nothing. Nothing at all."

"Then why are you sitting over there?"

"Because I don't trust you. You *manipulated* me, Dick."

He heard the Dick with joy. Dick could really do no harm. It was Lord Belami he had to be wary of.

"You *arranged* for Pronto to get me up to his clothes-press," she continued. "You put on that fine rant with Gilham for my benefit, to fool me."

"No, to give you a graphic demonstration of the truth since you wouldn't let me tell you to your face." Receiving no counterattack, he switched to her banquette and reached for her hands.

"Darling, what could I do? I had to get Lady Gilham out of her house that night to let Réal in to rifle it."

"You didn't have to take her dress off!"

"She took it off herself."

"You didn't have to take her to a private room at an inn."

"Where else could I take her in the middle of the night in the winter? You knew when you agreed to marry me that I sometimes have to do unusual things in my work," he pointed out as his fingers crept up her arms, pulling her closer to him by small degrees.

"Not so unusual for you, in this particular case," she countered.

"To embrace any woman but you is unusual for me," he said ardently, "and highly distasteful. It was the last thing in the world I wanted to do."

"You were doing it pretty well for someone who didn't want to do it," she said, her anger dwindling to pique.

"I can do it much better if you'll let me show you," he said in an insinuating voice as sweet and smooth as honey.

Her breath caught in her lungs, causing a strangling sensation as his arms enfolded her. He pulled her onto his lap, where he was soon doing it much more enthusiastically, till her head spun in dizzying circles.

"Dick, don't. We shouldn't," she said, reluctantly lifting her head to smile down at him. His face was shadowed, but the streak of light from the window cast its prominent features into relief. She gazed, unable to believe that wonderful Belami wanted her.

"Yes, we should. Often," he disagreed softly and put one warm hand on her throat to lower her lips to his. They were soft, yielding, infinitely sweet. He felt proud and exhilarated to claim her for his own.

"We're going to get married tomorrow, darling," he said when he released her. "I'm not taking any more chances of losing you."

"First you'll have to sweet-talk Auntie back into agreement." She laughed, knowing this had been done at the Pavilion.

"I'd kiss her, too, if I could find her lips," he said.

"We'd better stop. We're nearly home, and she'll be peeking out the window," she said, sliding from his knee.

"No, she isn't," he said, looking to the illuminated saloon windows.

"Silly, she peeks out the dark windows of the study. She's not a tyro at spying, you know. There, see the white curtain is jiggling."

Knowing they were under surveillance, they got out of the carriage the minute it stopped and walked sedately to the front door.

The duchess greeted them with her gargoylish smile. "You'd better get right home and start packing, Belami," she said in lieu of a greeting.

"Am I going somewhere?" he asked, startled.

"To Fernvale."

"With all due respect, your grace, Deirdre agrees with me that we want to get married here in Brighton. Tomorrow," he added, and felt a little quake inside. There was no saying how Charney would take this news.

She hardly heard him. "Excellent. I'm so happy for you both, but it can't be tomorrow."

"With a special license . . ." he began, and was summarily interrupted.

"We'll get one at Fernvale. That is where the marriage will take place as soon as you have handled a little business for me, Belami."

"Our minds are made up," he insisted. "If *you* insist on returning to Fernvale, there is only one thing for us to do." He gave Deirdre a peremptory glance to ensure her cooperation.

"I would prefer to be married at home, Dick." On her face was a dreamy smile. "In a white gown, in the chapel at Fernvale. I don't want a scrambling do."

"Yes, as I said before, there's only one thing to do. We'll have to change our minds about getting married tomorrow," he said with what the duchess considered a most mawkish smile. And Deirdre was suspiciously pink around the lips, too, she noticed.

"Then it's settled. Deirdre and I will lead the way to Fernvale, and you may come along behind in your rig."

"That's not . . ." Belami began in a belligerent voice and was again interrupted.

"Did you tell him about my brother?" the duchess asked her niece.

"No."

"I see. It seems to me ten minutes was plenty of time for it. It took you ten minutes to execute the few steps from the Royal Pavilion. I cannot think how you got jam on your face, Deirdre, but you are very red around the lips. Belami as well," she added, scrutinizing him.

Dick felt the old urge to either strangle the harpy or to stalk from the premises at once. But even while he glared, she continued with her intriguing tale.

An aging gentleman at death's door, with a batch of relatives scrambling for his fortune, an affair with an actress, some suggestion that Sir Nevil Ryder might be using undue influence to gain the purse, and other temptations, kept him listening, even considering the possibility of delaying the wedding a few days. It would allow Bertie to attend, which inclined him to agreement. Mama loved a wedding above anything.

"Since Deirdre wants to be married at her home, I suppose we can put the wedding off till we reach Fernvale," he decided before he left.

"I knew you would see reason," the duchess congratulated him.

"I trust the same may be said for you, madame," he answered smoothly. "I have just given you a few days' grace. Might you not give me five minutes alone with my fiancée?" His charming smile beguiled her into folly.

"Till midnight," she decreed. The clock on the shelf read one minute to twelve.

Her gait as she hobbled out the door hadn't been so lively

since the day she interred the late duke and came into her own realm.

It seemed a sad thing to marry Deirdre off and set her up for a life of subjugation, but as she bent her rachitic spine to look into the keyhole, she saw that the future marchioness was much too far gone to regret it.